What people are saying about
A Bride So Fair

"Carol Cox has proven herself as a top author in the Christian romantic suspense genre with *A Bride so Fair*. She blends gentle humor, suspense, and appealing characters within the setting of the Chicago World's Fair. A fascinating glimpse and a fun ride.
—Hannah Alexander, author of *Double Blind* and *Hideaway Home*

"I've been a fan of Carol Cox's books since her first publication. She has a way of putting the reader right into the setting of the story. In *A Bride so Fair* I smelled, tasted and experienced what went on at the World's Fair in Chicago 1883 as a backdrop to a suspenseful love story. This series is a keeper!
—Colleen Coble, author of *Anathema*

"Join the fun as award-winning author Carol Cox takes readers on a wild ride through the World's Fair in late 1800 Chicago. A novel filled with memorable characters, the charm of yesteryear, and a plot that keeps you turning the pages, this is one you won't want to miss!"
—Diann Hunt, author of *For Better or for Worse*

"Intrigue, history, and love all rolled into a fascinating story."
—Lois Gladys Leppard, author of the Mandie Books

"Carol Cox has skillfully woven a heart-tugging romance and page-turning intrigue around a fascinating historical setting, bringing all three to life."
—Linda Windsor, author of *Wedding Bell Blues* and *For Pete's Sake*

A BRIDE SO FAIR

CAROL COX

BARBOUR
PUBLISHING

ISBN 978-1-59789-492-0

This book is a work of fiction. Names, characters, places, and incidents are either products of the author's imagination or used fictitiously. Any similarity to actual people, organizations, and/or events is purely coincidental.

All scripture quotations are taken from the King James Version of the Bible.

For more information about Carol Cox, please access the author's Web site at the following Internet address: www.CarolCoxBooks.com

Cover Design: Müllerhaus Communications Group

Published by Barbour Publishing, Inc., P.O. Box 719, Uhrichsville, Ohio 44683, www.barbourbooks.com

Our mission is to publish and distribute inspirational products offering exceptional value and biblical encouragement to the masses.

 Member of the
Evangelical Christian
Publishers Association

Printed in the United States of America.

Dear Reader,

Some time ago I came across a history of the United States printed in the 1940s. Intrigued, I thumbed through its pages and found my attention caught by a passage about the World's Columbian Exposition, held in Chicago in 1893. Those brief paragraphs sparked my interest and set me off on a trail of research where I discovered a fascinating moment in America's history.

After winning the honor of hosting the great fair, Chicago opened its doors to the world and invited people from every nation to come to the White City. And come they did! Over 27 million visitors passed through the gates during the fair's six-month duration. Along with sightseers, the fair also drew those who would prey on the unsuspecting, which gave me the basis for this story.

By the time it was all over, America had established its position as a forward-thinking, cultured nation, and innovations such as the Ferris wheel and the Midway, hamburgers and carbonated soda, Cracker Jacks and ragtime music had become American institutions.

Thank you for joining me in reliving the moment that ushered in the twentieth century in America. I hope you will enjoy this excursion into the past as much as I have. Please visit my Web site at www.CarolCoxBooks.com. I'd love to hear from you!

Blessings,
Carol Cox

To Kevin, one of the best brainstorming partners around.
And to Samantha, who helped me unravel Mrs. Purvis's secret.
I love you both!

CHAPTER I

S top, thief!" The commanding bellow cut through the pleasant chatter of the crowds strolling the grounds of the World's Columbian Exposition.

Emily Ralston shielded her eyes against the noonday sun and scanned the gaily dressed fairgoers on Government Plaza, trying to spot the source of the commotion.

A lanky youth burst through a cluster of women and children on the far side of the plaza, scattering them like tenpins. Shrill exclamations followed him as he bolted past the ladies to the middle of the open area, where he slowed and glanced quickly from one end of its broad expanse to the other.

A stocky man in shirtsleeves charged through the same group, evoking more outraged squawks. He stopped short, gasping like a winded horse while he scanned the crowd.

"Hey, you!" he bellowed and started off in hot pursuit of the boy. In his haste, he collided with a young matron holding a small girl in her arms, nearly toppling them to the ground. The man halted long enough to steady the pair, although the infuriated look he cast in the boy's direction showed his longing to continue the chase.

At the man's angry shout, the fleeing youth looked over his shoulder and picked up speed. Emily saw him snap his hand to one side and watched a paper container arc through the air and disappear behind a potted palm.

Emily recognized the signs of someone doing something he shouldn't. She balanced on the balls of her feet, poised for action. She could never keep up with the long-legged adolescent if she tried to follow him across the fairgrounds, but there was more than one way to foil a troublemaker.

The boy changed course and pounded across the pavement in her direction. Emily smiled. She waited until the last instant before he reached the spot where she stood then stepped into his path.

"Stop right there!" she demanded.

The boy's eyes flared wide when he saw her blocking his escape. His feet scrambled for purchase as he veered abruptly to the right. Just as he passed, Emily darted forward and nabbed him by the ear.

"Ow!" The lad looked down at Emily with an astonished expression. "Leggo my ear!" He made as if to wrench himself out of her grasp, but a quick twist of her wrist brought him to his knees.

Emily allowed herself a brief moment of smugness. It wasn't the first time she had been victorious against an opponent larger than herself. Growing up at the Collier Children's Home had given her plenty of time to learn how to equalize a difference in size.

The stocky man raced up to them, puffing like a steam engine. "Thank you, miss," he gasped. "That was quite a catch."

Taking command of Emily's captive, he seized the boy by his upper arm and jerked him to his feet. "Where are the goods you stole, you young guttersnipe?"

The look of alarm slid off the boy's face, to be replaced by a cocky grin. "I don't know what you're talking about."

"Of course not," the man mocked. "Why were you running, if you hadn't just stolen a package of Cracker Jacks right off the counter of my stand?"

Emily felt her jaw go slack. Cracker Jacks? She had risked her own safety for nothing more than a container of the new popcorn, peanuts, and molasses confection?

Looking more confident by the second, the boy shook his head. "I was just walking along, and you started shouting and chasing me." He shrugged. "I thought you must be crazy. No one could blame me for running when someone so much bigger than me was on my tail."

His captor looked at Emily with a glint of humor shining in his eyes. "It doesn't look to me like it takes all that much in the way of size to get you under control." His grin faded, and he gave the boy a shake. "Now where are the Cracker Jacks you stole?"

The boy shrugged again. "I'm telling you, you've got the wrong person."

Emily broke into the exchange. "Then what was that I saw you throw away?"

The youth paled, and the vendor turned his attention back to Emily. "You saw him throw something?"

"Behind that potted palm over there." Emily walked briskly toward the plant and reached behind it, retrieving a paper package that rattled when she shook it. She returned to the waiting pair and held out the parcel. "Is this what you're looking for?"

The man took it with a grateful smile. "Thank you, miss. I'll be obliged if you'll stay around until I summon one of the Columbian Guards so you can tell him what you saw."

Emily shook her head. "I'm sorry. I work at the Children's

Building here on the fairgrounds, and my lunch break is nearly over." From deep within the massive Manufactures Building, she heard the clock in its alabaster tower chime the three-quarter hour. If she wanted to keep her job, she'd better get back to work and look sharp about it.

The man's face fell. "If you don't, it will be my word against his. I left my nephew watching my stand so I could catch this young rascal, and who knows what kind of mess he'll have made of things by the time I get back? The least you can do is help me out."

Emily wavered. Her supervisor took a decidedly dim view of tardiness, but the smug expression on the boy's face decided her. "All right, but only for a moment."

It took far longer than that for the guard to finish taking her statement. With the thanks of the vendor ringing in her ears, she set off once more toward the Children's Building. In the distance, she heard a clock chiming the hour.

"Oh no." She glanced from side to side, taking note of the throngs of people dotting the broad walkways. None of them seemed to be paying a bit of attention to her. Taking heart from this, Emily hiked up the hem of her skirt, planted her hand on top of her hat to keep it from blowing off, and sprinted headlong across the plaza, paying scant attention to the gleaming white buildings as she raced over the bridges spanning the lagoon to the Wooded Island and then to the far shore. From there, a quick dash put her at the front of the Children's Building.

She slumped against the outer door with one palm pressed against her heaving chest. When she managed to catch her breath, she pushed the arched door open and stepped inside. If she could assume her seat behind the reception desk before—

"Your lunch hour ended precisely three minutes ago."

Emily skidded to a halt and turned to face the gaunt woman

standing against the opposite wall. "I'm sorry, Miss Strickland. I—"

"If you plan to continue working here, Miss Ralston, I would suggest you make it a point to be punctual." Her supervisor's cold stare left no doubt about her disapproval.

"Of course, ma'am." Emily ordered her knees to quit shaking and tried her best to appear composed as she hung her straw boater on the hat rack and walked toward her desk. Lucy Welch, her blue eyes shining with sympathy, rose from the heavy wooden chair to let Emily take her seat.

Emily cast a grateful look at her friend; then she turned to bestow a wobbly smile upon the woman and boy who stood waiting in front of her desk. "How may I help you?"

"Could we finish here, please?" The young matron tapped her foot and looked daggers at Emily. "I would much rather be outside viewing the fair instead of waiting for you all to sort yourselves out. I'm not certain I want to leave Alexander here if this is any indication of the competency of your staff."

At the edge of her vision, Emily saw Miss Strickland's rigid posture grow even more erect. She fumbled with the heavy black book that lay open on her desk. "I apologize for the delay. I wouldn't have been late, except—"

"Excuses are unacceptable." Miss Strickland's harsh voice broke in. "I don't tolerate tardiness for any reason."

Emily clamped her lips shut to hold back the explanation she longed to give. She ought to have known better than to tarry long enough to give the Columbian Guard her version of what had transpired, but she couldn't find it within herself to let that boy get away with stealing the vendor's merchandise.

She looked up at the boy's mother and forced a smile. "If you'll just give me some information, I'll check Alexander in and you can be on your way." She entered his name and his mother's in the ledger then pinned a numbered tag to the boy's back and handed his mother a claim check bearing the same number. "Please keep this in a safe place. You'll need it when you come back to pick up your son. Miss Welch will take Alexander to the gymnasium. I'm sure he'll enjoy that."

She beckoned to Lucy, who had been hovering in the background, then turned back to the boy's mother. "Enjoy your time on the grounds. He will be well cared for."

Looking somewhat mollified, the woman slipped the ticket into her reticule and turned to leave. Just before she reached the door, it swung open. A man in the uniform of the Columbian Guards smiled and held it open for her; then he stepped inside. His glance wavered between Miss Strickland and Emily before he approached the reception desk.

She stared up at him, panicking at the thought that her attempt to do the right thing was going to cause her even more difficulty. "I already told the other guard everything I know."

Miss Strickland raised her eyebrows and moved toward the desk with a firm stride. "Bad enough to be tardy. What other trouble have you gotten yourself into?"

"It's no trouble of this young lady's making." The guard stepped to one side, and Emily realized a small boy encased in a heavy woolen coat stood behind him. The tall guard lifted the toddler into his arms and smoothed the boy's tousled blond hair. A smile lifted the corners of his dark mustache when the boy sniffled and snuggled against his shoulder.

Then he turned the smile on Emily, and she felt as if a giant vacuum had sucked all the air out of the room. She stared open-mouthed until Miss Strickland prodded her between her shoulder blades. Emily sat bolt upright and felt her face flame. "How may I help you?"

Before the guard could respond, Miss Strickland leaned toward Emily and looked her straight in the eye. "I expect a high degree of professionalism from you, Miss Ralston. Your attitude reflects on the entire staff of the Children's Building. Please keep that in mind." Her heels clacked against the floor as she crossed the open court that occupied the center of the building and disappeared down one of the side corridors.

Emily drew her first easy breath since the larcenous boy had crossed her path. She knew perfectly well what she had to do, and she could do it much better without her supervisor looking over her shoulder. She nodded a greeting at a couple who entered with two small children in tow then turned back to the waiting guard. "I'm sorry for the interruption. What can I do for you?"

The dark-haired guard hiked the child higher on his shoulder. "This little fellow seems to have lost his family."

Emily took a closer look at the little boy, noting the tear streaks on his cheeks. He couldn't be more than three years old. She felt her heart go out to him. Standing to put herself on a level with the child, she adopted a cheerful tone. "We have lots of things for you to do until we find your parents. Would you like to stay here while this nice man tries to find them?"

The youngster buried his face in the guard's neck and shook his head. "I want Mama."

Emily swallowed hard. She reached up to rub his back with a gentle touch. "What's your name?"

The boy sniffled again then raised his head and looked at her. "Adam."

"All right, Adam." At least he was old enough to tell her that much. Emily turned toward the desk and pulled the ledger over to her. "I'll write your name down here in this book, and then a friend of mine will come to take you to a room with lots of toys.

You can play with them until your mama comes for you. Doesn't that sound nice?"

Adam rubbed his nose with the back of his hand. Emily could see his lower lip quiver.

She dipped the pen in the inkwell and wrote "Adam" on the next blank line. She hesitated a moment with the pen poised in the air. "Do you know your last name?"

Adam shook his head.

"Do you know your mama's real name?"

He gave the same response.

The guard drew nearer and said in a low voice, "Some people found him over by the north bandstand. When the performance was over, everybody walked away but this little guy."

The father who had just entered with his family stepped forward. "Excuse me, but I couldn't help but overhear. I thought I recognized the boy. My family stopped to hear the performance at the bandstand, too. We saw his mother leave. I thought at the time it was awfully peculiar for her to go away and let such a young child stay there on his own."

The guard turned an intense gaze on the man. "You saw her leave?"

"That's right. In a hurry, too. She was practically running."

"Could you give me a description?" The guard set Adam down beside Emily, and the two men moved a few feet away.

Emily checked the couple's children in, half her attention on the task at hand, the other half focused on the story the father told while the guard made notes in a little notebook he pulled from his pocket.

"She was a nice-looking woman," the man said. "Blond hair, dark blue dress."

"With a gored skirt and a lovely shirred bodice," his wife put in. "Very up-to-date. Her hat was trimmed with matching silk ribbon and ostrich feathers."

Her husband chuckled. "Trust a woman to notice all the details of fashion."

Emily handed two claim checks to the children's mother and rang the small brass bell on her desk to summon Lucy.

Lucy appeared a moment later and gave all three children a bright smile. "Are you ready to come with me?" She bent to take Adam's hand, but Emily motioned her away.

"Just those two for now," she said. "Come back in a few minutes, and I'll explain."

The couple took their leave of their children. "We'll be back when your mother has worn me out seeing all the exhibits she's interested in," their father joked.

When the door closed behind them, the guard walked over and knelt beside Adam. "I'll go out and look for your mother now. You can stay here with Miss. . ." He looked up at Emily.

"Ralston," she supplied.

"Miss Ralston." He gave her another one of those smiles that made her stomach do flip-flops. "She'll make sure the people here take good care of you."

The little boy's chin wobbled, but he turned to Emily and placed his hand in hers. "Hello, Miss Rost—Ralt—"

Emily smiled down at him. "Why don't you call me Miss Emily?"

Adam nodded, his expression solemn. "Miss Em'ly," he repeated. His quick acceptance sent a rush of maternal feelings through her.

"Why don't we take off your coat?" she suggested. "It's lovely weather today, and I think you'll feel much better without it. I'll make sure we keep it safe so you don't lose it, all right?"

Adam hesitated then allowed her to pull the heavy coat off. Emily bit her lip at the sight of the sailor suit he wore, with its middy blouse and knee pants. This child was just too precious for words!

While she tried to make Adam more comfortable, the guard left to go search for the child's parents. A moment later, Lucy hurried back into the reception area. "What was it you couldn't tell me before?"

"You'll have to wait a little longer," Emily told her. "Adam, this is Miss Lucy. She'll take you to those toys I told you about."

The little boy studied Lucy then reached out to take the hand she extended and toddled off beside her.

Free of responsibility for the moment, Emily propped her elbow on the desk and rested her cheek on her palm. She stared at the front door, lost in thought.

"He is a handsome fellow, isn't he?" Lucy's voice came from right behind her.

Startled out of her reverie, Emily jerked upright and banged her elbow on the edge of the desk. She yelped and glared at Lucy.

"Sorry." Lucy's unrepentant grin belied the sincerity of her apology. "I didn't mean to make you jump. . .that much, at least." Her grin faded. "And I truly am sorry about what happened with Miss Strickland. I tried to cover for you when I saw you were late, but she came in and caught me at it." She wrinkled her nose. "I should have known it wouldn't work."

Emily sighed. "It's all right. It was my fault for not being back on time. I knew Miss Strickland wouldn't be happy about it, but she positively glared at me!" She rubbed her sore elbow and winced. "I hope she doesn't fire me. I don't want to lose the first job I ever had."

"First paying job, you mean. You've been a hard worker ever

since I've known you. And don't worry about Miss Strickland. Did you know she has already gone through six receptionists in the four months the fair has been going on? I got that from Ruthie Lawson in the Day Nursery." She looked over her shoulder and lowered her voice. "And they weren't all fired by Miss Strickland, either. Some of them got so fed up with her demanding ways that they up and left. People just don't do that on a whim, as hard as jobs are to find these days."

"But that's my point. People are hungry for jobs right now. She knows she doesn't have to keep me here."

Lucy snorted. "Listen to me. While you're sitting here checking children in and out of the building all day, I have a chance to talk to the other employees. You are the best receptionist they've had yet. Everyone says so."

Emily hoped her friend was right. The thought of losing her job was always an underlying fear. With the silver crash, masses of people were unemployed, making it harder than ever to find work. But even if jobs were as plentiful as the sand on the shores of Lake Michigan, she would hate to leave the Children's Building. Providing a safe, nurturing place for children to play and learn while their parents saw the fair was a task she could embrace with her whole being, and taking part in such a worthwhile endeavor filled her with immense satisfaction.

She had to admit that Lucy was usually right in her assessment of any gossip she managed to overhear. Maybe she could relax. . . just a little, anyway.

Something pulled on her sleeve, and she realized Lucy was shaking her arm.

Emily blinked. "Did you say something?"

"Back in dreamland again?" Her friend sighed then took on the air of a patient teacher. "I said you never answered my question about the guard. Don't you think he's handsome?"

Emily reached for a stack of papers. "I suppose so. I didn't really notice."

Lucy snorted again. "Of course you didn't." She moved toward the back of the building. "Call me when you need me."

The front door swung open again, and Emily whirled around, wondering if the guard had accomplished his mission so quickly. Her heart sank when she saw the slender man who stood before her dressed in a double-breasted serge jacket and flannel trousers.

"And how is my favorite receptionist today?"

Emily pressed her lips together and didn't answer. She watched as Raymond Willard Simmons III crossed the floor with a swagger that reminded her of a strutting peacock.

What would it take to make him quit stopping by? Emily dreaded his unannounced visits almost as much as she dreaded arousing Miss Strickland's ire. If only she could tell him to leave her alone! But Raymond's father was one of the fair administrators, and upsetting Mr. Simmons would upset Miss Strickland. That was something Emily did not intend to do by choice.

She tried to arrange her features in a pleasant expression while Raymond pulled a paper bag from behind his back like a magician producing a dove from his hat.

"Something to satisfy your sweet tooth." He set the bag on Emily's desk with a flourish. When she made no move toward the gift, he opened the bag and withdrew a caramel, holding it out for her inspection. "From one of the finest candy makers in Chicago. I hope that when you enjoy them, you'll think of me."

Emily kept her smile in place, though what she would really enjoy doing was telling him never to darken the door of the Children's Building again. "Thank you, Mr. Simmons."

His broad smile drooped. "I thought we agreed we knew each

other well enough to use our Christian names. Aren't you going to call me Ray? That's what my family calls me... and my closest friends." He said the last few words in an intimate whisper that was probably intended to make her heart melt. She ground her teeth instead.

"It really wouldn't be proper." Emily put all the primness she could muster into the statement.

Raymond moved closer and rested his elbows on the desk, putting his face on a level with hers. "Perhaps that's true here at the fairgrounds, where my father and I are seen as leaders. But away from the workplace, I see no reason to maintain such formality." He moved his hand toward hers. Emily immediately began straightening the papers on her desk.

Raymond didn't appear to notice the slight. "What about going to dinner with me tonight? It's time you got away from the fairgrounds and that dreary boardinghouse and saw something of Chicago. We could eat at the Palmer House—"

"Without a chaperone? That would hardly sit well with your family, would it? What would they think if word got back to them that you had been seen in public with a young lady they've never met?"

Raymond's face fell, and Emily knew she had scored a hit. His position as a member of one of Chicago's leading families meant everything to him, and he would do nothing to bring about his parents' disapproval or to risk their social standing.

Three couples entered and formed a line behind Raymond. Emily lifted her chin and tried to look as businesslike as possible. "I really must get back to work, Mr. Simmons."

Raymond straightened and gave her a sour look. He opened his mouth as if to say more but settled for a nod and exited, leaving Emily free to enter names and distribute claim checks.

Alone once again, Emily tapped a stack of papers against the desk to square their edges then set them neatly in the upper left-hand corner of her desk. Spotting the bag of caramels Raymond had left, she set it in her bottom desk drawer, out of sight. She didn't want Miss Strickland to find things in less than perfect order.

While she continued to straighten her work area, her mind turned back to the little boy the guard had brought in. There was nothing unusual about one of the Columbian Guards bringing a lost child to the Children's Building—it had happened several times already in the two weeks she'd worked there. But something about that little tyke tugged at her heartstrings.

If she could feel such a connection toward a child she had just met, his mother must be frantic. Emily paused in the act of scooping up an armload of file folders. A frown tightened her forehead. Why would anyone go off and leave a child that age alone? And to leave in such a hurry, practically running, the man who witnessed it had said.

She pulled open the file drawer and slid the folders into their places. A woman running through the crowded fairgrounds would be unusual enough to draw notice from any number of people.

Emily wrinkled her nose. She had probably drawn a fair amount of notice herself with her undignified dash across the plaza earlier.

CHAPTER 2

E xcuse me. Could you please direct me to the Agriculture
Building?"

Stephen assessed the weathered man before him, taking in the calloused hands and the deep grooves splaying out
from the corners of his eyes. He looked every bit a farmer. No
wonder he was interested in the agricultural exhibits. "It's quite a
hike from here, but it isn't difficult to find." Stephen pointed in
a southeasterly direction. "You'll need to stay on this path along
the east edge of the lagoon. Beyond that, you'll pass between the
Manufactures Building and the North Canal then circle around
the Grand Basin. The large white building to your left on the far
side of the basin will be Agriculture."

"Many thanks." The man turned to look at the small boy
behind him, jiggling from one foot to the other. He looked back
at Stephen and lowered his voice. "And is there a public comfort
station on the way?"

Stephen ran his fingertips across his mustache to hide his grin. "That's in the opposite direction, but it's much closer. It's right back there, near the Midway entrance at the end of the California Building." Once he made sure the father and son were headed in the right direction, he strolled on toward Fisheries and the U.S. Government Building, keeping a watchful eye for any disturbance in his domain.

None seemed to be on the horizon today. Calm reigned in the area he patrolled. Another day with crime held at bay. The sun shone low in the western sky, casting long shadows and dappling the walkway under the mulberry trees. One more day of patrolling the fairgrounds. One day nearer to its closing in October.

A sense of melancholy settled over him. Throughout the months of his employment there, the fairgrounds had become as familiar to him as the campus of Cornell University, where he had spent the past four years. Hard to realize that in a few more weeks, the great exposition would close its doors for the last time. No longer would he be able to meander along the walkways on his daily rounds, taking in the dazzling panorama, then returning to the apartment he rented from his uncle to dream of the buildings he would design himself one day.

Stephen circled toward the lake, noting that both the weather bureau and the lifesaving station seemed secure. He rolled his shoulders, as if that would help to shake off his gloomy feelings. It had been a good summer when all was said and done, with an interesting job that gave him an unsurpassed opportunity to study the works of some of the greatest architects of the day. Not a bad way to spend the summer after his college graduation, despite his father's opinion that he should have joined his uncle's firm without delay.

Stephen leaned against the railing that led out to the North

Pier, amused by the satisfaction he felt when he surveyed the placid scene before him, as if the fairgoers who flocked past him owed their pleasure to something he had done, rather than the drive and genius of Burnham and Root. He sharpened his gaze and took in the gargantuan Manufactures and Liberal Arts Building, trying to imagine the work that went into designing so elaborate a project. At the moment, something of that scope was beyond his reach, though he vowed that wouldn't always be the case.

But he had been a part of the magnificent undertaking, even in a small way. He shifted his position, turning to view the shoreline to the north, home to many of the exhibits from foreign lands. It felt good to know he had played a role in maintaining the safety of the millions of visitors at this world-renowned exposition. There had been moments of excitement, no doubt about that, but most of his days were as uneventful as this one, with the lost boy at noontime being the only disruption to the even flow of his routine.

An image of the fair-haired toddler formed in Stephen's mind. He'd been quite stoic for such a little guy, even though his tear-filmed eyes signaled his distress at being on his own in that teeming multitude. It was a good thing a concerned onlooker had called Stephen's attention to the situation so he could take the boy to the safety of the Children's Building for the rest of the afternoon.

Stephen turned his back on the lake and retraced his route. How long had it taken for the child's mother to come for him? And which of his fellow guards had little Adam's mother approached? Stephen wished he had been the one to talk to her. All through the afternoon, he had kept on the alert for a woman answering her description, but his efforts had been in vain. It was a pity. He would have liked to know what had made her run off like that.

Running. That was how several witnesses had described the way she left Adam. And that was where this particular incident parted company from the other cases he had encountered of children lost on the grounds.

Stephen drew his eyebrows together. Running meant she wanted to get to—or from—a place in a hurry. What could be her reason for dashing off like that? More important, why would she bolt off and leave her child alone?

It didn't make sense. Once again, he wished he could have talked to her and learned the rest of the story.

He crossed the bridge that lay just beyond the western pavilion of the Fisheries Building, intending to make a quick circuit of the Wooded Island before his shift ended. He passed a mother carrying a small child, who nestled against her shoulder. The sight brought back the memory of the way Adam had snuggled against him earlier. He seemed like a sweet child—and well cared for, too. Nothing indicated that being left to fend for himself was part of his normal routine. Stephen hoped not. The boy was in knee-length pants, but he couldn't be more than three or four years old, far too young to be on his own in any situation. Yet today he had been. Which brought Stephen back to his earlier question: Why did Adam's mother run away?

He checked his watch and hurried to join the other guards in front of the Woman's Building as they formed ranks and prepared to march to headquarters at the end of their shift. While they changed into civilian clothes at the guard station, he asked each one whether they had seen a woman matching the mother's description. No one had.

Stephen considered the puzzle while he pulled on his navy sack coat and straightened the collar. At least Adam had been able to await his mother's return in the charge of people who genuinely cared about children and were dedicated to providing a pleasant environment for them. The only exception being, in Stephen's mind at least, that supervisor. There always seemed to be one person in any group whose goal in life was to make everyone around them miserable, and Miss Strickland did her best to fill that role in the Children's Building. Stephen had run into her before, and each encounter left him feeling as if he'd just been doused with ice water. Thankfully her duties seldom involved interacting with the children.

He'd been glad when she left the reception area this afternoon. As frightened as Adam was then, he wouldn't have been helped one bit by her testy attitude.

The girl at the reception desk, though, was a different matter altogether. Stephen set his bowler hat atop his head and felt his lips curve upward at the memory of her winsome smile and the compassionate way she dealt with Adam. When she looked up at Stephen, her emerald eyes sparkled in the light that streamed through the mullioned windows and seemed to set her deep auburn hair ablaze.

She couldn't have been working in the Children's Building long. He didn't recall seeing her on any of his earlier visits, and someone like her would have stuck in his mind, no doubt about it. He would have to come up with a good reason to visit the building—and its pretty receptionist—again.

What excuse could he give? He could hardly wait around until another lost child crossed his path. A happy thought struck him. He would go in there the following day and see what had become of Adam. It would set his mind at ease to know the little boy had been reunited with his mother, and perhaps he could learn the reason she gave for taking off like that.

And he'd be able to look into those sparkling green eyes again. A grin spread across his face. He could hardly wait for tomorrow.

———

"I can't believe we spent the entire day here and didn't see even half the exhibits!" The speaker, a heavyset woman, sagged against Emily's desk and fanned herself with her handkerchief. "I am utterly exhausted. My Albert says we must have walked for miles, and I believe he's right. Thank goodness someone had the foresight to set up this facility for the children! We never would have been able to do as much as we did with our Billy along."

Emily gave her a sympathetic smile. "It is huge, isn't it? We'll be glad to keep Billy again another day, should you decide to come back and see the rest of it."

Lucy entered the reception area holding Billy's hand. At the sight of the stocky woman, he whooped and dashed toward her. His mother scooped him up and pressed her lips against his cheek. "Say good-bye to the nice ladies, sweetheart. Perhaps you'll see them again soon." The little boy waved over his mother's shoulder as she made her way to the front door.

Emily sat upright and kept a smile on her face until the heavy door swung shut behind them; then she leaned back in her chair and stretched her arms wide. Lucy slumped on one corner of Emily's desk and rubbed her lower back.

"I'm glad this day is over," Lucy sighed. "That was quite a crowd of children we had today. And the racket they made!"

Emily rolled her shoulders to loosen her tight muscles. "I won't argue with you there. It's getting pretty quiet now that most of them have been picked up. How many do we have left?"

Lucy yawned. "Only three or four. It seems like there are always a few stragglers."

Emily sat up and ran her fingertip down the entries in the ledger. Her finger stopped at one group of names. "Three of them belong to the same family, so they'll all leave at one time." She flipped the page and started scanning the neat lines of writing.

"And that lost little boy, Adam," Lucy added.

Emily clapped her hand to her mouth. "We've been so busy this afternoon I nearly forgot about him. Is he all right?"

"Every time I've seen him, he's been playing quietly by himself. He doesn't seem to be overly distressed, just rather subdued."

The front doors burst open, and a young couple entered. "Sorry we're late," the man puffed. "We decided to take a turn on the Ferris wheel, but we had no idea it would take so long."

He pulled three claim checks out of his vest pocket and handed them to Emily. She passed them to Lucy, who headed back to fetch their youngsters.

"Don't worry," Emily told the pair. "They're nearly the last ones here, but we certainly wouldn't go off and leave them."

Lucy returned straightaway with the couple's son and two daughters, who launched themselves at their parents with happy squeals. They left in a chattering group, each child determined to outdo the others in telling what they had done while their parents were gone.

With the children gone for the day, the other workers filtered out while Emily put the finishing touches on her ledger. A few minutes later, Iris Hunter, who had charge of the kindergarten where the younger children were instructed and amused, appeared with Adam walking beside her, his heavy coat slung over one arm. When he spied Emily, his face lit up in a shy smile.

Iris stopped at Emily's desk. "I need to leave. My husband's parents are coming over for supper. Would you mind looking after this one until his parents come?"

"Of course." Emily waved Adam toward her and pulled him into her lap. "You go ahead, and we'll take care of him."

With a grateful smile, Iris bent over Emily's desk to sign the time sheet and then departed. The moment the door closed behind her, Emily looked up at Lucy. Her best friend's expression of concern reflected Emily's own feelings.

"Now what?" Lucy asked.

Emily looked down at the ledger. A neat column of check marks indicated that each child had been picked up. All except for the lone entry near the top of one page, the entry with no last name. With no family information, they had no way of contacting the mother or any other relatives. A knot formed in the pit of Emily's stomach.

She stared back at Lucy. "I have no idea. I don't think this has ever happened before. I know it hasn't since you and I have been here, at any rate." She fixed her gaze on the ledger as if it could give her the answers she sought.

What could have happened? Not all parents were prompt about picking up their children. With some it might be attributed to inattention to the time, although most were simply overly optimistic about how long it would take to see as much of the fair as they wanted. But never in Emily's experience had there been anyone who just didn't bother to show up.

Adam snuggled closer against her and laid his head on her shoulder. Emily rubbed her cheek against his downy hair.

Then again, his mother hadn't been the one who brought him in. Perhaps she didn't know where to look for him.

No, that didn't make sense. How often had Emily seen parents dash through the front door, frantic with worry, only to slump in relief at learning their child was safe and sound and having a wonderful time with others his own age? Apparently someone had told each of them where to look. What was different in this case?

Emily's heart went out to the absent mother, as well as to the little boy. Could she have come back to the bandstand only to find him gone and spent the rest of the day searching for him? If so, what must be going through her mind right now? And what could Emily and Lucy do to help reconnect mother and son?

"Here comes Miss Strickland," Lucy said suddenly, sounding uncharacteristically relieved to see their supervisor. "We can ask her."

The tip of Miss Strickland's thin nose twitched when she noticed Emily and Lucy still in the building. "Don't think you can win your way back into my good graces by dawdling at your desk past quitting time, Miss Ralston."

Emily drew herself up. "On the contrary, we have a problem."

Miss Strickland's sharp features tightened even more. "Don't just throw out a vague statement—be specific. What sort of problem do you mean?"

At her harsh tone, Adam's eyes grew wide and he shrank back against Emily's shoulder. She pulled him closer to her and stroked his hair. "This little boy's mother hasn't come for him yet."

"Didn't you take down all the information required when you checked him in? That's why we ask for the names and addresses of the parents, so we'll have something to go by in case of an emergency."

Emily bristled at the implication that she hadn't been doing her job thoroughly. "He's the one the Columbian Guard brought in just after lunch, remember?"

The corners of the supervisor's mouth tightened. "Oh dear. Nothing like this has ever happened before." She looked from side to side, as if casting about for an answer. "We've taken him in and given him shelter during the day, but the responsibility of the Children's Building does not extend to offering round-the-clock care."

Emily chose her words carefully, not wanting to lose her temper and risk offending the prickly supervisor. "I understand that, but what should we do?" She saw tears puddling in Adam's eyes and felt her throat grow tight. If she didn't watch out, she would be crying herself, and that wouldn't help the situation a bit.

Lucy stepped up beside Emily and tilted her chin. "We can't very well set him outside on his own after the building is closed."

"Well, hardly!" Miss Strickland responded in a crisp tone. "Leaving children to fend for themselves is not the sort of thing the Children's Building is known for. Use your heads, both of you. There is only one thing to do: Summon the authorities. They'll know how to deal with an abandoned child."

Emily felt her body grow rigid. "Authorities? You mean the police?" At Miss Strickland's nod, she added, "But what will they do with him?"

Miss Strickland sniffed. "They'll send him to an orphan asylum, no doubt. That's what those places are meant for." She looked at the girls' stricken faces and demanded, "What is the matter with you? We can't very well keep him here, can we? The asylum will have staff members who are perfectly capable of caring for the boy. He'll be as safe with them as if he were in his own home. Safer, most likely, seeing that his mother ran off and deserted him."

When neither of the girls moved to comply with her demand, she clapped her hands together sharply. "Don't just sit around like a pair of statues. Do as I say, and be quick about it!"

Lucy and Emily exchanged glances after she stalked off. "We don't have to do it right this minute, do we?" Lucy asked.

Emily shook her head. "Of course not. We can wait a bit longer. We ought to give his mother at least a few more minutes to show up."

The girls watched the minutes tick by. Emily continued to cuddle the boy, all the while wondering where on earth his mother could be.

Lucy finally broke the tense silence. "Miss Strickland will be back here any minute. We have to do something."

Adam sniffled and wrapped his arms around Emily's neck. "Don't want to go away. Want to stay with you."

Emily held him close and looked at Lucy, feeling utterly helpless. "We can't send him off like that, not to one of those places."

Lucy shook her head slowly. "No, but what else can we do?"

Emily looked to make sure none of the staff were nearby and lowered her voice to a whisper. "We can take him home with us."

"To our boardinghouse?" Lucy's tone betrayed her skepticism.

"He won't be a bother." Emily looked at the sweet face staring up at her and felt the little boy's trust wind its way around her heart. "Look at him, Lucy. Knowing what those places are like, is there any way you can send him to one of them?"

Lucy looked doubtful. "I guess it won't cause any problems."

"Of course not," Emily said with an assurance she didn't feel. She looked down at the little boy cradled in her arms, and her heart knew she was doing the right thing, even though her mind told her otherwise. This child had already been abandoned once today. She couldn't bear the thought of doing it to him again.

Gently she slid the boy from her lap and stood him in front of her so she could look into his face. "It doesn't look like your mama is going to be back right away. Would you like to go home with Miss Lucy and me?"

Adam gave her a long, searching look and then nodded.

"All right." Emily stood up and smoothed her skirt. "Now that we're all agreed, how will we manage it?"

With their decision made, Lucy seemed set for action. "I'm ready to leave. I only have to sign out." She scrawled her name on the time sheet on Emily's desk and grabbed her hat from the hat rack.

Emily retrieved her reticule from her desk drawer and pulled her straw boater from its hook, realizing as she did so the gravity of what they were about to do. She fumbled with the hat pins until she had anchored the boater firmly upon her head.

Drawing a deep breath, she took Adam by the hand and moved to the door. She had her hand on the doorknob when Miss Strickland's strident voice carried from the next hallway.

"Are you still here, Miss Welch?"

"Emily and I are just leaving," Lucy called. She reached around Emily and yanked the door open then shoved Emily and Adam outside onto the pavement. She pulled the door back toward her to screen the two of them from view.

Emily could hear Miss Strickland's voice growing closer. "Did you deal with that abandoned child as I told you to?"

"It's all taken care of," Lucy called. "He just left. We'll see you in the morning." She pulled the door closed behind her and met Emily's gaze. "What?"

"How could you say that? I never intended to lie to her."

Lucy shrugged and pulled Emily and Adam along with her, past the wooden chairs lining the walk outside the front entrance and across the walkway that ran along the south side of the Woman's Building. "It wasn't a lie—not exactly, anyway." When Emily didn't respond, she jutted out her chin and added, "It is all taken care of, isn't it? And he did just leave the building, didn't he?"

CHAPTER 3

Y ou're late." Ian McGinty looked up at the two men framed
in his office doorway. "I expected you hours ago."

The taller of the two shut the sturdy door behind
them, and the pair swaggered across the floor, closing the space
between them and his desk with a leisurely gait.

McGinty clenched his teeth and felt his jaw throb. Idiots, both
of them. The quality of his subordinates needed improvement, no
doubt about it.

"I take it that means you got what I sent you for?" With an
effort, he kept his voice even. He hated having to associate with
this sort of riffraff.

He eyed their smug faces. Too full of themselves by far. They
had no idea how brainless they really were. But putting intelligent,
ambitious men into a subordinate position only meant trouble.
Men with any more brains than these two would soon be scheming
to find some way to take over his operation.

The taller one, wearing a jacket that seemed too small to contain his broad shoulders, chewed on a matchstick and parked himself on the corner of McGinty's desk.

"We found her." The match bobbed in the corner of his mouth when he spoke.

McGinty leveled a stare at the man, who eased himself off the desk and shuffled his feet.

McGinty nodded. "Go on."

Seeming to notice his employer's chilly demeanor for the first time since entering the room, the big man cast a nervous look at his friend, who cleared his throat and took up the tale.

"Like Flynn said, we found her. The house was empty when we got there, but that kid you have keeping an eye on her told us he saw her heading toward the fairgrounds. We caught up with her there."

The duo's obvious pride in their accomplishment sent a wave of cold anger flooding through McGinty. "On the fairgrounds?" He maintained his even tone with an effort. "With thousands of people around?"

The smaller man's head bobbed like a cork in the water. "And let me tell you, it took us awhile to find her in that crowd. That's partly why we're behind schedule."

"I'm the one who spotted her." Flynn puffed out his chest, stretching his jacket tight across his broad frame. Me and Mort split up—"

"That was my idea," Mort put in.

"—and followed her when she took off."

"Took off?" The muscles in McGinty's jaw tightened. He could feel a vein in his temple start to throb. "And why would she do that?"

Flynn shrugged. "She must've seen me just before I spotted her."

"That's the beauty of my plan," Mort bragged. "With Flynn so much taller than most people in the crowd, she focused on him. She had no idea we were both after her."

The throbbing in McGinty's temple intensified. "So she ran. And you both went chasing after her, in full view of all those people." He made it a statement, not a question. As thickheaded as these two dolts were, he had no doubt they had done exactly that.

"No, boss, it wasn't like that." Flynn hastened to set the story straight. "Neither one of us was running. We just followed along in the direction she was going and kept her in sight."

Mort chuckled. "She kept looking over her shoulder to see where Flynn was. With her distracted like that, it let me get up close to her before she even knew I was there. We were out of sight of everyone when we grabbed her."

McGinty waited, but the storytellers seemed to have reached a stopping point. He looked at each man in turn. "So where is she now? Why didn't you bring her back with you?"

Flynn shuffled his feet again. "That's where things went a little different than we'd planned."

Bile rose in McGinty's throat. "You didn't let her get away. . ." What irony to think that after all his well-laid plans, his empire might be toppled because of one fool woman.

And these two incompetents.

"No, no." Mort's pride was obvious. "She isn't going anywhere, boss, no worries about that. After she spotted Flynn, she headed out to the Midway. My guess is she thought she could lose him and slip out one of the exits." ·

He snickered. "It didn't quite work out that way. By the time she noticed me, she'd just passed the Japanese Bazaar. We cornered her back by the fence; then one of us got on either side of her and held her arms good and tight."

McGinty's hands knotted into fists. "She didn't scream?"

"She looked like she was goin' to, but when Flynn squeezed her arm again, she changed her mind. Even if she had, there's so much noise going on back there on the Midway no one would have noticed."

A smug look crossed Mort's face; then he took up the tale again. "Flynn saw a storage building off to one side, so we ducked in there when no one was watching. I held on to her while Flynn blocked the door."

The big man rolled his shoulders and grinned. "Yeah, she settled down right away after that."

"We asked her whether she was carrying something that didn't belong to her," Mort said. "She told us she didn't know what we were talking about."

"Get to the point." McGinty's voice cut like a lash. "Did she have it, or didn't she? And where is she now?"

Flynn shrugged. "She's dead."

McGinty bolted straight up from his chair then lowered himself back into it, feeling as though all of the wind had gone out of his sails. "What happened?"

Mort glanced at McGinty then lowered his gaze to the floor. "Well, Flynn moved away from the door—"

"To help him make her talk."

"—and that's when she made a break for it. She took off for the door like a scared rabbit. Flynn grabbed her, and a couple of seconds later, she went limp."

Flynn spread his hands wide. "I don't know how it happened, boss. She was fighting me like a wildcat, but I didn't hit her or nothing."

McGinty pressed his palms flat on the surface of his desk.

"You're sure she's dead?"

Mort nodded. "Absolutely."

"And what about the papers I sent you to look for?"

Flynn shook his head. "Nothin' in her bag, and she didn't have them on her, either. We checked." He and Mort exchanged quick grins; then he looked back at McGinty. Flynn's face paled, and the grin melted from his face. He cleared his throat. "She didn't have them, boss. We made sure of it."

McGinty paused before he spoke, letting the silence drag out until the tension in the room reached a palpable level. "Why are you so late getting back?"

"We heard people moving around outside the storage shed." Mort eyed him carefully as he spoke. "We had to lay low until it was clear."

Flynn nodded violently, as if eager to make amends. "Then we took the long way back here. We wanted to make sure nobody followed us, just in case."

McGinty left them sweating through another long silence while he mulled the situation over. He was reasonably sure she had taken the papers, but he couldn't be positive. If she did have them and had hidden them, there was a chance they would never turn up. But he couldn't be certain of that.

So what was his next move? Shut down the operation and move on? No, the business he had spent years building up was far too lucrative to throw it all away on the possibility of one woman's treason. She may or may not have been a threat. He'd never been quite sure. But threat or not, she was gone now, and. . .

He looked up at the nervous pair. "Where's the boy?"

The two of them exchanged blank looks.

McGinty planted his hands on his desk and rose to face them. Mort took a quick step away from the desk and raised both hands in front of him. "You sent us after the woman. No one said anything about a kid."

McGinty flexed his fingers and watched the small man dance another step backward. "She has a child, you cretins." He'd had enough of holding back his anger. His head felt as if it were ready to explode. He opened his mouth and let out a roar that rattled the panes in the windows: *"Where's the boy?"*

Emily and Lucy, with Adam between them, hurried past the Woman's Building and pushed their way through the crowds heading for the Midway as they pressed on toward their goal, the Fifty-ninth Street exit. Even in the early evening, throngs of people still poured in through the turnstiles, making the foot traffic more like a logjam.

Emily clung tightly to Adam's hand, fearful she might lose him in the crush and knowing how horrible it would be for him to be alone on the fairgrounds twice in one day. As if feeling her anxiety, Adam tightened his grip on her fingers, and his steps lagged.

Emily looked down at him, concerned he might be frightened at the prospect of going off with two strange women, but the look on his face was one of exhaustion, not rebellion. She stopped long enough to pick him up; then she went back to shouldering her way through the mob in Lucy's wake.

A family burst through the nearest turnstile and stopped squarely in front of her.

"I want to see the displays first," the mother announced.

A young boy with an eager expression on his face protested, "Come on, Ma. The Ferris wheel is right down there." He pointed toward the Midway, where the giant wheel loomed high above the grounds. "Can't we do that first?"

The pretty matron hesitated and looked up at her husband, who smiled. "Shall we?"

"I guess it would give us a chance to get a good view of the way the fair is laid out," she said. Without waiting to hear more, the children set off ahead of their parents, shrieking gleefully.

Lucy leaned over and shouted to be heard above the din. "That would be fun, wouldn't it? We'll have to try that on one of our days off."

Emily eyed her friend. In contrast to her own feeling of imminent doom, Lucy seemed perfectly cheerful, as though they were taking part in some adventurous game.

But it wasn't a game. Emily found it hard to push down her increasing sense of panic.

What were they doing? Adam didn't belong to them, and they had no right to take him along with them. What if his mother showed up at the Children's Building before Miss Strickland left and was told her son had been turned over to the Chicago police? Emily glanced over her shoulder, wondering what would happen if the woman suddenly appeared and accused them of abducting her child.

Near the gate, they joined the line getting ready to push through the exit. Emily let her steps lag.

Lucy turned around, a frown creasing her forehead. "What's wrong?"

Emily hitched Adam up higher on her shoulder. "I'm not sure we've thought this through. What do you think will happen when his mother returns and is directed to the police and finds out they've never heard of Adam? We could lose our jobs for doing this."

Lucy tugged at Emily's sleeve, drawing her out of the swirl of activity until they reached an island of relative quiet. "But that isn't the way it's going to happen. You'll be up at the reception desk tomorrow morning, as usual. When his mother comes looking for him, you'll just tell her he's perfectly safe, right there in the building. She'll be so grateful she'll never think to wonder where he spent his time when the building was closed."

Lucy grinned at Adam, who gave her a sleepy smile in return. "Besides, think what he's already been through. Which is more important, following Miss Strickland's orders or protecting him from even more upheaval?"

It sounded logical enough. Emily had vivid memories of her first day at the children's home and wouldn't wish that experience on any child, certainly not one as sweet as Adam. And she couldn't deny that she and Lucy had done their share of bending the rules at the Collier Home. But then, the prospect of getting caught meant a demerit or reprimand, nothing more. In their current situation, the consequences would be far more severe.

What had they let themselves in for? Miss Pierce, the head matron, always warned her about her tendency toward impulsive behavior. Had she or Lucy considered the consequences of their actions before committing to this foolhardy plan? Hardly.

Lucy tugged at her arm again, this time urging Emily toward the exit. "Come on. We don't want to be late for supper."

Emily wavered then followed her out the gate, feeling as though she had just crossed an invisible line. There would be no turning back now.

They walked on, parallel to the fence that separated the Midway from Fifty-ninth Street. "Keep your chin up," Lucy admonished. "You'll feel better once we get back to the boarding-house and have a hot meal. After we put Adam to bed, we can talk about it more, if you still want to."

Emily nodded wearily. "That sounds like a good—" She

stumbled to a stop and stared at Lucy. "What are we going to tell our landlady?"

Lucy blinked twice then looked off into the distance. From the years they'd known each other, Emily recognized the signs of a maneuver to gain time for Lucy to think up a plausible answer. "I'm sure she won't mind."

Emily knew false bravado when she heard it. She shifted Adam to her other arm. "Mrs. Purvis may be a little eccentric, but don't you think she'll notice a new arrival? I'm not so sure this is a good idea, Lucy. Maybe we should go back to the Children's Building now and—"

"And what? Tell Miss Strickland we didn't do exactly as she said? Can you imagine what she would do? We wouldn't have jobs to go back to tomorrow morning." She paused a moment to let the implications of that sink in. "Besides, she's probably already left for the night. We really don't have any choice now." She nudged Emily's elbow, and they started walking again.

"She'll know he isn't ours. How, exactly, are we going to explain him? And what if she tells us to leave?" Emily could hear the note of panic in her own voice. "Do you want to risk winding up in a place where the landlord expects more than just rent from us in order to let us stay there?" She had heard all too many stories about the risks of young girls making their own way in the world.

Emily could tell by the look on Lucy's face that her friend didn't want to face that possibility any more than she did. They trudged along a few moments in silence. Adam's head drooped onto Emily's shoulder. Fine wisps of his hair tickled her neck, and she reached up with her free hand to smooth them down.

Lucy's face cleared. "We'll tell her just what happened—most of it, anyway. His mother didn't return to pick him up, and he's staying with us until tomorrow. Surely she won't turn us out of her house for that. It isn't like it would be an inconvenience for anyone. After all, we're the only boarders she has right now."

Emily shot a glance over her shoulder but didn't see an irate mother in hot pursuit. Her mind raced madly for a better way to explain Adam's sudden appearance to Mrs. Purvis, but she came up with nothing. "I guess that's all we can do. We'll tell her the truth and hope for the best."

Emily's jitters hadn't subsided by the time they reached the boardinghouse on South Blackstone Avenue. After carrying Adam most of the way, her arms felt as if they were about to fall off.

"Open the door," she ordered Lucy in a tense whisper. "He's almost asleep. If I can get him upstairs to my room, I can lay him on the bed. If Mrs. Purvis doesn't see him right away, it will give us more time to decide how to break this to her."

Yet another question popped into her mind: Where was Adam going to sleep? Emily sighed. It was one more thing she hadn't thought about before she proposed this harebrained scheme. She waited for Lucy to swing the door open wide then stepped inside the entry hall. Lucy followed and started to pull the door closed, but a gust of wind caught it and slammed it shut.

"Is that you, girls?" The cheery voice came from the direction of the kitchen.

Emily gasped and carried Adam toward the foot of the stairs, but not quickly enough.

A bright-eyed woman of middle age bustled to the entry hall, her cheeks flushed and rosy. "The biscuits are done to a turn, and I'm just ready to take the chicken out of the— Why, who's this little mite?"

Taken completely off guard, Emily stared at Lucy, who stared back. She started to speak, but the explanation stuck in her throat.

Their lack of a response didn't seem to bother Mrs. Purvis in the least. She walked toward Emily and beamed at the sleepy youngster in her arms. "Well, well, aren't you a handsome young gentleman?"

Adam's eyes blinked open; then he stuck one of his fingers in his mouth and smiled around it.

"What a little charmer!" Mrs. Purvis exclaimed. "Is he staying for supper?"

Still unable to form any words, Emily could only nod. Lucy moved next to her. "Actually, he'll be staying for the night."

"If that's all right with you," Emily added quickly.

"No one came to pick him up at the Children's Building, and—"

"And you could hardly leave him there, could you?" Mrs. Purvis patted Adam on the head then headed back toward the kitchen. "I'll just set one more place at the table."

A broad smile spread over Lucy's face. "That went well, didn't it?"

Emily gritted her teeth at her friend's incurable optimism and started toward the stairs again. When she reached the bottom step, Adam squirmed to get down.

Emily set him on the first step and rubbed her weary arms. She led Adam upstairs to wash up for supper, grateful for the momentary reprieve but knowing she couldn't expect the rest of the evening to go as smoothly.

Much to her surprise, it did. Mrs. Purvis was full of information and prattled away about a new family moving in down the street. Thankful to find the conversation focused on any topic but their current situation, Emily nodded encouragement while she cut Adam's serving of chicken into bites small enough for him to manage. He ate his chicken and half a biscuit with gusto before his eyelids began to droop again. Finally he laid his head on the table next to his plate and fell asleep with the rest of the biscuit clutched in his dimpled fist.

"I suppose I ought to take him up to bed now." A wave of exhaustion swept over Emily at the knowledge she still had to figure out the accommodations for her little visitor.

Mrs. Purvis hopped up from her chair. "Go on upstairs, dear. I'll fetch some blankets and fix him a pallet on the floor."

By the time all was said and done, the landlady not only had made up a temporary bed for Adam but had helped Emily get the sleepy child out of his clothes and into the camisole Emily decided to use as an improvised nightshirt.

"It's a little big," Emily said doubtfully.

Mrs. Purvis shook her head. "It will do for tonight. He's so tired he won't be bothered by that at all." She grabbed hold of the end of Emily's bed to pull herself to her feet and started toward the door. "Are you coming back down?"

"In a little while. I want to make sure he's asleep first." Emily pulled a small rocking chair close beside the pallet and watched the little boy's chest rise and fall in a gentle rhythm. She reached down to push the pale hair off his forehead.

Was this what it would be like in a normal family, with the mother keeping a nighttime vigil at her child's bedside?

Adam whimpered in his sleep, and Emily patted him gently until he quieted.

He had a mother and a family of his own, she reminded herself. What was she thinking, to take him off like this? This was hardly helping his mother find him.

But what was the alternative? Emily remembered Miss

Strickland's pinched face and her thin lips snapping out the words, "Call the authorities."

She shuddered, feeling surer about her decision. Like it or not, God had brought him into her life. Turn this precious child over to uncaring strangers to be placed in a foundling home?

Never in her life!

CHAPTER 4

Y"ou'll go in first?" Emily stood to one side of the door to the Children's Building, keeping Adam close beside her.

Lucy nodded. "Just as we planned. I'll go find Miss Strickland and keep her occupied while you check Adam in and take him upstairs to the kindergarten."

Acid touched the back of Emily's throat. "I can't believe we're doing this. I have a feeling it's only going to get worse."

Lucy made an impatient gesture. "You worry too much. All we have to do is get him inside and wait for his mother to come claim him."

Emily helped Adam into one of the wooden chairs that lined the walk on each side of the entrance and pulled Lucy a short distance away. "How can you be so sure she is going to show up? It doesn't make any sense that she would leave him overnight and then come back the next morning."

"Maybe she was taken ill and expected someone else to come

get him, but they didn't follow through. Today someone in his family will come looking for him." She gestured toward the little boy. "Just look at him. No one would go off and abandon a sweet child like that. His clothes are clean and in good condition. You can tell just by looking at him that he's loved very much."

Despite Lucy's admonition, Emily couldn't shake free worry's grip. "And what happens when Miss Strickland sees him here after you led her to believe he'd been turned over to the authorities?"

Lucy shrugged. "You know what Miss Strickland is like—she's more concerned with keeping things running smoothly to make herself look good to the fair administrators than with paying attention to the children themselves. She probably forgot what he looked like two minutes after she left. We get a lot of children who come back several days in a row while their parents make a leisurely tour of the fair. If she notices him at all, she'll just think he's one of them."

Emily nodded, though inside she wasn't so sure. "I guess we don't have much choice, do we? All right, go ahead."

Lucy slipped inside the building, and Emily caught the door before it could swing shut completely. She leaned forward and peered through the narrow crack, watching while Lucy circled the courtyard, checking one corridor after another. At the third hallway, she stopped and gave Emily their prearranged signal.

Emily took Adam by the hand and hurried him through the open court and up the stairs to the room at the southwest corner of the second floor. "Adam is here again," she announced.

Iris Hunter looked up. "I'm surprised to see you instead of Lucy."

Emily cast about for an answer that would satisfy the other woman and still remain within the bounds of truthfulness. "She had to attend to something. I told her I would bring Adam up here."

Iris smiled and held out her hand. "Good morning, Adam. I'm glad to see you again." She looked back at Emily. "Will he be coming here for an extended period?"

"I don't know. I guess we'll just have to take it day by day." While Iris got Adam involved with a toy train, Emily dashed back down the stairs to the reception area.

Safely seated at her desk, she entered Adam's first name in the ledger then paused. What if Miss Strickland made one of her impromptu examinations of the book? She would certainly notice a child with only one name.

Emily thought a minute then added "Bentley" to his entry. She tucked the ticket inside her reticule, relieved to have averted that potential avenue of discovery. She couldn't shake the feeling of skating on dangerously thin ice, but if she continued to be careful, maybe she and Lucy wouldn't be caught.

The front door opened to admit a family with six little girls, and soon Emily found herself too caught up in her daily routine to worry about a catastrophe that hadn't materialized yet.

Before she knew it, the morning had passed. Lucy stopped at her desk with the string of her reticule looped over her arm. "Are you ready to go to lunch?"

Emily shook her head. "There's no one to relieve me right now. You go on ahead. I'll just have to take my break late again today."

Lucy pulled a long face. "All right. I'll bring you one of those hamburger sandwiches, just in case you aren't able to get away at all."

Emily smiled her thanks then turned to greet a young couple bringing in a baby.

"Are you sure, Albert?" the young mother asked. "I don't know about leaving him with strangers."

Her husband looked embarrassed. "It will be a chance for a day all to ourselves. We haven't had one in months." He reached for the baby, but his wife held the infant tight in her arms.

Emily rose and came out from behind her desk. "Ma'am, you may leave your baby here with perfect confidence. Our staff is carefully selected and highly trained. Would you like to see our crèche?" She led the couple to a set of glass doors where they could see a roomful of infants in the charge of sweet-faced nurses wearing snowy caps and aprons.

The woman watched for a few moments; then she relaxed visibly. "It would be good to have a day without any responsibilities." Her wistful tone of voice was unmistakable. She turned to her husband. "If you're certain. . ."

A few moments later, Emily had entered the child's information and handed the parents their ticket, assuring the nervous young mother once more that their little son would be happy and healthy when they returned to pick him up. The baby's father gave her a grateful look as he ushered his wife out the door.

Emily knew that when they returned, they would find their baby happy and content and themselves rested after a carefree time together. She felt privileged to be part of such a fine undertaking. Conceived as the brainchild of the Board of Lady Managers, this was no mere "hat check for children," as some dubbed the child care offered at the Paris Exposition of 1889, but a showcase of the most modern child-rearing methods available.

Her stomach growled. Emily pressed her hand against her waist, suddenly feeling ravenous. Checking to make sure no one else was around, she bent over to open the bottom desk drawer where she had stashed Raymond Simmons's bag of caramels. The candies were no substitute for a square meal, but at least they would help stave off her hunger pangs until she was able to take her break.

Pulling one from the bag, she popped it into her mouth and sank her teeth into the chewy morsel. *Mmm.* The sweet, creamy flavor was just the thing to assuage her appetite. She closed the bag and was in the act of returning it to the drawer when she heard the front door open.

Oh no! Emily stayed bent over in her chair and chewed frantically, hoping to reduce the gooey mass to a size she could swallow without choking. She heard the sound of footsteps crossing the floor, growing nearer, coming to a stop on the other side of her desk.

"Miss Ralston?" The deep voice held a note of concern.

Emily jerked upright and looked straight into the dark brown eyes of the guard who had brought Adam to the Children's Building the day before. Her heart stopped; then it started racing madly. Had they already found out about her and Lucy's subterfuge? Had he come to arrest her?

She gulped involuntarily, squeezing the caramel down into her throat. She opened her mouth to make a reply, but all she could manage was a strangled gurgle.

The merry light in the guard's eyes dimmed. He leaned over the desk, a worried frown knitting his brows. "Are you all right?"

Emily could do no more than nod while the sticky wad of caramel worked its way down her throat at a snail's pace. Once she could draw a breath, she gulped for air and tried again. "I'm fine, thank you." The words came out in a high-pitched squeak.

She watched the corners of his mustache tilt upward slightly. Her cheeks grew warm, and she knew her face must be turning a shade of red dark enough to match her hair. She cleared her throat.

"I'm fine." It sounded better that time. Emily squared her shoulders and tried to put on an air of unruffled calm, hoping to present a demeanor far different from that of someone who, less than twenty-four hours earlier, had absconded with a child who didn't belong to her. "How may I help you?" Thoughts raced through her head behind what she hoped was a mask of serene respectability. Did they know? Why else would he be here?

The guard smiled and looked straight into her eyes. Emily's knees went weak, and she felt grateful to be sitting down. Facing one of the fair's law enforcement officers for the first time since the previous day's escapade, all she needed was for her legs to give way and let her crumple into a heap on the floor. She might just as well confess the whole thing now and get it over with.

Instead, she maintained her smile and waited for him to speak, wishing her heart would slow its pace so she could catch her breath.

"I was working in this area of the fairgrounds today," he said in that deep voice that sent a tremor rippling through her limbs. "I thought I would stop in and find out what happened to the little boy I brought in yesterday."

Rather than slowing down, Emily's heart picked up speed until it bounded like a racehorse galloping down the final stretch toward the finish line. Was this a casual inquiry on his part or a carefully worded question designed to trap her into admitting what she and Lucy had done? She looked down at her desk to hide her confusion and found inspiration there.

"Let me check the ledger." She leafed back through the pages, running her finger down each column of names to give herself a moment to frame an answer that wouldn't be an outright lie. "His name was Adam, wasn't it?"

"How many lost children were turned in yesterday?"

Emily heard the rumble of laughter in his voice and looked up, startled. Once again, heat flooded her face. "Actually, he was the only one."

The guard smiled. Emily could see the hint of a dimple near the left corner of his mouth, where it wasn't completely covered up by the mustache.

"So you do remember him." His eyes still shone with good humor. "Did he have to wait here long before his mother came back to pick him up?"

Emily scrambled for an answer, reminding herself of the need for caution. He might have been one of the handsomest men she'd ever laid eyes on, but he was also a Columbian Guard, one of the authorities whose duty would be to see Adam placed in a foundling home if he ever learned the truth.

She sat up straighter and fixed a bright smile on her face. "Thank you for checking. Everything turned out all right—he left late yesterday afternoon." There. That wasn't exactly a lie, not really. Emily flinched inwardly when she remembered her response to Lucy's similar statement the day before.

A crease formed between the guard's dark eyebrows. "It took her that long to come for him? I wish I'd gotten a chance to talk to her. Did she give any explanation for running off and leaving him the way she did?"

"We, uh, didn't question her." The answer popped out without conscious planning on Emily's part. Her stomach knotted. Though technically true, the statement was intended to mislead. It seemed as though this sort of misdirection came more easily every time she opened her mouth. How had she become so adept at lying?

The guard nodded, evidently accepting her answer. Emily kept the smile plastered on her face, wondering when he would leave.

Instead, he cleared his throat and glanced around the building then looked back at her. "You gave me your name yesterday, but I didn't tell you mine. My mother would call that a deplorable breach of etiquette. I'm is Stephen Bridger."

The sudden shift to personal topics took Emily off guard. She extended her hand, and her smile was genuine this time. "I'm happy to meet you, Mr. Bridger. And I won't tell your mother."

Stephen Bridger laughed, and Emily joined in, as if they shared a delightful secret.

"Do you enjoy working with the children here?"

"Yes, I do." Emily's relief at the change of direction knew no bounds. "Since I check them all in and out, I don't spend as much time with each of them as the others who work in the crèche or the kindergarten, but it makes me feel good to know I'm part of a program that keeps them happy and safe while their parents are gone."

Struck by a sudden inspiration, she gestured toward the glass doors. "Would you like to see the babies in the crèche?"

She regretted the impulsive question as soon as the words left her lips. What an idiotic thing to ask such a stalwart specimen of masculinity! To her surprise, he stepped toward the doors with apparent eagerness.

Emily glanced around. Seeing no one entering the building to drop off or pick up children, she decided it wouldn't hurt to leave her desk for a few moments. She followed him, watching him observe the children with every appearance of enjoyment.

He pointed to a toddler rolling a ball across the floor. "Look at that little fellow, walking already. His parents must be proud of that one." He smiled at Emily, and her knees threatened to mutiny again.

She reached out to steady herself against the wall. What was it about this man that had such a disconcerting effect on her?

He looked into her eyes, as if totally unaware of the havoc his nearness wreaked on her equilibrium. "I've taken up too much of your time and should be getting back to work myself. I'd better be on my way."

They walked back to the reception area, with Emily praying her legs wouldn't buckle. When they reached her desk, she gripped the back of her chair and watched him continue to the exit. She waited until the door swung shut behind him; then she slumped into her seat. Lucy was right. He was an attractive man, no doubt about it.

Did he experience any of the same tingling sensations she did when he was with her? The question brought her up short. He hadn't come to the building to see her but to check on Adam. She shouldn't try to make any more of his visit than that.

Emily settled down to work again and reached for a sheaf of reports that needed to be filled out before the day was over. She tallied the number of children who had been checked in and out of the Children's Building the day before and listed that on the report, followed by a breakdown of the numbers by age groups.

While part of her mind concentrated on entering the numbers correctly, muddled thoughts raced through the rest of her consciousness. Would she see Stephen Bridger again? Could he feel even a glimmer of the same attraction that took hold of her every time he came near?

And if he did, would he still feel the same way if he knew the truth about Adam?

~

The day settled back into its normal routine. Emily worked on her reports in between greeting parents as they dropped their children off to experience the wonders the Children's Building had to offer and returned hours later to pick them up again.

But in all that time, no one came for Adam.

Near the end of the day, Lucy managed to break away from her other duties to stop by Emily's desk for a whispered conversation. Her blue eyes danced in that mischievous way Emily knew so well. "You won't believe what just happened."

Emily raised her eyebrows and waited.

Lucy leaned closer. "Miss Strickland just spoke to Adam."

Every muscle in Emily's body tightened. She swiveled around to look behind her, expecting the supervisor to round the corner and descend upon them at any moment. When Miss Strickland didn't appear, she turned back to Lucy. "What do you mean? Do we still have our jobs?"

"You should have seen it. She didn't connect him with yesterday's lost boy at all." Lucy covered her mouth with her hand to stifle her giggles. "She was taking a group of dignitaries on a tour of the building and stopped to show them the kindergarten. She called Adam over to her and asked whether he was enjoying his time here."

Emily's heart pounded so hard that she could hear the rush of blood in her ears. "What did he say?"

Lucy laughed out loud then muffled the sound with her hand. "Our perfect little gentleman? He nodded very politely and said, 'Yes, ma'am.' Then he went back to playing with his toys. Miss Strickland just beamed and told the group it showed what a good job the Children's Building is doing."

Emily gasped. "That's all?"

Lucy nodded, and her grin widened. "I told you she wouldn't recognize him. If she sees him here again, she'll only remember him as the boy who made her look good."

Relief flooded Emily. She laughed aloud then quickly sobered. "And she may very well see him again. Do you realize it's almost closing time, and no one has come for him?"

Worry colored her voice. "Something is dreadfully wrong, Lucy. That boy has a family. He has been well cared for and raised to be a little gentleman. No one would just go off and abandon him like that. Maybe we should have followed Miss Strickland's orders and—"

"You know we couldn't have done that."

"But we can't just keep taking him home with us day after day. His family must be looking for him. How are we ever going to get them back together?"

Lucy waved her hand as if brushing away a fly. "That's something we'll have to figure out later. We have no choice but to take him home with us again tonight. Right now, our goal is to get him out of here sight unseen. I'll go get him."

"What about Miss Strickland?" Emily could feel all her uneasiness return.

"That shouldn't be a problem. I expect she's still preening in front of all those dignitaries. But I'll hurry just in case she decides to lead them through here."

She was back in a moment with Adam in tow. The girls gathered their things and slipped out the front door without attracting anyone's attention.

Emily drew in a deep breath of moist air. They had managed to elude detection again. How many more times could they expect to get away with it before discovery brought judgment crashing down upon their heads?

She bent down to place herself at Adam's eye level. "Did you have a good time today?"

He nodded enthusiastically. "We made people."

"Iris Hunter let them play with modeling clay," Lucy translated.

Emily grinned and ruffled the boy's hair; then she took a moment to straighten his collar.

Lucy tapped her on the shoulder. "Look over there."

Distracted by the collar, whose corners insisted on turning up instead of lying flat, Emily barely paid attention. She smoothed the collar into place then stood next to Lucy. "What? Where?"

Lucy pointed toward the walkway that skirted the lagoon in front of the Woman's Building. "Over there. The man in the navy suit walking this way. He almost looks like your Columbian Guard."

Emily craned her neck, trying to spot him through the heads of the crowd. "His name is Stephen Bridger, and he isn't 'my' Columbian Guard."

When she caught sight of the man, she drew in her breath sharply. She took hold of Lucy's arm in a grip that made her friend wince. "That isn't almost like him. That *is* Mr. Bridger."

Lucy grinned. "He may not be your guard yet, but I'd say he's certainly interested in you. Exciting, isn't it?"

"Exciting?" Emily's voice grew shrill. "Lucy, are you out of your mind? What do you think he's going to say when he sees. . ." She trailed off and pointed at Adam.

Lucy followed her gesture. "Oh."

Emily grabbed Lucy's elbow again and maneuvered her so she was standing between Adam and the oncoming guard. Such a little boy would be hard to see behind all those passersby, but she couldn't afford to take any chances. If only they could manage to get away without attracting Mr. Bridger's attention.

"He's coming this way!" Lucy wore a look of irrepressible triumph. "I told you he's interested in you. He probably wants to talk to you without worrying about interrupting your work."

At that moment, Stephen Bridger spotted Emily and waved.

Emily's mind whirled. He had seen her. There was no point in her trying to evade him now. What if they walked quickly in the opposite direction? No, that wouldn't work. If Lucy was right and he wanted to talk to her, he would follow them. He hadn't shown any indication that he'd seen Adam, but once he reached them, discovery would be imminent. Unless. . .

She whirled toward Lucy. "You have to get out of here. Both of you."

Lucy's jaw sagged. "What do you want me to do?"

"I don't know." Emily flapped her hands at her friend like a farmer's wife shooing a chicken. "Just take Adam someplace where you'll both be out of sight until I can get away. I'm sure it won't take long."

"All right." Lucy looked from side to side. "But where?"

Emily watched as Stephen Bridger neared the south corner of the Woman's Building. They only had a few seconds to make this work. "Duck around the back of the Woman's Building and head for the Midway. There are tons of people milling around there."

She urged Lucy on her way with a series of little nudges. "Hurry. I'll walk over to meet him and hope he doesn't notice you."

CHAPTER 5

The milling crowd of fairgoers made it difficult to see clearly. Stephen watched Emily turn to speak to a blond girl he remembered seeing at the Children's Building the day before. Was she planning to hurry away before he got there?

And could he blame her if she did? Seeking out a young lady's company so often on such a brief acquaintance was hardly typical of him, but he couldn't expect her to know that.

Was he making a total fool of himself? He had wrestled with that question all day and still wasn't sure of the answer. He had known other girls before, but there was something special about this one, something that made him more concerned about the possibility of losing her than with following the rules of etiquette.

Emily's blond companion turned and headed in the other direction. Stephen held his breath, certain Emily would join her. Then she turned and—wonder of wonders—began walking his way. Stephen quickened his pace, able to breathe again.

She gave him a smile as dazzling as sunlight on the lake. Stephen tipped his bowler. "Good afternoon. I was hoping to catch you before you went home, but I didn't expect the timing to work out so well." He stopped talking, not wanting to seem presumptuous.

Emily fidgeted with the string of her reticule as if waiting for him to continue. That, at least, was encouraging. Hoping his nervousness wouldn't be too obvious, Stephen took a deep breath and plunged in. "Would you care to go for a stroll?"

Emily's eyes flickered to one side before she met his gaze again. "I'm sorry. I'm supposed to be meeting a friend soon. On the Midway." She looked at the watch pinned to the front of her blue cotton blouse. "In just a few minutes."

So she already had plans for the evening. He should have expected that and not assumed she would be free to spend time with him. Still, she hadn't shut him down completely. It wouldn't hurt to try again. "Perhaps another time, then?"

Her smile wavered then held steady. "Yes, perhaps."

The light in her eyes gave him more hope than her lukewarm words. Taking heart, he pressed his advantage while he had an opportunity. "May I escort you to the Midway? We could visit a bit until your friend—"

"Ah, there you are." A slim man about Stephen's age stepped up to Emily, taking no notice whatsoever of Stephen. A summer spent as a guardian of the law allowed Stephen to assess him in a glance, from the polished boots to the natty glen plaid suit to the derby hat tilted at a jaunty angle. He had a pleasant enough face, but something about his demeanor set Stephen's teeth on edge. If he could compare it to appraising the soundness of a building, he would have said the man had a shaky foundation. *I don't even know his name, but already I don't like him.*

But if this was the friend she expected to meet. . .

Stephen cleared his throat, ready to take his leave. He might not think the fellow was good enough for Emily to wipe her dainty shoes upon, but far be it from him to insert himself into a situation where he wasn't welcome.

"Good afternoon, Mr. Simmons." The smile remained on Emily's lips, but the light in her eyes faded, and Stephen noticed a tightness in her voice.

She took one step away from the newcomer and nearer to Stephen. "May I present Mr. Bridger?"

Simmons shot a glance Stephen's way but didn't acknowledge the introduction. Looking back at Emily, he said, "I was hoping you would reconsider our dinner engagement. I'm sure my sister and one of her friends would be happy to go with us. That would ensure the demands of propriety have been met and serve to let you meet some of my family at the same time."

Stephen's stomach tightened. Did the two of them have some sort of understanding? Emily seemed ill at ease in Simmons's presence, but could it be due to some sort of lovers' tiff?

"No, I'm afraid not." Emily held her ground. To Stephen's delight, she moved even closer to him. "In fact, Mr. Bridger was just escorting me toward the Midway."

Simmons took a good look at Stephen for the first time. An image shot into Stephen's mind, that of two dogs circling each other, each gauging the other's weak points. The vision was over in a flash. Simmons straightened the lapels of his jacket. "Don't let me keep you, then. I'll see you later. . .Emily." He stalked away to be swallowed up in the crowd of fairgoers.

Stephen held out his arm, absurdly pleased when she tucked her hand into the crook of his elbow. They walked toward the Midway at a leisurely pace, with Emily keeping silent as if deep in thought and Stephen wondering what he had just witnessed. The possibility of having witnessed a lovers' tiff kept playing through his mind like one of the scenes from Mr. Edison's kinetoscope.

Emily had seemed happy enough to use him as an excuse to send that Simmons fellow on his way, but was Stephen's role that of a welcome rescuer or just a convenient means of escape?

"I hope I wasn't the cause of your changing your plans."

When Emily looked up at him, he could see moisture along her lower lids. She gave him a wobbly smile. "Not at all. You've been a great help, and I'm very grateful to you."

Encouraged, Stephen searched for a suitable topic of conversation. "Do you and your family live in Chicago, or did you come here specifically to work at the fair?"

It seemed a long time before she answered. "I've lived in Chicago all my life."

Stephen thought she was about to say more, but she didn't continue. The crowd grew thicker as they neared the avenue that bisected the mile-long Midway, slowing them down to a snail's pace. Stephen welcomed the delay, glad for every additional moment he could spend with Emily.

In a moment or two, she would be meeting her friend, and any more opportunity to talk would be lost. Stephen gathered up his courage and waited until they walked under the viaduct where the Illinois Central rumbled overhead, making quiet conversation impossible. "I know we've only spoken a couple of times," he began, "but would you think it bold of me if I asked to call on you at home?"

He felt Emily's fingers stiffen on his arm and wondered if he had just ruined his chances by pushing too quickly. Emily ducked her head then looked up at him. "I'm not sure that would work."

His spirits flagged. "I'm sorry. I didn't mean to make you feel uncomfortable."

"It's not that. It's just that. . .I don't have a family, you see. I live in a boardinghouse."

The simple admission touched Stephen's heart. "I think I understand. I wouldn't want to do anything to make you feel like I'm trying to stretch the bounds of propriety. My question about coming to call on you still stands, though. Do you think your landlady would be willing to act as a chaperone?"

Her laugh held a brittle note. "She might be willing to do that; however, you must understand she is a little odd."

Stephen's protective instincts rose to the fore. "In what way? Are you safe there?"

This time her laugh sounded more genuine. "Oh, I feel quite safe. It's just that. . .well, she has her little quirks. Nothing dangerous, you understand, but I'm afraid you might feel ill at ease there."

"If you're comfortable there, I'm sure I can handle a few little quirks." He waited for her response, feeling as though his future happiness was riding on her answer.

Emily looked up at him with an expression he couldn't read. "Let me discuss it with my landlady. I should make certain it's all right with her before I invite a visitor." She looked at a point past his right shoulder and waved. She smiled up at him, a look of relief spreading over her face. "I just saw my friend over there. Thank you so much for escorting me." She withdrew her hand from his arm and hurried away before he could say anything more.

He watched her weave her way through people to join the blond girl he'd seen earlier. The two ducked into the entrance to the Irish Village and disappeared from view.

Now what was that all about? If the two of them had planned to come to the Midway, why had Emily sent her friend off in the first place, instead of walking over together? His first thought, and a pleasing one, was that Emily had sent her friend off so she could talk to him. The idea encouraged him, but a gloomier thought reared its head. If that were the case, why did she cut things short and rush off so quickly at the end?

And how did Simmons fit into all this? Unwillingly he revisited the question: Had he been her knight in shining armor or rather a pawn in some sort of lovers' quarrel?

Emily hurried up to the place where she had spotted Lucy, under an archway beneath a banner reading *"Céad Míle Fáilte."*

Lucy kept her gaze focused over Emily's shoulder. "He's still watching you. Come this way." She pivoted, revealing Adam standing behind her, neatly hidden from the view of anyone on the Midway. Keeping him in front of her, Lucy led Emily farther into the Irish Village. They slipped between two cottages and walked into an open area.

Emily had to force herself not to look back. She concentrated on keeping her pace slow and casual. This had to look like a pair of friends enjoying a happy excursion, not some sort of furtive escape.

"I'm glad you saw me," Lucy told her. "We never talked about how we were going to reconnect once I left. I didn't know how I would ever find you."

"I wasn't sure myself. I had no idea what I might be getting into when he volunteered to walk over here with me. I just kept watching for you, hoping I could spot you before he saw Adam."

Lucy beamed. "And you did." She stopped as if to inspect a display of handmade lace then casually glanced back toward the archway. "He's gone. You can relax."

Emily felt the tension drain from her shoulders.

"So what did he want?"

Emily gave a little shrug, her shoulders tightening again. "I'm not sure. I was afraid at first that he might have some inkling about Adam, but that didn't seem to be the case at all. I think. . ."

Lucy prodded Emily's ribs with her elbow. "Well?"

Emily swallowed hard. "He asked if he could come calling."

Lucy gripped Emily by her arms and bounced up and down like a jack-in-the-box. "I knew it! And he's such a handsome man. Oh, this is so exciting!"

"No, it isn't. Have you forgotten he's a Columbian Guard? I don't dare encourage his attention." But hadn't she done just that by implying he might be able to come calling? What had she been thinking?

"Better him than that awful Raymond Simmons."

The reminder brought Emily up short. "You won't believe this. Guess who came up to us while Stephen and I were talking?"

Lucy gaped at her. "You're joking."

"I wish I were. We hadn't said more than a couple of sentences before Raymond showed up and asked if I'd consider going to dinner with him if he provided a chaperone." She flinched at the memory. "It was so embarrassing, Lucy. He acted as if Stephen wasn't there, even after I introduced them."

Lucy's eyes twinkled. "Stephen, eh? As I recall, you refuse to call Raymond Simmons by his Christian name, even though he has asked you to do so any number of times."

Emily blinked. Stephen's first name had rolled off her tongue so naturally that she hadn't even realized her slip until Lucy mentioned it. For a moment, she allowed herself to think what might have happened if she hadn't nearly been caught trying to smuggle a child off the fairgrounds. "If circumstances were different, he would be walking me to our boardinghouse right now. It's exciting, it's frightening, it's. . . I don't know how to explain it."

Lucy hugged herself and bounced up and down on her toes. "Didn't I tell you? He's interested!"

"But I can't let things go any further right now." Speaking the words brought Emily's rising spirits back to earth with a thud. She pointed to Adam, who stood watching a troupe of Irish dancers. "Not until this is resolved and I'm free to see Stephen without worrying what might happen."

She swallowed the lump in her throat and knelt down to talk to Adam. "What did you and Miss Lucy do while you waited for me?"

Adam popped his finger out of his mouth. "We looked at the castle."

"The Libbey Glass exhibit," Lucy explained.

Emily smiled, remembering the breathtaking Midway exhibit built to resemble a palace. "Anything else?"

The little boy shook his head solemnly. "No. We hided."

Emily shot a questioning glance at Lucy, who told her, "I'd been keeping an eye out for you. I saw you and your guard coming under the viaduct, so we slipped back under the archway and waited. I told Adam it was a game to see if you could find us." She bent down to join Emily at the little boy's eye level. "And she did, didn't she? I told you she was good at playing hide-and-seek."

Adam's rosebud lips curved in a shy smile. He pointed across the busy walkway. "Can we see the animals?"

Emily followed his gesture and saw the building opposite where a caged lion looked down at the crowds from his perch above the doorway and a boldly colored sign invited all and sundry to enjoy the wonders of Hagenbeck's Animal Show. Her heart went out to their young guest. After having his world turned topsy-turvy and being pulled from pillar to post the past couple of days, he deserved a little fun.

She hesitated long enough to glance at her watch again. "I'll tell you what—we're going to be late for dinner if we don't hurry home right now. We don't want to do that to Mrs. Purvis when she's worked so hard to prepare a good meal for us, do we?"

Adam shook his head but looked wistfully toward the animal exhibit.

"I'll do my best to bring you back to see the animals another day. Will that be all right?"

Adam sent one last, longing glance at the garish display; then he nodded. "All right, Miss Em'ly."

Emily scooped him up in her arms and gave him a big hug. Then she set him back on his feet and stood up. "That's a big boy. I'm very proud of you, and so is Miss Lucy. Now let's go see what Mrs. Purvis has fixed for our dinner, shall we?"

Adam nodded eagerly. "Yes. I'm hungry."

CHAPTER 6

S uch a good boy." Mrs. Purvis watched Adam fold his napkin neatly beside his plate.

Emily reached over and tousled his hair. "Yes, he is, isn't he? Somebody has done a good job of teaching him manners."

Mrs. Purvis tilted her head toward the boy, who leaned back in his chair and rubbed his eyes. "Anything new?"

"Nothing." Emily met the landlady's gaze. "I'm really not sure what to do next."

Lucy arranged her fork on the rim of her plate. "I guess we didn't think it through very well."

Her words triggered an onslaught of self-recrimination that Emily had tried to stave off all day. *We didn't think at all, or we wouldn't find ourselves in this mess.* She looked back at Adam, whose head now rested atop his folded napkin. His eyes were closed, and his breathing was steady.

Emily dropped her voice to a whisper, just in case he was still awake enough to attend to her words. "I don't understand. Where's his mother, and why hasn't she—or someone—come for him?"

Lucy scooped the last morsel of apple pie from her plate with her fork and popped it into her mouth. "I thought you liked having him here. He isn't a bit of trouble."

Emily stared at her friend, appalled. "It isn't like we've taken in a stray puppy. He's a person with a family and a home. . . somewhere."

But people came to the fair from the world over. What if his home was hundreds of miles away? How long would it take for other relatives to hear about his mother's disappearance and start searching for Adam? If they didn't expect word from her anytime soon, it might be weeks before they realized she was missing, maybe even after the fair ended. What would be done about reuniting Adam with his family then?

Mrs. Purvis broke into Emily's gloomy thoughts. "You girls did what you thought was best. God hasn't abandoned any of us, least of all that little mite. He knows every hair on our heads, so He's well aware of where Adam comes from and how to get him back together with his family."

Emily looked at her pie and picked up her fork; then she laid it down again, her appetite diminished by worry. "We thought it was best at the time, but was it really? Did we do wrong by not turning him over to the authorities right away?"

An unspoken question lingered in her mind: *How much trouble are we going to get into for what we've done?*

She pushed the thought away, not wanting to dwell on it. She scooted her chair back and lifted Adam into her arms. "I'm going to get you ready for bed, sweetheart," she crooned into his ear. "And we're going to have to do something about getting you some more clothes soon."

Mrs. Purvis smacked the palm of her hand on the table, making Adam flinch in his sleep. "I meant to tell you when you came home. I knew you didn't have any clothes for him, so I talked to that new neighbor down the street. Her boy is just a little older than Adam. Don't worry—I only told her I had a little fellow visiting me who left home unexpectedly and was a little short on clothing. She offered to give me some her son had outgrown." A beatific smile wreathed her face. "Isn't it wonderful how God blesses us?"

She accompanied Emily upstairs, stopping near the top of the landing to tap along the wall in a slow circle. She repeated the performance one step higher. "Do you hear any difference, or do both of those sound the same to you?"

Emily's eyes widened. She and Lucy had whispered and giggled about their landlady's tendency to rap on the walls and baseboards, but up to now, Mrs. Purvis hadn't drawn either of them into this strange preoccupation. She chose her words carefully. "I don't believe I hear a difference. Do you?"

Mrs. Purvis shook her head, looking vaguely disappointed. She left Emily at the door of her room and continued down the hall, returning moments later with a stack of little boys' clothing, which she set at the foot of the bed. "Here you go, and don't you fret. God will sort this out; just you wait and see."

After she left, Emily pondered the likelihood of divine intervention while she helped Adam out of his clothing and into a nightshirt just his size. "Father, I know You have a plan, but I sure wish I knew what it was. We're in a real mess now, and I don't see any way out."

She tucked Adam in and scooted the rocking chair over so she could sit close beside him. Was it really as simple as Mrs. Purvis seemed to think? Emily watched the gentle rise and fall of Adam's chest and continued her conversation with the Lord. "I wanted to do the right thing by protecting him, but I didn't take the time to think first. Can You really straighten all this out after I've tangled it up so badly?"

She squeezed her eyes shut. Hot tears seeped through her closed eyelids and trickled down her cheeks.

Miss Pierce, the matron at the Collier Home, always told her to look on the bright side of things. Was there a bright side to this situation? She tried to think of some assets. Adam was healthy. That was definitely a good thing. And no one, Miss Strickland in particular, had discovered his whereabouts yet.

On the other hand, neither had his family. Emily leaned her head against the back of the chair. What if Adam's relatives were looking for him at this very moment? Could she be keeping this precious child from going back home just because she didn't want to suffer the consequences of her actions?

She pushed the disquieting thought away and forced her attention back to the plus side of the ledger. Mrs. Purvis seemed to think everything would turn out all right, and Mrs. Purvis was a woman of deep faith.

Who went around knocking on walls at every turn.

Emily sighed. Which side of the ledger would that fall on?

By the time Emily went back downstairs, Lucy and Mrs. Purvis had nearly finished washing up the supper dishes. Emily picked up a dish towel and helped dry the remaining plates; then the three women sat down at the kitchen table as if they'd been following the same routine for years.

"We don't normally have children come to the building for more than two or three days at a time," Emily said, as though there had been no interruption in their earlier conversation. "He's been there two days now. What are we going to do when people start asking questions?"

"I can think of a perfectly good answer to that." Mrs. Purvis's eyes sparkled. "You can leave him here with me during the day while you're at work."

"Oh, I wasn't hinting." Emily felt her face flush. "I wouldn't dream of imposing on you."

"It's no imposition at all. He's a lovely little boy, and I'd be glad of the company."

"Well, if you're sure. . ." Emily could hardly contain her relief at the thought of not having to sneak Adam in and out of the Children's Building every day.

"I'm quite sure. It will be good for all of us." The landlady's cheery tone made it obvious she considered the matter settled.

Emily's mouth stretched wide open in an unexpected yawn. She clapped her hand over her mouth, embarrassed. "I guess I'd better go to bed. All the worry seems to be catching up with me." She scooted her chair back from the table and stood.

Lucy looked at her with guileless eyes then turned to Mrs. Purvis. "You've been such a dear to us. You wouldn't mind if someone came calling on Emily, would you?"

"Lucy!" Emily's exhaustion disappeared in an instant.

Lucy gave her a grin, one that meant she wasn't about to be dissuaded from her self-appointed task.

Mrs. Purvis's eyes gleamed. "You have a gentleman friend? I didn't know."

"I don't—"

"Oh, don't be modest," Lucy cut in. "He's interested in you, and you know it. Moreover, you're interested in him, whether you admit it or not."

Emily sank back into her chair, holding her flaming cheeks between her palms.

Mrs. Purvis fluttered like a proud mother hen. "Don't be embarrassed, dear. It's perfectly fine to entrust your little secret to me. As a matter of fact. . ." Her voice trailed off, and she bustled over to one of the cupboards. After rooting around inside it for a moment, she pulled out a piece of paper and pressed it to her bosom as she crossed the kitchen to sit down opposite Emily.

She lifted her head with the air of someone about to make a momentous announcement. "God has blessed me in many ways, even after my dear Randolph passed away. He has given me the means to remain in my own home by taking in boarders, and He put this fair practically in my backyard so I've had a steady stream of them this summer. Along with that, I've discovered a new gift that brings me a great deal of pleasure." She laid the sheet of paper on the table and unfolded it with a flourish. "Look here."

Emily saw a brief notation listing several names, nothing more. She looked up cautiously at her landlady. "I'm not sure I understand."

Mrs. Purvis gave a tinkling laugh. "It's a short list, I'll admit, but it's a beginning. You have to understand what it represents to fully appreciate it." She leaned forward across the table as though she was about to share a delightful secret.

Despite her misgivings, Emily found herself drawn by the older woman's excitement. To her right, Lucy leaned forward, and the three of them huddled together like a group of schoolgirls.

"These young ladies." Mrs. Purvis tapped two of the names on the list. "They both came to stay with me, just as you have done. And while they were here, each of them discovered her true love."

Emily heard a croak and realized it came from her own throat.

A broad grin split Lucy's face. "So you wrote their names down?"

Mrs. Purvis nodded eagerly. "I discovered something wonderful this summer. I've been given a gift, you see, the ability to recognize the potential for young love. This list is a record of my successes so far, and I expect to add to it very soon."

The croak became a gurgle. Emily pushed away from the table. "Maybe having Mr. Bridger come calling is not the best thing to do."

Mrs. Purvis reached up to take her by the hand. "Nonsense. God has given me this ability to know when He is drawing two hearts together. I would be honored to meet your young man and give you my opinion."

"He isn't my young man." The protest sounded weak, even to her own ears.

Lucy clapped her hands. "Oh, go on, Emily. What have you got to lose? The next time he asks to see you, let him know he's welcome here. We'll have a grand time."

Emily turned on her, not bothering to hide her exasperation. "Have you forgotten we have to keep him from seeing Adam?"

"Do it late enough, and Adam will be asleep. That won't be a problem at all." Lucy held up her hands as if she had just made an end to a simple problem.

Mrs. Purvis bobbed her head. "That would be perfect. The little fellow is always nodding off by the time we finish supper, and once he's asleep, he never wakens before morning. It will be an ideal way for you both to get to know each other better in a perfectly respectable setting."

Anticipation warred with anxiety. Emily had a feeling something exciting was about to happen. But would it be a joyful excitement or the kind engendered by a train wreck? She thought about what Lucy had said about it being safe with Adam asleep. That made sense, but she had no idea what she would do with her caller once he arrived.

How should she amuse him? What on earth should she say? She had never been good at the small talk some girls seemed to find so easy. A picture formed in her mind of her and Stephen sitting in the parlor without a word being spoken between them.

But Mrs. Purvis would be there. Maybe she would be able to help keep the conversation moving. Or perhaps she would get up and start tapping along the wall. Emily grinned. It might not be what Stephen expected from the evening, but at least they wouldn't lack for entertainment.

She might as well give in. There would be no living with Lucy until she surrendered. "All right. The next time he asks—if there is a next time—I'll tell him he may call on me here."

Ian McGinty put the finishing touches on the Hanover knot in his tie and studied the effect in the cheval mirror. He pulled it a shade tighter and examined the results with a critical eye, wanting to be sure every detail was correct.

Rosalee should have been here to take care of that for him. How many evenings had begun with him standing in the hallway just inside her front door, with her examining him from head to toe? She had a faultless eye for detail and didn't miss a thing. When he was with Rosalee, he could relax, knowing his appearance was impeccable. Her own appearance would add the finishing touch, making him appear more dashing and debonair than any son of an Irish laborer had a right to look.

Rosalee had never enjoyed their evenings out as much as he did, with her constant fretting about being snubbed by the other women. She couldn't say that about the men, though. They might put on an air of disapproval while their wives were nearby, but he'd seen the looks of admiration—and more—in their eyes whenever Rosalee walked into a room on his arm. He knew every one of them envied him.

But Rosalee wouldn't be on his arm tonight, or ever again. For a moment, the rage that was kindled when he'd learned of her death threatened to envelop him.

Those fools! He should have had them dispatched as soon as they'd admitted their idiotic failure. He still might, once they found the boy. It was one thing to make a calculated decision not to surround himself with people of nearly his own intelligence. With them, he would always have to be on the lookout for the threat of a takeover. But he couldn't have complete idiots, either. All he'd asked for was Rosalee's return, but they couldn't even give him that. He should have taken care of the matter himself.

How had things gone so completely awry? Some of it had to be Rosalee's fault. She should have known his men were under orders to bring her back but not to harm her. His lips tightened. Unless she had some reason to believe returning to him would be the greater risk—in which case, she might have had the evidence, after all.

He picked up a handkerchief she had dropped on her last visit to his home and pressed it under his nose. It still bore the scent he liked, a blend of lavender and roses, almost as if she had used it and left the room moments before. He closed his thick fingers around the delicate cloth and allowed memories of their times together to wash over him. She knew how to listen, Rosalee did. She knew more about him than anyone.

Maybe too much. His hand tightened. He'd never been certain what had happened to those papers Arthur Long tried to use to threaten him. To his knowledge, Rosalee hadn't been around during that conversation. But ever after, her eyes had shadowed at any mention of Long's name. Had she somehow come into possession of those papers and decided to use them to destroy him? Impossible, he would have said, and yet his young informant swore Rosalee had set up a meeting with Gerald Cavender, on the district attorney's staff. Thus Mort and Flynn's mission to intercept her and recover the evidence, if it was in her possession.

But those idiots claimed she didn't have anything like that on her. Which might mean things were even worse than he imagined. Had she passed the information on to someone else? If that was the case. . .

His hands gripped both ends of the handkerchief, rending the fragile fabric in two. If that was the case, it would make her a traitor, and she knew he never suffered betrayal. He cast the fragments of linen aside. Maybe that explained her ill-timed bolt for freedom.

He needed to clear his head, to think things through. He hadn't gotten where he was today by failing to consider a situation from every possible angle. What if she'd passed the information along? Who would she have given it to?

A sudden thought seized him. What if tonight's gathering proved to be a trap? Some of his highborn acquaintances made no secret of their aversion to dealing with someone of his reputation. He turned the notion over in his mind and discarded it. His hostess would never agree to have one of her soirees disrupted by anything so distasteful as an arrest.

He slicked back his hair, checking to be sure the part was exactly straight. It might not hurt to check with one of his connections to see if anyone was talking about him in the district attorney's office. He sorted through a mental list of those likely to be at tonight's party. He could pass along a subtle request to look into it.

Subtlety. That was something those ruffians who'd man-handled Rosalee would never understand.

McGinty looked at his well-appointed bedroom, so different from the warehouse office where men like Mort and Flynn did business with him. He smiled. If a person planned to move in two different circles, he had to have two sets of contacts. And he must remember never to mix the two if he planned to stay out of trouble.

The delicate maneuvering involved reminded him of the steps of a complicated dance, and it was a dance he had followed for a long time. But here a misstep wouldn't just mean a social faux pas; it could spell disaster.

His reputation in Chicago's underworld, carefully forged over the years, was one of ruthless determination that struck fear into the hearts of underlings and any who might cross him. But his wealth meant acceptance by the upper class, those high ranking in business and politics who were key to his security.

He picked up his walking stick and headed for the stairs. If he could find out that nothing was being said, that no whispers of suspicion followed him, he could relax a little. Enough, at least, to allow him to go back to business as usual.

Before he reached the front door, he set his top hat on his head and paused for one last look in the hallway mirror. He swung the door open, pleased to see his carriage waiting at the curb. It took skill and a gift for organization to keep things operating like a well-oiled machine, and he possessed both of those qualities in ample supply.

The driver let him into the carriage and closed the door behind him. McGinty settled back against the plush seat, relaxing as he always did in the carriage's luxurious interior. Not bad for a boy who got his start in the slums of New York, always on the lookout for ways to better his lot. That was why he'd made the move to Chicago during the rebuilding after the Great Fire. His recognition of an unparalleled opportunity let him step up to a whole new level and become a man of substance in a place where no one knew about his beginnings or questioned where his money came from.

Then, as on other occasions, taking a chance had paid off. Through sharp thinking and hard work, he had built a comfortable life for himself. It had taken him years to get to this place, and now he meant to enjoy it. Everything was going as planned.

Except for Rosalee's death.

By the dim light of the carriage lamp, he saw the tail of a thread he hadn't noticed before protruding from his jacket cuff. He tugged on the thread but stopped when he felt the hem of the cuff begin to give way. He tucked the loose end back inside his sleeve and made a mental note to send it to his tailor for repair. Odd the way a small thing like one loose thread could prove the undoing of all his careful grooming.

His lips tightened as his mind made the connection. Just the way that missing evidence had the potential to unravel his whole existence.

CHAPTER 7

Sunlight reflected off the mighty Statue of the Republic, sending golden shards of light across the waters of the Grand Basin. Stephen continued his patrol around the Court of Honor, watching the crowd for any sign of trouble and taking special note of the number of couples who strolled in and out of the magnificent white buildings.

Since the fair's beginning, he had enjoyed looking at these masterpieces of architectural design on his solitary patrols. Now he realized such awe-inspiring sights were meant to be shared.

Take this setting, for instance. He stopped at the east end of the basin and gazed out through the Peristyle to the pier that jutted out into the waters of Lake Michigan. The sight never failed to fill him with a mixture of peace and amazement. How much more enjoyable it would be if he could see Emily's reaction to all this.

He moved to the north side of the basin and continued his

circuit, following the south edge of the imposing Manufactures Building that dwarfed all the other structures put together. God had blessed him by allowing him to have a job that let him spend the bulk of his time outdoors. How differently Emily's time was spent, cooped up in the Children's Building day after day. Perhaps she would agree to let him escort her around the grounds in the evening or on one of her days off.

His mood brightened, thinking of the things he'd like to show her. There was the Ferris wheel, of course, and the view from the roof of Manufactures. His pace picked up as he added to his mental list.

Knowing every nook and cranny of the grounds, he was familiar not only with the places favored by the public but also with those that would offer a place for a twosome to hold a quiet conversation while still remaining in the public eye. The Wooded Island, for instance. Now there was a place ripe with possibilities— the fragrant rose garden, the benches placed at strategic intervals, positioned so one who took refuge there could listen to the soft lapping of the lagoon against the shoreline. And then there were the fairy lights that dotted the island's edge.

He could imagine himself strolling with Emily along the shady paths, then sharing a bench until night fell and the fairy lights came on, their gentle glow so much softer than the stark white incandescent lights that outlined the major buildings and set the night ablaze.

It was easy to picture Emily in that setting, those brilliant emerald eyes, the curve of her chin, the mass of auburn hair that lay swirled around her head. Her eyes would gleam in the moonlight's glow when she turned her face up to look at him. And perhaps, in that sylvan setting, he might dare to steal a kiss.

Hold on there! Stephen made a mighty effort to rein in his imagination before it galloped away with him. He was getting ahead of himself to imagine any such thing. Why, they hadn't even been able to talk on more than a superficial level yet. But that was about to change.

He strode across the bridge that led toward the Grand Plaza with a spring in his step, wishing he could click his heels and give a loud whoop instead. It hadn't been any coincidence that he'd been able to intercept her on her way to work that morning—he'd been keeping a close watch on the walkway between the Woman's Building and the smaller Children's Building, nestled near its side. He recognized her companion as the blond girl she had met at the Midway the day before and was pleased to see the Simmons fellow was nowhere in sight. He changed direction so his course would intersect with hers.

Emily looked up when he drew near, and a smile lit her face. Though he watched her carefully, he detected none of the reserve he had noticed the day before. Emily introduced her friend as Lucy Welch, who won Stephen's undying appreciation by giving him a quick hello, then taking herself off to the Children's Building and leaving him alone with Emily.

"Did you get a chance to talk to your landlady?" The question popped out without any conscious planning on his part. She laughed before he could worry about having offended her.

"As a matter of fact, I did. She's looking forward to meeting you."

Stephen made a mental note to do something nice for this perspicacious landlady. They only had a minute more to visit before they parted at the door of the Children's Building, but the smile Emily gave him before she went inside was enough to stir hope and carry him through the remaining hours until he could see her again.

He glanced at his pocket watch and shook it to make sure it was still running. Surely more time had passed than that. The glories of the fairgrounds that usually thrilled him with their beauty suddenly seemed tame and bland, and his thoughts centered on the time he would be able to spruce up and get ready to make his appearance at the address she had given him on Blackstone Avenue.

Why had he suggested waiting until after supper? He would much prefer escorting her home when she finished her workday. Then he remembered the way she'd relaxed when he brought up the idea of waiting to visit until after the evening meal. Though he didn't understand why, that slight alteration seemed to make all the difference in the success of his request.

All right, then, he would wait. Emily was worth waiting for. They would spend the evening together, and that was the main thing.

But he didn't promise to be patient about it.

"Bridger!"

Stephen stopped short and looked around to see where the voice had come from. A little distance away stood Bill Watson and two of their fellow guards. Bill gestured to him to join them.

Stephen quickened his pace when he saw the stern expression on each of their faces.

"What's going on, fellows?"

"Colonel Rice sent me to find you," Bill told him. "He wants us over on the Midway double-quick. They've found a woman's body."

Emily turned from side to side in front of the mirror that hung over her dresser, careful not to disturb the sleeping boy on the pallet nearby. She wished the mirror was larger. Only seeing a small section of herself at a time, she couldn't get a true picture of how she looked. Did the cream-colored shirtwaist go with the forest green skirt as well as she hoped?

Giving up on trying to gauge the success of her outfit, she looked straight into the mirror and adjusted the pins in her thick auburn hair. Emily wrinkled her nose. She had long lamented her thick, unruly hair. It was difficult to make it stay up when its weight was so heavy it threatened to pull loose at any moment. If only it would hold fast tonight!

She leaned closer to the mirror and pinched her cheeks and bit her lips to bring out the color. She wished she could do more, but she would just have to make do with what she had. Either Stephen would like her for herself, or he wouldn't.

She studied her reflection again. Lucy had a pin that might be just the touch she needed for the shirtwaist. With one last glance to make sure Adam slept soundly, she stepped out into the hallway. Lucy would be in her room right now, having promised to stay upstairs in order to give Emily as much privacy as possible during Stephen's visit.

"One chaperone is enough," she'd told Emily at dinner. "But you have to promise to tell me all about it after he leaves, every last detail."

Emily was halfway to Lucy's room when she heard a knock on the front door, followed by a quick patter of feet. She stopped to listen, barely able to breathe.

Mrs. Purvis's voice floated upstairs. "Emily dear, your young man is here."

Emily's heart fluttered so badly she didn't have the presence of mind to remonstrate about Mrs. Purvis's reference to Stephen as her young man. She wavered a moment, looking at Lucy's door, then shook her head. No time to get the pin now. She would go as she was, and that would have to be good enough. She hoped Stephen wouldn't be disappointed.

If the light in his eyes when she descended the stairs was any indication, disappointment would not be a problem. Emily held on to the railing the last few steps in case her traitorous knees gave way.

"Good evening." The rich timbre of his voice sent a delightful shiver skittering up her spine. "Thank you for letting me come."

Emily stared into eyes the color of rich, dark coffee and realized she needed to speak. "Thank you for coming," she responded demurely. "Would you like to come into the parlor?"

"Yes, do." Mrs. Purvis waited for them in the doorway, her eyes as bright as buttons. "I've made some nice lemonade, and there's a plate of oatmeal cookies waiting for us." She herded them toward the parlor like a sheepdog nipping at the heels of a pair of wayward lambs.

Emily took a seat on the gold damask settee and wondered if Stephen would sit on the chair opposite. To her delight, he joined her on the small couch. Mrs. Purvis carried in a tray laden with a pitcher of lemonade and three glasses. She set the tray next to the plate of oatmeal cookies on the low table in front of the settee, then settled herself in the chair opposite, apparently prepared to play her role as chaperone to the hilt.

She tilted her head like an inquisitive robin and fixed her eyes on Stephen. "So you're one of the fine Columbian Guards who make sure the fair runs smoothly?"

Stephen's face tightened, and Emily wondered if he found something offensive in the question. It wasn't the reaction she would have expected from him.

"That's right," he finally said.

Mrs. Purvis poured lemonade into the glasses and handed one to Emily and another to Stephen. "And do you like your job?"

All expression faded from Stephen's face while he reached out to take two cookies from the plate Mrs. Purvis held out to him. "Most of the time."

Emily took two of the tasty cookies for herself, more to give herself something to do than because she felt hungry. Up to now, she would have described Stephen as the most easygoing man she'd ever met and never at a loss for words. What was wrong?

The silence lengthened, and Emily wished for something clever and captivating to say. Or for Mrs. Purvis to start tapping on the walls. Or for the floor to open and swallow her up. Anything to end this oppressive silence.

Mrs. Purvis cleared her throat gently, and Emily looked over to see her making a go-ahead gesture. She scrambled for something to say. "It seems odd to know we'll all be looking for employment in a matter of weeks, once the fair is over. Are you planning to pursue a career in law enforcement?"

Stephen set his glass of lemonade back on the table with more force than necessary. He used a napkin to wipe up a few drops that splashed over the rim. "No, I'm afraid that isn't where my interests lie. The Columbian Guards were looking for college graduates, and I had just earned my diploma from Cornell University. I took the job in part to be able to see the exposition firsthand and partly so I could study the buildings."

Emily nibbled at her cookie. At least he was talking now. "Study the buildings? I'm not sure I understand."

He smiled, looking once again like the man who could turn her to jelly with a mere glance. "I didn't make myself clear. I graduated with a degree in architecture. Spending my days on the fairgrounds gives me the opportunity to see firsthand some of the best design work of the most noted architects in the nation."

With a laugh, he added, "By this time, I think I know every one of them inside and out. For instance, do you realize the Manufactures Building covers over thirty acres? More than forty, if you count the galleries. It's the largest building every constructed to date. And the way it's designed boggles the mind—why, there isn't a single supporting pillar under the roof of the central hall." He cut off the flow of information and gave her a sheepish smile. "But you probably aren't interested in all that." He leaned against the arm of the settee, and his face clouded over again.

Emily cringed inside as the silence stretched out. What had she done? He had seemed eager enough to come calling, but now that he was here. . .

Emily caught her breath. She should have known—it wasn't him; it was her. Seeing her here, away from the buildings that dazzled him so, he saw her for what she was—a plain girl unlikely ever to measure up to anyone's expectations.

Perhaps she could at least make an attempt to discuss this topic he evidently loved. "The buildings are marvelous, aren't they? They look as though they're built to last several lifetimes."

Stephen winced. "No, they were never intended to last longer than the duration of the fair."

Emily slumped back against the settee. She had done her best, but it obviously wasn't good enough.

Stephen took another sip of lemonade then set the glass down on the table and rose to his feet. "I think I'd better leave."

Emily gasped at his abrupt announcement and blinked rapidly to hold back the tears. She knew she wasn't a scintillating companion, but she'd never expected to be brushed off like this. Even Mrs. Purvis seemed taken aback.

Stephen looked over as if sensing her distress. "Please forgive me. This is not going at all the way I'd planned. I know I'm poor company tonight, and it's all my fault. Something happened at work."

Emily laced her hands together in her lap, wondering if she dared grasp at the hope that she wasn't totally responsible for the disaster their evening had become. "What's wrong?" she asked.

Stephen hesitated then resumed his seat. "It isn't a pleasant topic of discussion."

Emily gave him an encouraging smile. Anything had to be more pleasant than thinking she had ruined all hope of furthering their relationship.

"I'm really not sure. . ." He looked over at Mrs. Purvis, who nodded at him.

"Of course, dearie. I've found it's best to talk about things that bother us. The Bible does say we're supposed to bear one another's burdens and not try to carry them all on our own."

Stephen gave a half smile and looked down at his hands. "A woman's body was discovered on the fairgrounds today."

"Oh, how awful!" Emily cried.

Mrs. Purvis made a tsking sound. "An older lady, was it? Probably too much excitement. I know when I've visited the fair, there's so much going on my heart takes to pounding something fierce. It must have been too much for her, poor dear."

Stephen shook his head. "No, she was actually quite young. And the circumstances we found her in were rather peculiar. One of the workers on the Midway went to get some supplies from a storage building. When he opened the door, the man noticed—"

He broke off and looked at his hands again. "He noticed something seemed to be amiss. He looked around a bit and found the woman's body laid out along one wall."

"How dreadful!" Emily thought about the scene he'd described and added, "But what was she doing in the storage room?"

Stephen's hands curled into fists. "That's the question we'd all like to have answered. She wasn't one of the workers. No one recognized her or remembers seeing her around there before."

Mrs. Purvis leaned forward, her eyes shining with compassion. "The poor thing. Was it from natural causes?"

"We don't believe so." Stephen paused as if deciding how much to tell them; then he added, "There were no marks on her body, but her neck was broken."

Emily couldn't think of a thing to say in response. Questions tumbled through her mind, but she didn't feel right about peppering Stephen with them when he was so obviously disturbed by this tragedy. Her heart warmed despite the grim news. It took a tender spirit to be so distraught about the death of a stranger.

He sat still, head bowed, with his forearms resting on his knees. Emily wished she could reach over and smooth away the furrows that lined his forehead.

He looked up at her then. "There is something that puzzles me."

Emily gave a slight smile and tilted her head to one side. "Yes?"

"The little boy I brought to the Children's Building the first day we met—you remember him, don't you?"

Emily sat perfectly still and reminded herself to breathe. "Of course. What about him?"

Stephen turned so he faced her squarely. "Tell me again what happened when his mother came to pick him up."

Emily clenched her fingers together and resisted the urge to jump up and flee from the room. "I don't understand. Why are you asking?"

"The woman we found matches the description I was given of the boy's mother—the blond hair, even the details about her dress and hat." Stephen's face twisted. "Colonel Rice, the head of the guards, said it appeared to him she'd been dead about two days. That would put it around the time I brought in the little boy. I can't help but be struck by the resemblance, but it can't be his mother, since she came back to get him." He paused and waited for an assurance she couldn't give him.

Emily raised her eyebrows, attempting an expression of pure innocence.

"Just for my own peace of mind," he continued, "it would help to know more about the boy's mother. We haven't identified the woman we found yet. The resemblance is so remarkable that I wonder if she might be a relative, maybe even a sister. You told me the boy left with his mother that afternoon. Can you give me any more details?"

Emily squirmed. "That isn't exactly what happened."

Stephen's eyebrows drew together. Emily began to feel like a cornered rat. The snare she had laid for herself was tightening. "What do you mean?" he asked in a stern voice.

"I didn't say his mother picked him up." Emily twisted her fingers together and looked from side to side as if an avenue of escape would open up before her. She glanced at Mrs. Purvis for help, but the landlady looked as defeated as Emily felt. "I said he was in good hands."

Stephen's expression darkened, and Emily's heart sank. It wasn't going to work. She should have told him the whole story from the very beginning. She closed her eyes to shut out the sight of his suspicious gaze. It was time to tell him the truth. All of it. She opened her mouth, ready to confess what she and Lucy had done.

Before she could utter a word, the door to the parlor opened. All three of them turned to see Adam, barefoot in his nightshirt, rubbing his eyes with the back of his hand.

"Miss Em'ly, I had a bad dream."

CHAPTER 8

Stephen felt as though his eyes would bulge right out of his head. He looked at the child in the doorway. It couldn't be, and yet. . . He saw the same blond hair, the same trusting blue eyes, the same cherubic face that had snuggled against his shoulder only two days before.

And he'd called her Miss Em'ly.

Footsteps clattered down the stairs and across the floor. Emily's blond friend skidded into the doorway and stared at him with a horrified expression.

"I'm sorry," she said to Emily. "I didn't realize he was gone until I went in to check on him and found he wasn't in his bed. I came down as soon as I knew." She raised her arms and let them drop against her sides.

Of all the day's strange events, this had to rank at the top of the list as the strangest. Stephen looked at Emily. "Would you care to explain this to me?"

She stared back at him, her lips moving soundlessly. Mrs. Purvis hopped to her feet. "Why don't I make us all a nice cup of tea? It's good for relaxing after a shock." She scuttled off to the kitchen with remarkable speed for a woman her age.

Emily's friend picked Adam up and sent an apologetic look their way. "I'll put him back to bed. You go on with your evening. Don't worry about a thing."

Stephen blinked. Had the whole household gone mad? He looked back at Emily, reading the guilt on her averted face.

At last she turned and looked him squarely in the eye. "His mother never did come back. Lucy and I brought him home."

Stephen scrubbed his face with his hands then spread his arms wide. "What do you mean? You can't just waltz off with a child who doesn't belong to you."

Emily's brow puckered, and her lower lip trembled. Her chest heaved in a shuddering gasp before she continued. "Miss Strickland, the supervisor, wanted us to turn him over to the authorities, but we couldn't do it."

"But why?" Stephen shook his head, wishing he could clear out all the confusing thoughts that seemed to have taken up residence. "They're the ones who are equipped to—" He broke off when Emily leaned toward him, tears filming her eyes.

She spoke in a voice so low he had to strain to hear it. "I told you I didn't have a family. I grew up in the Collier Children's Home. So did Lucy. We've known each other since we were little. Yes, we were cared for there. We each had a place to sleep and clothing to wear, and we never missed a meal. But you have no idea what loneliness is like when you know other children have a mother and father to love them and tuck them into bed at night, and the best you can do is go to sleep on a cot in a room full of other children as lonely as yourself."

Her voice sounded near to breaking, but she went on. "We—I—couldn't let that happen to Adam."

"But I came back to check on him the next day. Why didn't you tell me then?"

"I wanted to, but I didn't know what you would do. I thought you might feel you had to take him away, and I couldn't bear that."

Stephen stared at the woman who was dangerously close to laying claim to his heart. Her eyes, her hair were still as lovely as before, but he felt like reaching up and pulling out his own hair by the handful at her obvious lack of understanding. "But he has a family."

"Do you think I haven't thought of that?" Her voice rose nearly an octave.

"Well, you obviously didn't think enough."

She shrank back as though he had slapped her. Remorse smote Stephen. He longed to reach out and draw her into his arms, but he steeled himself and continued. "Do you realize the position you've placed me in? Now I have to consider that this woman really was Adam's mother. How am I supposed to explain this to my superiors?" He stood, and she quailed back against the settee. Self-loathing filled him for intimidating her like this, but he had to make her see reason.

He sat down again and took her hand. "You have to understand. There are reasons we have rules and policies in place. You've put us both in a bad situation."

She pulled her fingers from his grip and covered her face with her hands.

"I can't cover this up," he told her. "I'm going to have to tell my boss that there's a connection here. If this is a murder, it has to be investigated as such. And since she left her child—remember the way she ran away from him?—she must have known she was in danger. This totally changes the direction we'll need to pursue.

I can't leave my superiors in the dark."

Emily lowered her hands to her lap and looked up at him. Tears filled her eyes and spilled over to trickle slowly down her cheeks. "I don't want to ask you to go against your principles, but please consider this: To all appearances, this little boy has lost his mother in a far more final way than we ever dreamed. You don't know what that's like, but I do. He's happy here, and he has a place to stay where he's cared for and has all the attention he needs. Please, can't we put his welfare above the rules?"

A part of Stephen wanted to acquiesce. It would be so simple to ease the torment he could read in her eyes, but he knew where duty led him. He stood again and stepped away from the settee.

"I can't."

Emily rose and followed him. "We'll look for the rest of his family. When you find out who his mother is, we'll know where to find them. I'm not trying to keep him forever. I just want him to be happy until he can get back to the people who love him. Won't you do this. . .for Adam?"

Stephen held his hands up, bringing her to a stop. His head told him to follow regulations; his heart said something quite different.

As if sensing his inner turmoil, Emily added, "Think it over, at least. Promise me you'll do that. One more night won't make a difference."

"All right." Stephen wondered what this capitulation would cost him. "I'll give you that much, but I can't promise what my decision will be."

───※───

Ian McGinty scrutinized the latest reports from his various business enterprises. Attention to detail—that's what divided the winners from the losers. A shiver rippled the skin between his shoulder blades, and he stepped away from the desk long enough to stir the fire in the grate. Autumn was on its way in earnest.

The thought did nothing to cheer him. He hated the cold, and the roughly built warehouse did little to keep the damp chill at bay. He would suffer the cold less, of course, if he kept his working hours to the daytime as most people did. But he had always enjoyed the night, seeming to catch a second wind when the shadows grew darkest. This, combined with the need for little sleep, helped give him the extra edge he'd needed to surpass the competition and stay well ahead of it.

His office door opened, and one of his underlings stuck his head inside the room. "They're here."

The two he had sent after Rosalee stepped inside. Maybe they brought good news this time. McGinty half rose from his seat and looked past them to see if the child followed. He looked up, a frown tightening his forehead.

The pair shook their heads in unison. "No luck," Flynn told him.

Mort stepped forward. "We took the key you gave us and went in the back door of her house. We went through it from top to bottom, but the place looks like she just left for the afternoon."

"No sign of the boy?"

Flynn shrugged. "Nothing yet."

McGinty narrowed his eyes. They both wore far too casual an air for two men skirting the brink of disaster.

"We checked with the neighbors," Mort said, "and the old lady next door who took care of the kid sometimes. Nothing there. We even looked up the little spy you had keeping an eye on your lady friend. He gave us some more places to try, but nothing there, either. Nobody has seen the kid, boss. It's like he just vanished."

McGinty kept them waiting while he stared at the opposite wall, turning over different scenarios in his mind. Finally he spoke. "The fairgrounds."

"Huh?" Deep creases furrowed Flynn's forehead.

"She must have had him with her."

Mort wagged his head. "We never saw no kid, boss."

"You weren't looking for him, either, were you? She saw you, and she ran. You told me that yourself." McGinty spoke his thoughts aloud, following the line of reasoning as it came together in his mind. "Did she tuck him away somewhere? Put him in someone else's care? If so, the child could be anywhere."

He laced his fingers and tapped his thumbs together. "But did she have time for that?" He thought over the scenario they had described to him and shook his head. He didn't think so.

McGinty straightened in his chair. If she'd given him to someone, the boy was gone without a trace and the trail was cold. Unless. . .

"You." He pulled a couple of bills from his wallet and tossed them toward Mort. The short man snagged them and turned a puzzled look on McGinty. "What's this for?"

"First thing in the morning, go get yourself a decent-looking suit of clothes. Make yourself look respectable. Then you will present yourself on the fairgrounds and act as though you've lost a child. Ask someone where you should look. There must be some procedure they follow."

Mort pocketed the money and stood as if awaiting additional orders. Flynn eyed him jealously. "Why don't you let me go?"

McGinty fixed him with a withering stare. "You're a bit too heavy-handed for this. I want the child back in one piece." He turned his attention back to Mort. "Be careful. This may be your last chance to find the boy."

After they left, McGinty sat lost in thought. It might work. It *had* to work.

CHAPTER 9

Good morning, Emily."

Emily, who had been sliding a folder into its place in the filing cabinet, whirled at the sound of her name. She felt her smile fade when she saw the man standing there.

"Good morning, Mr. Simmons." She took her time closing the file drawer, wishing he would take the hint and leave. Her hope went unfulfilled; he still stood there when she turned back around again.

He walked over to the desk and extended one arm, presenting her with a nosegay of fall flowers. "Lovely, aren't they? But the moment you take these in your hand, their beauty will be eclipsed by your own."

Emily felt her stomach churn. When he pushed the small bouquet toward her, she put her hands behind her back and shook her head. "I can't accept these."

He looked startled. "You took the caramels I left the other day."

"I apologize. I shouldn't have done that." She stooped down to retrieve them from the bottom drawer and thrust them toward her unwelcome visitor.

Raymond Simmons's hand closed around the bag, a bewildered expression across his face. "I don't understand."

Emily picked up her pen and rolled it between her fingers. "I'm sorry if I have given you the false impression that your attentions are welcome."

Raymond's face darkened. "Are you saying your affections are engaged elsewhere?"

Emily opened her mouth then shut it. She could feel the heat creeping up her neck and knew her face must be turning pink. When Raymond's scowl deepened, she felt sure he'd noticed it, too.

"Is it that fellow I saw you talking to the other day? Who is he? I've never seen him before."

His voice took on a conciliatory tone. "These are difficult times, Emily. You need someone who can give you security. How much do you know about him? Does he even have a job?"

"He is currently employed here on the fairgrounds. . .just as you are," she added pointedly.

"In what capacity?"

Emily drew herself up and lifted her chin. "As one of the Columbian Guards."

Raymond's loud guffaw made Emily want to slap him. "My dear girl, you do realize that means he will be unemployed in a little over a month. What then? Are you willing to tie your fortunes to someone who may not have two nickels to rub together by the fair's end?"

His voice became smooth again. "I'm sure he is attracted to you. After all, you do have a very comely face. But what are his intentions in the long run? Men these days are taking advantage of innocent young women. Think about it, my dear. As a guard, he spends his days roaming over the entire fairgrounds. He may have half a dozen women dangling from his string, and you're just another bauble to add to his collection."

Emily drew back and narrowed her eyes. Smiling as though he knew he'd struck a nerve, Raymond pressed his advantage. "What do you know about his background? Any man can look good in a uniform."

Emily could feel her whole body tremble. In another moment, she *would* slap him if he didn't move out of her reach. "I'm going to have to ask you to leave, Mr. Simmons. I have work to do."

A quick tap of heels sounded along the adjacent corridor. Miss Strickland rounded the corner and came to a quick halt when she saw only Emily and Raymond in the reception area. "I heard voices. It sounded like an altercation of some sort."

Emily smoothed her skirt, hoping she appeared calmer than she felt. "There is no altercation. Mr. Simmons was just on his way out."

Miss Strickland bestowed a toothy smile on Emily's unwanted suitor. "So nice to see you, Mr. Simmons. Please give my regards to your father."

Raymond looked as if he wanted to say more, but he did no more than give a quick nod to each of the women before he left.

Miss Strickland crossed her arms and stared at Emily until she wanted to shrivel up and crawl away. "Those flowers he was carrying. Were they for you?"

Emily nodded and cleared her throat. "He tried to give them to me. I wouldn't accept them."

"Why?"

"It wouldn't be fair to give him the impression that I welcomed his attentions."

Miss Strickland sniffed. "You'll never have another opportunity like this in your life. How many chances does a girl like you have to meet a man such as Mr. Simmons, much less attract his notice? The Simmons family is well respected in this city, and you are a nobody. You should be pleased he even deigned to notice you. To turn him down the way you did—it's absolutely foolish."

Emily stood still under the onslaught, trying not to look as though Miss Strickland's words cut like blows from a lash. When she saw Emily wasn't going to respond, the supervisor raised her arms in the air. "I wash my hands of this. I've thought from the beginning that you were a foolish girl. This confirms it. If you don't have the sense to welcome such an opportunity when it comes your way, I have nothing more to say on the matter."

She stormed off, and Emily sank down onto her chair, grateful the other woman had left before she could see the anguish her words had caused.

A girl like you. A simple phrase, but one that opened up a wound Emily had struggled with all her life—a deep wound she usually kept hidden under the surface but one that never completely healed, because she knew it was true.

Memories of her time at the Collier Home flowed through her mind in an unwelcome stream: seeing children being adopted and taken home to loving families or being reclaimed by parents who had left them there out of necessity after some family crisis.

But no one ever came for her.

She rested her elbows on her desk and pressed her palms against her cheeks, praying no one would come in to drop off or pick up a child until she regained her composure. Tears coursed down her cheeks as she remembered how she used to build up her hopes then watch some other child find a home. She knew it was because they were prettier, cleverer, or more appealing in some way she could never hope to be.

Finally she had accepted reality and given up the dream of one day meeting a family willing to accept her into its bosom.

The tears kept flowing. At least she had a few people who cared for her. She wouldn't trade her friendship with Lucy for anything. And Mrs. Purvis was an absolute gem, almost like a mother to her. Look at the way she'd offered to take Adam under her wing. That in itself was a blessing, relieving Emily from having to worry about his well-being all day. Not that she didn't love him—his unreserved trust had already won her heart—but the strain of trying to keep him from being discovered had worn on her more than she cared to admit.

And it was better for Adam, too. He needed all the security he could get, especially after she'd had to tell him his mother would never be coming home again. Spending his days with Mrs. Purvis would be almost like time spent with a grandmother. So much nicer than being just one in a crowd of other children or being the target of Miss Strickland's wrath, should she learn of his presence in the building.

Emily shuddered. She could only imagine the invective the supervisor would have unleashed upon them both if that had occurred. She couldn't bear to think of a little boy trying to deal with that. It was hard enough to cope with the woman's harsh tongue herself.

But as much as Miss Strickland's hateful words hurt, Emily knew she was right. Because of some flaw she could not identify and had no idea how to correct, she would never be good enough, no matter how hard she tried.

Yet according to the minister at the church that the children from the Collier Home attended every Sunday, she was accepted by God just as she was. That promise registered in her consciousness for the first time when she was twelve. She welcomed Jesus into her heart as her Savior with unbridled joy and clung to the promise that He loved her, even if no one else did.

Considering her recent string of half-truths, though, she wondered just how happy He was with her right now. The loneliness she usually managed to hold at bay opened before her like an abyss. She still clung to the hope of heaven, but it seemed everything she wanted in this life was on the other side of that vast gulf.

Including Stephen.

For a fleeting moment, she'd dared to hope that he might be interested in her and that his interest might flower into something more. But that hope had died when he saw Adam the night before. She remembered his compassion when he spoke of the dead woman and the way his features had taken on a stony, shuttered look when he learned of Emily's duplicity.

Could she blame him? How could he trust a woman who told him less than the truth? Maybe she hadn't out and out lied, but she'd certainly led him to believe something that wasn't true, and wasn't that the same thing?

Emily retrieved her reticule and fished inside it until she found her handkerchief. She used the square of cotton to blot her cheeks and wipe the tears from her eyes. She knew her ruse had ruined the possibility of building a deeper relationship with Stephen. But she had to think of Adam, not just of herself. She might not matter, but that precious little boy did. What would Stephen decide?

Lord, please let him make the right choice. The trouble was, things had gotten so mixed up that she didn't know what the right choice would turn out to be.

───

Stephen walked south along the walkway in front of the Choral

Building, observing the fairgoers within his view. He passed a boat landing on his left and looked across the lagoon to the Wooded Island, where couples strolled along shaded walkways. The placid scene acted like a balm to his troubled spirit, something he sorely needed, ever since the scene at the boardinghouse the night before when little Adam appeared in the doorway asking for Miss Em'ly.

Even more shocking than seeing the child again had been the realization that Emily had deliberately misled him as to Adam's whereabouts.

What had she been thinking? He still didn't understand. The proper thing would have been to notify him or one of the other Columbian Guards, who would have passed the word to the Chicago police, who in turn would have taken the boy to one of the city's foundling homes.

Policies were set in place for a reason, based on logic and order. But everything fell apart when one individual took it upon herself to circumvent the expected sequence of events and try to deal with the issue in her own amateurish way.

He continued on past the Transportation Building, strikingly different from its dazzling white neighbors in autumn shades of red, orange, and yellow. Before him on his left, the Mining and Electricity buildings capped the south end of the lagoon.

Had he been wrong about Emily? From the moment they met, he thought there was something different about this girl, something special. Despite their brief acquaintance, he felt drawn to her in a way he couldn't deny. At first he'd been certain that attraction came straight from heaven. But what communion did light have with darkness? Surely God wouldn't want him to consider being yoked with anyone who handled the truth so lightly.

Did he really want to consider the possibility of linking his lot to a woman when he would never be sure she was speaking the truth?

His route led him toward the Hayward Restaurant, where delicious aromas wafted out to scent the afternoon air. Stephen's stomach rumbled, and he looked toward the dining establishment longingly. He couldn't stop now, not while he was on duty. His stomach protested again.

When he reached Terminal Station, he turned left and entered the Grand Plaza. Sunlight glinted off the golden dome of the Administration Building in the center of the broad expanse.

Off to his left, he saw the white and gold Menier Chocolate Pavilion, where more delectable smells trickled out to tantalize him. Maybe it wouldn't hurt to duck inside for just a moment and pick up something to stave off his hunger until the end of his shift.

Just as he reached the door, a slender, sandy-haired man emerged, and Stephen recognized his friend Seth Howell.

The young pastor broke into a smile when he caught sight of Stephen. "Hello there! I haven't seen you for a while."

Stephen sent up a silent prayer of thanks. Seth was just the person to help him sort through this dilemma. Coincidence? Stephen didn't think so.

Ignoring the rumbling of his stomach, he fell in step with Seth as he strolled across the plaza. "What brings you here?" he asked his friend. "I thought your days of pushing people around the grounds in rolling chairs were over once you became an old married man."

Seth grinned. "I thought I'd surprise Dinah and meet her when she takes her lunch break."

Stephen eyed the paper bag Seth carried in one hand. "So the chocolates are for Dinah?"

Seth laughed. "Sorry. They're already spoken for."

All right, then, he couldn't hope for any chocolates. But maybe he could get some answers to the questions that had been plaguing him. "Do you expect her to come out soon?"

"It'll probably be a little while yet. I got here early to make sure I didn't miss her."

Stephen looked around the busy plaza and took a deep breath. "If you don't mind talking while you wait, I'm in need of some godly counsel."

Interest sparked in Seth's eyes. "I'm honored you consider my advice in that category. Why don't we go over there"—he pointed toward a spot near the entrance to Terminal Station—"so you don't have to compete with the music they're playing in the bandstand."

They found a spot with a clear view of the doors of the Administration Building. Seth eyed Stephen for a moment then held out the bag of chocolates. "I guess it won't hurt if you eat just one."

Stephen hesitated only a moment before he reached into the bag and helped himself. He could think better if he wasn't quite so hungry. The smooth confection melted over his tongue.

"Now what's on your mind?" Seth asked.

Stephen paused to savor the last taste of the sweet chocolate before he answered. "I find myself in a bit of a moral dilemma."

Seth gave a barely perceptible start. "Tell me about it."

"I met this girl," Stephen began. He stopped when he saw his friend's wary expression. "No, it isn't what you think. You see, there's a child involved."

Seth's jaw sagged, and Stephen hastened to add, "It isn't mine."

The explanation didn't seem to clear things up. Seth stared at him, glassy-eyed. "I believe we're going to need more time to hash this out than I have available before Dinah comes along."

"I'm not doing this well at all." Stephen scrubbed his hand across his face. "The child isn't hers, either."

Seth reached into the bag and popped a chocolate into his mouth. "I think you lost me there."

Stephen went back over the whole story, beginning with taking Adam to the Children's Building and ending with his visit to the boardinghouse the night before, when Emily's subterfuge came to light.

Seth chewed slowly and held the bag out to Stephen once more. Stephen took another chocolate and waited for his friend to speak.

Seth stroked his chin. "Does she strike you as the kind of person who lies habitually?"

Stephen took off his hat and ran his fingers through his hair. "That's just it. Up until last night, I would have sworn there wasn't a deceitful bone in her body." He settled the hat back on his head and adjusted the chin strap. "I guess that just goes to show you can't trust first impressions."

Seth tilted his head from one side to the other. "Maybe, maybe not."

"What do you mean?"

"Do you have any idea why she would have done this?"

"She said she didn't want him to go to strangers." Stephen blew out a puff of air hard enough to stir his mustache. "What does she think *she* is? She met him after I did."

"It sounds to me like your problem may not be so much a matter of truth versus falsehood—although I'll admit it does sound like she stretched the truth a bit."

"I'd say she did more than stretch it," Stephen muttered.

"More like she snapped it in two."

Seth raised one hand. "Granted, but let's look at where her heart is in all of this. I think that's where the real issue lies. You're looking at this from a logical standpoint, and she's looking at it from an emotional point of view. You both want what's best for this little boy, don't you?"

Stephen pulled himself erect. "Of course I do."

"Then you both have ample reason for feeling the way you do. You're just coming at it from different directions."

"You mean I'm seeing this clearly through the eyes of logic, and her view is clouded with emotion?"

Seth smiled. "You have just described one of the big differences between women and men."

"You mean you can't ever expect them to look at things logically?"

Seth just grinned. "Tell me why she's so set against the boy going to an orphan asylum."

"She was raised in one herself. She says she knows what it's like, and she doesn't want him to have to go through the same thing."

Seth lifted one eyebrow. "Sounds pretty logical to me."

"But that's only part of the problem," Stephen protested. "If it was just a matter of her holding on to Adam, that might be an issue we could deal with. But now we have an even bigger problem."

"Which is?"

"Yesterday we received a report of a woman's body discovered on the Midway. It seems very likely that she was Adam's mother."

Seth pursed his lips and gave a low whistle. "That does complicate things."

"So that's why we have to follow the rules so carefully. This is a murder investigation, not a Sunday picnic."

Seth nodded. "I see what you mean. Of course, looking at it logically, that tells me that without a mother to come back and claim him at some point, if no other relatives step forward, this little boy is likely to spend the rest of his childhood in an orphan asylum, just like your Emily did."

"So you're saying she's right?"

Seth clamped his hand on Stephen's shoulder. "You're both right. God has given us minds, and He expects us to use them. He has also given us hearts to feel compassion. There's something about matters of the heart that tends to defy logic, whether it's the tenderness between a parent and child or the love between a man and a woman. But that doesn't make it any less valuable than looking at things from a purely logical point of view."

He offered Stephen another chocolate and popped one into his own mouth. Then he folded his arms. "Let's say this whole issue with Adam is resolved and nothing else stands between you. What then?"

Stephen paused for a moment, willing his mind to erase the doubts that had risen like a dense fog since the night before. He felt his mouth curve upward. "If that were the case, I'd probably be spending all my off-duty time over on Blackstone Avenue, getting to know her better and making sure she's really the one."

"Blackstone Avenue?"

"She's staying at a boardinghouse there."

Seth's lips began to twitch. "You've met her landlady?"

"Yes." Stephen looked at his friend curiously.

"Her name wouldn't be Ethelinda Purvis, would it?"

"It's Mrs. Purvis. I don't know about the Ethelinda part. Why?"

"How would you describe her attitude toward you? Would you say she was enthusiastic about you coming to call on Emily?"

Stephen shrugged. "She was nice enough. She called me Emily's young man when I arrived on the doorstep, even though it was the first time I'd come to call."

Seth threw back his head and laughed. "You might just as well give in now. You're a goner. Dinah was staying there when I met her. If Mrs. Purvis has given her approval, you can be sure your days as a single man are numbered."

Stephen's mind happily followed the train of thought created by Seth's flight of fancy. Then reality slapped him in the face like a splash of cold water. "But we're not past this yet. Emily wants me to keep quiet about Adam's whereabouts. How do I reconcile that with maintaining any kind of integrity as a guard. . .or as a man?"

Seth tilted his head. "Is there anything the boy can add to the investigation? Will the fact of his staying with Emily rather than going to an orphan asylum change things at all?"

"Who knows? He's just one piece of the puzzle. We don't know yet how that piece might fit with the others to give us a picture of what happened."

"Then consider this: That little boy has lost his mother. To uproot him again could cause him trouble for the rest of his days. Think long and hard about this before you do something that can't be undone and will wind up costing Adam a great deal more than it will cost you." Seth paused a moment, letting his words sink in. "Who's in charge of the investigation, by the way?"

"The Chicago police," Stephen answered. "I'm sure Colonel Rice will keep himself informed about the situation."

"Would he be willing to share information about the case with you?"

Stephen considered the question then nodded. "Yes, I'm certain he would. I was there to help with the preliminary part of the investigation, so I don't see why he'd have any problem talking to me about it."

"Do you think you can come to an agreement with Emily that if you find out making the boy's presence known is critical to the investigation, she'll let the police know about him?"

"I suppose so, although I don't know that for sure."

"Then as far as I can see, until this woman can be identified, you're dealing with an unknown person. The boy hasn't been of any help along that line?"

Stephen shook his head. "He can only tell us his first name and that he calls his mother 'Mama.'"

"Then until someone comes forward to claim her or file a missing persons report that matches her description, you're at a standstill. And from my own experience, I can tell you the police are so swamped with reports of missing persons that it's entirely possible they'll miss a connection. Without a name, without a way to connect this little fellow with his family, I don't see how the situation will be jeopardized by choosing to go along with Emily's plan."

Stephen frowned. "But what about the part in the Bible that talks about obeying authority? Don't I have an obligation to follow procedure here?"

"Remember that Jesus didn't always go along with man-made rules. I think you need to look beyond the rule book and see if there isn't a bigger issue at stake here."

"Then you're saying I should just forget about policy and go along with this wild idea of hers?"

Seth smiled and shook his head. "What I'm saying is, I believe this may be one of those times when a heart of compassion is more important than a logical mind." His gaze shifted, and a smile lit his face. "There she is."

Stephen turned to see a dark-haired young woman walking their way. He had been around newlyweds enough to know his talk with Seth was over. That was all right, though. He'd gotten the sound advice he'd asked for, though not in the form he expected. He appreciated Seth's counsel. . .and the fact that he could call this man his friend.

"How are you, Stephen?" Dinah Howell gave him a friendly wave then turned a radiant smile on her husband. "I didn't expect to see you here."

"I wanted to surprise you. Look, I brought. . ." Seth hesitated and glanced down at his hand, then crumpled the empty sack and palmed it to Stephen. Dropping a conspiratorial wink, Seth said, "I'll talk to you later. Let me know how things work out."

He cupped his hand under Dinah's elbow. "Why don't we go over to Menier Chocolates? I'll buy you a bag of your favorites."

⌒

"How may I help you?" Emily looked up at the small, slender man standing before her desk. Since he didn't have a child with him, he must be coming to claim one, but she didn't remember seeing him earlier that day.

He was dressed well enough; his suit looked brand new. Emily held back a smile. It wouldn't be the first time she had seen someone who had spent a month's salary to spruce up for a visit to the exposition. This man probably fit into that category. He seemed ill at ease in well-cut garments, shifting from one foot to the other and running his finger between his collar and his neck.

Perhaps he was uneasy about coming alone to pick up his youngster. Most men either came in with their wives or waited outside. Emily wondered if he had left his wife in one of the chairs outside to let her rest a bit from the rigors of sightseeing. If so, that made him a very caring man.

"They told me this is where they bring lost children."

"They? Oh, you mean one of the guards?"

"Yes, ma'am, that's right."

Emily felt relieved. That meant neither he nor his wife had been inside the building earlier. No wonder she didn't recognize him. "Yes, it is. Have you lost your child?"

He shifted his gaze then looked back at her. "Yeah. I mean, no. My brother's kid was lost, and I'm trying to help find him."

"I see. But we haven't had any lost children brought in today." Concern stirred at the thought of a child wandering around the fairgrounds on his own. "How long has he been missing? We should alert the guards so they can be on the lookout for him."

The man backed up a step and patted the air with his hands. "No, we don't need to do that. This happened a couple, maybe three days ago."

Emily started. "And you're just now looking for him?"

The man shrugged and gave her an ingratiating smile. "My brother and his wife had a fight while they were here, and she got so mad she took off. He thought she had the kid with her; she figured he had the boy with him. When she got over being mad and came back home, they realized the last time either of them saw the little guy was here. Crazy, isn't it?"

Emily caught her breath. Could he be talking about Adam's parents? The snippets of information they had managed to glean so far started coming together to form a picture. It would make sense. If his mother had been angry at his father, she might have taken off in exactly the way this man described.

Or maybe she wasn't running away at all. Perhaps she'd spotted her husband after their argument and wanted to go over to him to give him a piece of her mind. In that case...

Emily's throat went dry. The woman was later found dead on

the Midway. Who would make a better suspect than her husband, this man's brother? She looked up at him again, hoping he couldn't read her thoughts.

The man shrugged his shoulders. "Don't get mad at me. I'm not the one who had the fight. I'm just trying to figure out where we should start looking for the boy. So what do you do with lost kids if no one comes to pick them up?"

Thoughts whirled through Emily's mind at a lightning pace. She had no proof he was talking about Adam, though everything within her assured her it must be so. But something about this man set warning bells clanging in her head. She looked at the way he fidgeted, unable to meet her gaze for more than an instant or two. Just the way Johnny Meacham, the resident bully of the Collier Home, used to act when he was trying to convince the matron he wasn't guilty of yet another misdeed.

She made up her mind in an instant. She wasn't about to divulge Adam's whereabouts to someone who might return him to a dangerous situation.

But maybe she knew a way to answer his question and divert attention from Adam at the same time. She looked straight at the man and said, "In cases of children who are left at the fairgrounds, my supervisor insists we notify the authorities and let them take it from there."

The man blinked rapidly several times. "You mean the police?"

"That's right." Emily rose from her chair and moved to open the front door. "Let me help you flag down one of the guards. I'm sure he would be happy to put you in touch with someone who—"

"No, no. Don't go to any trouble. I appreciate the information, but I don't want to take you away from your duties. I'm sure you're a very busy lady. I'll take care of it on my own." He practically bowled her over in his haste to leave the building.

What was that all about? Emily closed the door and returned to her desk. Was he really looking for Adam?

Of course he was. How many other children had been left there without someone coming to pick them up? There was some connection; she knew it. But what?

She sank into her chair and stared at the far wall, deep in thought. If the man truly was Adam's uncle, that would make him the first connection they had found to the child since Stephen brought him in. And if he was, what right did she have to make the decision to keep Adam from him?

Something was wrong about the man; she felt sure of it. But what? True, he didn't look as though he belonged in the clothes he wore, but she remembered the plain clothing she wore growing up at the children's home. She knew better than to judge a person's worth by the clothes they wore.

But uncle or not, something about him didn't ring true. She had gotten into this situation wanting to protect Adam, and the child had wound his tiny fingers around her heartstrings more with each passing day. How could she turn him over to a man she didn't know and didn't trust?

CHAPTER 10

S tephen looked down at the diminutive woman walking at his side and felt a sense of contentment that seemed completely out of place, given their circumstances. Seth Howell's admonition to use a heart of compassion rather than cold, clear logic had struck a chord, and he respected the young pastor enough to take his advice seriously.

If nothing else, it removed the barrier between him and Emily, giving him a chance to consider the future without prejudice.

Her green eyes shone in the afternoon sunlight when she looked up at him. "I'm so glad you agreed to leave Adam in my care. I know it wasn't an easy thing for you to do, and I want you to know I do appreciate your willingness to go along with me in this."

Stephen shrugged, giving little outward sign of the internal battle he had waged in order to reach this point, even after talking to Seth. "Just remember the rest of our agreement. If it turns out that revealing Adam's location is essential to solving his mother's murder, we'll have to let the police know."

Emily sighed and nodded agreeably enough, although Stephen suspected she was waging an internal war of her own.

"I have to tell you, though, I have no idea how to go about finding his family. The initials on his mother's handkerchief don't help much, and we don't even know where they're from. They could be locals or from anywhere across the country. Where do we start?"

They walked a few more steps before Emily answered. "I may have learned something about them already."

His feet stopped of their own accord. He stood in the middle of the sidewalk and stared at her. What had she been withholding from him this time?

As if guessing his thoughts, she looked up at him from under her straw hat, her eyes wide and pleading. "It only happened this afternoon. I told you I would be completely open with you from now on."

Stephen nodded slowly. Trust was a difficult thing to rebuild, but after talking to Seth, he was willing to give her a chance.

They started walking again and made the turn onto Blackstone Avenue. They strolled past the brick houses lining the east side of the street while Emily related her encounter with the man purporting to be looking for a lost child. "He couldn't be talking about anyone else."

"I agree. Tell me again why you didn't let him know about Adam."

"There was something about him. I don't know how to explain it. But it was something wrong—I'd stake my life on that." The light coming through the birch trees dappled her pale green dress. "Is there any way we can find out more about this man without letting him know we're checking on him?"

Stephen turned the possibilities over in his mind. "Did he give his name?"

Emily shook her head. "No, and I was so confused by the whole affair that I didn't think to ask."

"Then I don't know how we could go about locating him any more than we could Adam's father." Side by side, they walked up the steps of the neat redbrick house.

Emily sucked in a quick breath and gripped his arm. "I have an idea how we can at least find out if he might really be an uncle. Who would know better than Adam? Let's ask him. He might be able to solve that part of the mystery."

———

They found Adam playing with a set of wooden blocks on the parlor floor. Lucy watched him from the settee.

Emily stumbled to a stop when she saw her friend. "How did you get home so quickly?"

Lucy grinned. "I didn't walk any faster than usual. You two just took your own sweet time."

Stephen liked the way Emily's cheeks grew pink at her friend's comment. But then, was there anything he didn't like about Emily? Though small of stature, she packed more force of character and determination to do right—as she saw it—into her small frame than most people twice her size. He studied the way her heavy auburn hair swirled against the back of her neck and wondered what it would look like if it were loose and tumbling down around her shoulders.

Mrs. Purvis bustled into the room and beamed when she caught sight of Stephen and Emily. Stephen jerked to attention and remembered Seth's comment. He eyed the landlady with a good deal more caution than on his previous visit.

"There you are," she warbled. "And just in time for dinner. You'll stay, won't you, Stephen, dear?"

He glanced at Emily, who looked up at him expectantly; then he smiled back at the landlady. "Thank you. I'd be glad to." If Seth was right, he had already passed muster, which might bode well for deepening his relationship with Emily.

Come to think of it, Mrs. Purvis had obviously given her approval to Emily, as well. And if Seth was correct, the woman was a keen student of human nature. Maybe he should look at that as another positive sign.

He walked over to where Adam knelt on the rug, intent on balancing a pile of blocks. Emily joined them. "You got some new blocks?" she asked.

Mrs. Purvis answered. "Another gift from the little boy down the street. His name is Matthew."

Adam looked up from his game and smiled. "Matthew's blocks."

"His mother brought him down and let the boys play together earlier this afternoon," Mrs. Purvis explained.

Emily's eyes flared wide. "Do you think that's wise?"

The older woman patted her on the shoulder. "They're a lovely young couple. Their little boy needs a playmate, same as our Adam. I'm not letting him out of my sight for a moment, so don't you worry a bit. Why don't the two of you sit down and relax a bit while I put the finishing touches on our dinner? It will only take me a minute or two." With that, she turned and headed for the kitchen.

Lucy followed her. "I'll set the table."

Stephen knelt beside Adam and pulled the little boy onto his knee. "I'd like to ask you something," he began. "What's your last name? Do you know?"

Adam looked at him.

Stephen tried again. "Do you know where you live?" When Adam frowned and looked around the room, he added, "I mean, when you're not living here."

Adam hunched his shoulders up around his ears. "At Mama's house."

This wasn't going at all the way he hoped. He looked at Emily for help, and she joined them on the rug. She smoothed Adam's hair back from his forehead. "What's your mother's name, sweetheart?"

Crystal droplets welled up in Adam's eyes. The answer came out in a ragged whisper. "Mama."

Stephen saw Emily press her lips together and blink rapidly before she asked, "What about your father?"

Adam slipped off Stephen's lap and squatted in front of his blocks again, ignoring both of them.

Emily looked at Stephen helplessly. "So much for my bright idea. If he can't tell us about his parents, we can't find out a thing about this so-called uncle."

He helped her to her feet and gestured her toward the far corner of the room, where he bent over and spoke just loud enough for her to hear. "I have a friend on the Chicago police force. I could ask him if he's heard anything about this." When her eyes took on a wary look, he hastened to add, "I will be discreet. I promise you that. I don't want anything happening to our Adam any more than you do."

It wasn't until he saw the corners of Emily's lips curve that he realized he had slipped into Mrs. Purvis's possessive habit of referring to the boy. The smile that lit up her warm green eyes, only inches away from his, made him feel as if the two of them existed in some remote spot with no one around but themselves.

If that were truly the case, rather than having a little boy playing with blocks on the nearby rug and Mrs. Purvis carrying food from the kitchen to the dining table, he would be sorely tempted to steal a kiss. He looked at her lips, so soft and inviting, and made an effort to keep his arms at his sides instead of reaching out and drawing her to him.

The look in her eyes changed, and he wondered if she sensed his inner struggle. Did she share any of those feelings? Maybe they could adjourn to the front porch to discuss Adam's situation out of his hearing. He was about to suggest that when Mrs. Purvis came back into the room.

"Dinner's ready." She included all three of them in her cheery smile. "I told you I'd have it fixed in a jiffy."

Adam jumped up, scattering blocks across the rug, and pelted across the room, where he dove behind a heavy overstuffed chair in the far corner.

Mrs. Purvis's jaw sagged. "Well, would you look at that?"

The look on Emily's face told Stephen she was just as astounded as he was. "Adam," she called. "Come on. It's time to get ready to eat."

The little boy remained in the recess behind the chair and stared at them with wide, frightened eyes.

Emily crossed the room and knelt down beside the chair. She held out her hand. "Come on, Adam," she coaxed. "Let's go have dinner."

Adam regarded her steadily. Finally he reached out and took her hand and allowed her to draw him out.

He fidgeted throughout the meal, showing little interest in the pot roast and green beans. Even a slice of Mrs. Purvis's apple pie failed to bring forth any enthusiasm.

Aside from Adam's odd behavior, Stephen felt the meal went

swimmingly. Mrs. Purvis regaled them with stories of life in Chicago before the Great Fire of '71.

Emily drank in the stories as though listening to tales about a foreign land. For the first time, Stephen began to realize the depth of her isolation behind the walls of the children's home. Someday, he promised himself, he would show her much more of the world and his little corner of it.

His thoughts continued as she walked him to the door after they finished eating. He collected his hat from the hall tree and lingered a moment, knowing it was getting late but not wanting to end their time together. He ran his hands around the brim of his hat and tried to think of something to say.

"I'm glad we had this evening to work things out." He leaned back against the doorjamb, enjoying the way the lamplight played across her face and hair. "It was nice of Mrs. Purvis to invite me to stay."

Emily smiled. "She's a dear, isn't she? I think she likes you."

Her casual statement brought Seth's joking comment to mind. Maybe what his friend had said about Stephen's bachelor days being numbered wasn't such a bad thing to contemplate.

In the distance, he could hear the muted rattle of dishes as Lucy and Mrs. Purvis cleared the table. But apart from that, he and Emily seemed to be set apart from the rest of the world.

The hallway suddenly seemed to shrink, and Stephen closed the space between them with a single step. Emily looked up at him, and he could see the pulse throbbing at the base of her throat. To bring the evening to a perfect conclusion, all he had to do was sweep her into his arms, bend down, and claim those inviting, petal pink lips.

But should he? He swallowed, his throat suddenly gone dry. Searching her gaze, he saw only welcome there. He reached toward her and watched her eyelids flutter closed, her lashes fanning across her smooth cheeks.

Not yet. His pent-up breath escaped in a long sigh, and he balled his hands into fists, feeling the hat brim crumple under his grasp. Not tonight. It was too much, too soon. They still had things to iron out between them, issues that had to be resolved before he took a step in a direction they might both regret.

Emily's eyes opened. She tilted her head to look up at him, questions lingering in those emerald pools.

"I'd better say good night." His voice came out in a rough whisper. "We'll tackle this problem together," he said, not sure whether he referred more to the situation with Adam or to his romantic dilemma.

Emily pressed her lips together and nodded but didn't speak.

Stephen took a step back. "We'll do everything we can to locate his family—I can promise you that."

He left her standing in the entry hall with the lamplight glinting off the sheen of moisture in her eyes.

———

Ian McGinty crumpled the stack of receipts in his fist and flung them away from his desk. He reached for another set. Surely business couldn't be that bad everywhere.

He flipped through the slips of paper, running a quick tally in his mind. The resulting sum made him feel as though someone had punched him in the stomach with a fist of concrete. The saloons were losing money, all of them. What about the gambling dens?

He pulled a slim ledger toward him and ran his finger down the column of figures on the last page. The news there was no better. Muttering an oath, he shoved the book away from him.

It teetered on the edge of his desk then dropped to the floor.

Planting his elbows on the desk, he stabbed his fingers through his hair and pressed the heels of his hands against his brow. He was losing money everywhere, in every area of business he controlled. The saloons, the gambling halls, the trafficking—income from every one of them was dropping at an alarming rate.

Not only that, but the number of people coming to him for loans had fallen off. A few business owners down in the Levee had been brazen enough to refuse to turn over their protection money when his men went to collect.

He took a long, slow breath and pulled himself together. This was no time to fall apart. He needed to assess the situation with the cold light of logic. He stared at the corner of his desk and forced himself to put his thoughts in order.

Someone was moving in on his territory. There was no other explanation for it.

But who? And how?

It couldn't be any of the men working for him. None of them had the brains for it. He sucked in a breath. And maybe that was where he had made his error. Perhaps the threat of strife from within had blinded him to the necessity of maintaining an alert system to warn of an attack from outside.

In his business, he couldn't afford to make a mistake like that. He needed to find out who was behind the decline, make a quick strike, and push them back out.

Who would do this? He shook his head. His name was known throughout Chicago as the person one didn't want to cross. Who would have dared to go up against the organization he had so carefully constructed?

He picked up his pen and studied it. It must be someone new, someone who'd come into the city full of arrogance, thinking they could topple McGinty off his seat of control.

That had to be it. The pieces didn't fit together any other way.

He tapped the end of the pen against the blotter. Their arrogance wouldn't last long. He would find out who they were, where they were, and wipe them out with such a crushing blow that no one would ever have the temerity to try the same thing again.

A knock rattled the door, startling him from his murderous thoughts. The door swung open, and Mort strolled into the room.

McGinty welcomed the opportunity to give vent to his dark feelings. "What do you want?" he barked.

Mort flinched visibly, and McGinty felt himself relax for the first time that evening. This was the way things were supposed to be.

The man's lips stretched into a fawning smile. "I found out a few things I think you'll want to know."

McGinty narrowed his eyes. "Don't stand there grinning like an ape. Tell me what you've got, or get out."

Mort pulled a handkerchief from his back pocket and mopped his brow. His hand trembled visibly when he tucked the square of fabric back into its place. "I went to the fairgrounds like you said."

McGinty's attention sharpened.

"I talked to a lady at the Children's Building. That's where they take the lost kids."

"Go on. Did you find the boy?"

"Not exactly."

McGinty brought his fist down, impaling the blotter with the pen point. "Quit blathering, man, and get to the point."

"I told her we'd been looking for my brother's kid for a couple of days. I asked her if he might have wound up there and what they'd do with him if no one came to pick him up."

"You didn't give her your name, did you?"

Mort looked deeply offended. "No, of course not. What do you take me for?"

McGinty forbore to answer.

"She seemed nice enough and all, but I kept thinking she was trying to hide something. She wasn't acting quite straight with me, if you know what I mean. You know how it is when someone doesn't keep a poker face and you can tell they've got a good hand? That's what it was like."

McGinty nodded, accepting the premise but wondering if his minion's card-playing skills were sharp enough to read this woman correctly. On the other hand, thin as the link might be, she was the only possible lead they had. He steepled his fingers and looked up at his subordinate. "But there's really no way to know for sure."

Mort lit up like one of Edison's incandescent bulbs. "Actually, boss, we do."

McGinty leaned forward. "What do you mean?"

"Like I said, I had a notion. So I hung around until she got off work; then I followed her home."

McGinty's interest quickened. Maybe he had underestimated the man's usefulness. "And what did you learn?"

"Not so much the first night, except that she lives in a brick house on Blackstone Avenue. Nice neighborhood. She was walking with a blond girl, and they both went into the same house."

McGinty drummed his fingers on the blotter. "Is there some meat in all this gravy?"

Mort flushed and went on talking. "I didn't want to stick around too long. There aren't a lot of people out and about on that street like there are on the fairgrounds, and I knew she'd recognize me if she saw me again. So I went down to Gilly's Pub and got that kid you had watching your lady friend's house. The kid's smart, and he keeps a sharp lookout. I showed him the house and told him to keep his eyes open.

"He watched the house until all the lights were out. Then he came back this morning and followed her to the fairgrounds. When she went inside the Children's Building, he knew it wasn't worth hanging around, so he went back to the house, just in case there was something to be seen."

Mort grinned. "That's where we hit pay dirt. He crawled back under the bush and sat tight. And it's a good thing, because what does he see? The door opens, and four people come out on the front porch. There's an old lady, a young lady, and two little kids. The young lady and one of the kids say good-bye and go off down the street, but the old lady and the other kid go back inside the house. He's there, boss, with the girl I talked to at the fair."

McGinty quashed the hope that surged up within him. "How do we know it's the right boy?"

Mort puffed out his chest. "The kid doing the watching recognized him. It's the same one, all right. We've got him."

McGinty felt as if a jolt of electricity tingled his fingertips. "Is he sure the boy wasn't just visiting?"

"He's sure. He stayed there and watched until the lady from the Children's Building came home. This time she was with some big guy."

"Her husband?" That would change his method of approach. Women weren't as easily intimidated when a strong, young husband was involved.

"Nah, the kid kept on watching until he saw the big guy leave. That's when he came to tell me, and then I came here to tell you." Mort wore a proud expression that reminded McGinty of a dog expecting a treat after performing some trick.

He ignored the man, focusing instead on thinking the situation through. He needed to check all the pieces and see if they fit together. Why did this young woman have the boy? Was she acting purely on the instincts of a good Samaritan? Or had a subtler plan been set in motion, one connected with the attempt to overthrow him?

His interest was piqued. He was no stranger to planting spies in various places to keep watch over his enemies. It would make sense for his new rival to do the same, even bribing an innocent-looking young woman to participate in a scheme to gain control over him by holding his son.

His son. The heir to whom he would bequeath all the earthly goods he had accumulated. Assuming he could hold on to them.

A flash of anger ignited at the reminder of his current vulnerability. If he didn't take care of this interloper, there might not be anything left to pass on to his son and heir. He slammed his fist into his open palm. He would have to deal with this threat and deal with it decisively, before he was ready to make the next move. There was no way he could take a child into his life right now.

And even then, once the invader had been soundly crushed, he would need someone to care for the boy. He couldn't very well have him underfoot day in and day out. McGinty ground the heel of his hand against his forehead while he sorted out this new dilemma. He knew plenty of available women all around the city, but none suitable for rearing a child. Not his child.

Leave him where he is. The thought hit him like a bolt out of the blue. The woman who had him worked in the Children's Building. She was used to caring for youngsters. If she chose to care for Adam for whatever reason, well then. . .let her.

A chuckle rumbled from his chest; then he threw back his head and laughed out loud, feeling more buoyant than he had all evening. If she—or whoever was directing her actions—thought to use the boy as bait, they would have a long wait before the fish took the hook.

They wanted the boy? They could keep the boy. The child would be available for him to pluck up whenever he was ready.

The thought of turning the tables on his faceless adversary pleased him. And while he was at it, why not move the competition to a higher level? The notion warmed him. Yes, that was exactly what he would do—let them know he was aware of their scheme and was keeping an eye on them in turn.

CHAPTER 11

"Look, it's a lion!"

Stephen leaned close enough to be heard over the ruckus of shrieking children. "It was a wonderful idea to bring him here."

"Actually, it was Adam's idea in the first place." Emily sent up a quick prayer of gratitude at being able to keep her promise to him. It had been well worth the effort. Her heart swelled at the sight of the little boy bouncing on the bench beside her. His eyes shone, and he wore the brightest smile she had seen since the day Stephen had brought him to the Children's Building.

So this was what he looked like when he was truly being himself instead of a lonely little waif. Stephen's gaze met hers over the top of Adam's head, and she knew he was thinking the same thing.

She put one arm around Adam's thin shoulders and pulled him into a quick hug, then released him so he could turn his attention back to the sights and sounds of Hagenbeck's Animal Show. On her other side, a stout woman claimed more room on the bench, moving so close that her elbows jutted into Emily's ribs.

Emily pulled Adam onto her lap and scooted a couple of inches to her left to give the woman additional space. With no barrier between her and Stephen, she found it easier to lean over and put her lips near his ear in order to be heard without shouting. "I'm so glad we both had our day off today so we could enjoy this together."

The corners of Stephen's mustache quirked up. "I had to pull a few strings, but I agree. I wouldn't have wanted to miss it."

Emily studied him under her lowered lashes. Did he mean he didn't want to miss seeing the animal show and enjoying it with Adam. . .or spending the time with her?

The woman beside her spread out even farther, and Emily slid over again. The move brought her elbow to elbow with Stephen. She glanced up at him again, not wanting him to think she was being forward. Apparently he didn't object at all to her nearness. The look in his eyes sent her heart skipping along at an uneven pace.

Emily pretended to focus her attention on the tiger riding on horseback. So Stephen had to make special arrangements in order to spend this time with her. She resisted the urge to wave her arms and whoop like the little boy in her lap.

Prince, the highly touted equestrian lion, circled the ring on horseback. Polar bears teetered across a tightrope, and zebras cavorted around the sawdust-covered floor.

Karl Hagenbeck himself presided over the grand finale, which was met with wild applause by young and old. With Adam between them, Emily and Stephen joined the crowd filing out of the arena and back into the bright September afternoon.

"Can we go again?" Adam begged.

Stephen laughed and ruffled the little boy's hair. The light breeze blowing toward the lake stirred the blond strands even more. He picked the little boy up and held him in his left arm, then cupped Emily's elbow in his right hand. "Tell you what, buddy. I'll just bet they have even more sights to see on these fairgrounds. Let's go look around and see what we can find."

They strolled the broad walkway of the Midway Plaisance, taking in the Javan Settlement, the German Village, and the Turkish Village opposite.

Emily stared in delight. "This is like going on a world tour without ever leaving home."

Stephen laughed. "I won't argue with you on that." When they passed under the next viaduct, he swept his arm out in an arc in the manner of a tour guide. "To your right, Egypt. Otherwise known as 'A Street in Cairo.'"

Camels carried footsore fairgoers past buildings topped with minarets. Young boys held up trays of trinkets and shouted at the passersby, offering their wares.

Emily gave the Old Vienna exhibit an appraising glance as they passed. "Maybe we should take Adam in and let him see some of the exhibits in these places. They might be very educational."

Stephen looked around, and she saw him try to wipe away a smile. "I don't know that Vienna will hold much appeal for a three-year-old, but there's an ostrich farm right over there."

"What a grand idea. Look, Adam!" She led the way, cutting across the stream of fairgoers to stand in front of the fenced enclosure housing the ungainly looking birds. The ploy proved successful in holding Adam's attention for a few moments, at least.

As they retraced their route, Stephen moved out into the middle of the walkway. "I have an idea of something this young man might be interested in. What do you say to that?"

He pointed toward the sky, and all three of them tipped back their heads to gaze up, up, up to the top of the great wheel that soared high above the Midway. Stephen turned to Adam. "What do you think?"

Adam's face took on a look of pure adoration. He nodded his head vigorously and jiggled in Stephen's arms.

"Is it all right with you?" Stephen threw an apologetic glance at Emily. "I should have checked with you first."

"I think it's a fine idea." She bounced on her toes and tried to curb her own desire to do a little dance of her own.

They joined the line that zigzagged up a series of steps to the loading platforms. As the line moved forward, Stephen set Adam down between them and turned to Emily. "There's something I've been meaning to ask you."

Torn between gazing raptly at the giant wheel and planning what she would tell Lucy about her great adventure, Emily barely glanced at him. "Yes?"

"My parents are coming to town tomorrow from Springfield. My father has some business in the city, and they've invited me to dine with them in the evening." Stephen cleared his throat. "Would you care to join us? I'd like for them to meet you."

Emily's lips parted, and she whirled around to study his face. He wanted her to meet his family? What did that mean? Or did it mean anything? Once again, she was made painfully aware that growing up in the orphanage had given her no point of reference for understanding such things.

"I hope you'll say yes. It's just going to be a casual family dinner." Stephen looked at her expectantly.

Emily knew she had to say something. She nodded her head then finally found her voice. "I'd like to very much," she said simply, warning herself she mustn't make too much of the invitation. Perhaps it was only a friendly gesture on his part and not an event of great significance.

They stepped up onto the loading platform at last, and a uniformed guard opened the door at the end of the long car the size of a Pullman sleeper. The three of them filed in along with the other passengers. Inside, two rows of circular padded seats ran down the center of the car, with room left over for those who preferred to stand. Emily took the padded seat at the nearest end and pulled Adam into her lap. Stephen stood close beside her.

Adam wriggled in her lap as if unable to contain his joy. Emily couldn't blame him; she felt like wiggling herself. How many times had she watched the great wheel make its circuit up into the sky and wished she could be one of those on board? And now she was!

The guard closed and locked the door and stood in front of it. An older woman to Emily's left fluttered her hands. "You're sure this is safe?"

The guard smiled. "Perfectly, ma'am. You have nothing to worry about. Just enjoy the sight of the fairgrounds and Chicago at your feet."

The beginning of their circuit was so smooth that Emily didn't realize they were ascending until she saw the dome of the Moorish Palace drop away below them.

Adam scrambled down from her lap and ran to the window. He peered out the glass, his face wreathed in utter delight. "Look, Mama, look! We're flying!"

Emily froze, uncertain she had heard him correctly. One look at Stephen's startled face told her she had. She left her cushioned seat and picked the little boy up. "That's right, sweetheart. We're going right up into the air."

Stephen stepped up beside her and took Adam, relieving her

of the child's weight and holding him higher so he could see even more of the panorama spread out before them. The elderly woman bestowed a pleasant smile upon them.

As though she were standing a distance away and looking at the three of them, Emily realized what the other passengers saw. They looked like a family.

Family. She had never been entirely comfortable with the word. Up to now, it had never meant more to her than a longing in her heart. But Stephen had a family.

And he wanted her to meet them.

Panic trickled into her mind. She didn't have any family for him to meet. The closest she could come to that was Lucy, more like a sister to her than a friend. And she had given Stephen her unreserved approval.

Emily looked at the little boy who had just called her "Mama." He had a family, too, or he used to. A thought stirred in her mind. If their efforts to find his family proved fruitless, could she keep him with her?

Up to now, she had seen their arrangement as a temporary one, but his innocent misstatement opened the door to feelings she hadn't known she possessed. Would she be willing to become Adam's family if his relatives could not be found?

In the next heartbeat, she realized she could open her heart to this little boy without the slightest hesitation.

By the time the wheel made its second revolution and began stopping at intervals to let passengers disembark and take new ones on board, Adam's wild excitement had subsided only a bit. When they left the loading platform and made their way back down the steps to ground level, he wrapped his arms around Stephen's neck.

Stephen gave him a tight hug. "Did you enjoy it?"

Adam's face shone. "Yes!" He pressed his cheek to Stephen's. "Thank you, thank you, thank you!"

Stephen grinned at Emily. "I think we can say our outing has been a success." He set Adam on the ground, and Emily took his hand.

"What a wonderful experience!" She turned back to watch the wheel glide up into the air at a stately pace. "I know we were up there quite a while, but in a way, it seemed it was all over in just a jiffy."

In a flash, Adam jerked his hand from her grasp and darted across the walkway, weaving in and out through the pedestrians and ignoring their startled cries. Emily hiked up her skirt hem and raced after him, with Stephen at her side.

A large basket, big enough to hold a man, stood in front of one of the buildings that lined the replica of a street in Cairo. Adam dove into the narrow space between the basket and the building and huddled into a tiny ball.

Emily ran up to him. "Adam, what's wrong?"

He looked up at her, wide-eyed. His lips moved, and she had to bend down to be able to hear him over the noise of the nearby crowd. "Tell me again," she urged.

"You said 'jiffy.'"

An image flashed into Emily's mind: Adam hiding behind the overstuffed chair in the boardinghouse parlor. What was it Mrs. Purvis had said just before that? Wasn't it something about having dinner ready in a jiffy?

She stared at Adam. "Why are you hiding here? Is it because I said 'jiffy'?"

He nodded solemnly. " 'Jiffy' means run and hide."

The fog of confusion began to dissipate. Emily took both of his hands in hers. "Did your mama tell you that?"

Adam nodded, his eyes still wide and frightened. Emily pulled him into her arms and cradled him, rocking back and forth. Why would his mother have done such an odd thing? The fog lifted further. It had to be some kind of code word, a means of telling Adam to seek protection without saying it outright.

She looked up at Stephen, who helped her to her feet with the tense little boy still in her arms. Emily held Adam tight, her thoughts in a whirl. His mother had known she was in danger even before that fateful day on the fairgrounds. What kind of straits would she have had to be in to feel compelled to set up a signal like that to ensure the safety of her child?

Emily pulled Adam away from her shoulder and turned his face to meet her gaze squarely. "I'm sorry. I didn't mean to frighten you. I promise I will not use that word again."

Adam gave her a long, measuring look. "Unless you mean run and hide?"

A smile curved Emily's lips. That would be an easy promise to make. She couldn't imagine a situation that would require its use. "Unless I mean for you to run and hide."

CHAPTER 12

Emily stood in the entry hall and clasped her hands against her stomach to quell the fluttering that threatened to unnerve her. She glanced at the mirror in the hall tree for what must have been the dozenth time since coming down from her room. "Do you think I look all right?"

Mrs. Purvis patted her shoulder. "You don't need to worry a bit. You'll do just fine."

Lucy smiled from her position by the front window. "You look beautiful, Emily."

Beside her, Adam nodded his agreement. "Beautiful."

Emily turned and pressed the tips of her gloved fingers against her cheeks. She hoped her friends were right and not just saying this to help allay her fears. She knew the royal blue dress and matching cape would not rank as the height of fashion, but up to now, the outfit had served her well as her "good" clothes. One good thing, at least, about growing up in the Collier Home—she and Lucy had both learned to sew at an early age, enabling them to copy some of the fashions they saw in *Harper's Bazaar.*

Lucy peeked out the window. "He's here," she called, her cheeks pink with excitement.

Maybe Emily should trade clothes with her friend and let Lucy go in her stead. She seemed far more exuberant about Emily's prospects for the evening. The nearer the time grew for the dinner with Stephen's parents, the greater Emily's sense of the hours ahead being an ordeal rather than a happy occasion.

A knock rattled the door. Mrs. Purvis and Lucy nearly knocked each other over in their haste to reach for the knob. Mrs. Purvis won the race, and Lucy stepped back and took Adam's hand.

Mrs. Purvis swung the door open, and Emily felt her breath squeeze from her lungs. "Good evening, Stephen." The landlady beamed. "Don't you look fine tonight!"

More than fine. Emily stared at her escort, resplendent in a black broadcloth suit.

Stephen thanked Mrs. Purvis; then his gaze roved around the entry hall until he found Emily. The gleam in his dark eyes told her he didn't find her appearance wanting.

"I won't keep her out too late." He addressed the words to Mrs. Purvis, though his eyes were still fastened on Emily.

"Take your time and enjoy yourselves." Mrs. Purvis smiled at him like a doting mother.

From behind the landlady, Lucy grinned and gave Emily a broad wink that made her cheeks flame. She hoped Stephen hadn't noticed.

She bent down to give Adam a hug and a kiss. "Good night. Miss Lucy will tuck you in tonight, and I'll see you in the morning."

Stephen joined her and reached over to shake Adam's hand.

"You be sure to take care of the ladies tonight, will you?"

Adam puffed out his chest and bobbed his head.

Stepping back, Stephen extended his arm to Emily. "Shall we?"

They walked outside, and Emily caught her breath when she saw not a cab but a carriage waiting at the curb. She looked up at Stephen, openmouthed.

"My uncle sent it for us," he explained. "We're having dinner at his house."

Emily clasped her hands to her stomach again. "But I thought—"

"Didn't I tell you my uncle lives in Chicago? I live in an apartment over his carriage house. When he heard we were planning to dine with my parents, he thought a meal at his home might make for a more relaxed atmosphere." He helped her into the carriage and seated himself beside her.

Stephen seemed content to make the ride in silence, while Emily sat rigidly upright with her hands knotted in her lap. What had she let herself in for? A meeting with his parents was one thing, but now there was an uncle thrown in for good measure. What other surprises did the evening have in store?

The carriage came to a stop in front of an elegant, two-story brownstone. Stephen helped her alight and made sure she was steady on her feet before leading her up the flagged walk to the heavy oak door.

A middle-aged woman in a dark gray dress took their hats and wraps. Emily half expected her to be introduced as Stephen's aunt, but he merely said, "Thank you, Grace."

"They're all back in the drawing room, Mr. Stephen."

He escorted Emily down the hall to the second door on the right. Two couples looked up when they paused in the doorway, and both men stood.

One of the women rose gracefully and swept across the room with her hands extended. "Good evening, my dear. We're so glad you could join us."

Stephen gestured with his free hand. "Aunt Martha, may I present Miss Emily Ralston. Emily, my aunt and uncle, Martha Charles and Bridger."

The older of the two women, shorter and a bit plumper than the first, was close behind. Stephen stepped over to her and gave her a hug. "Mother, I'd like you to meet Emily. Emily, this is my mother, Natalie Bridger, and my father, Thomas."

His mother stepped forward and enfolded Emily in a warm embrace. His father gave her a genial smile and said, "So this is the young lady who has gotten our boy in such a stir."

Emily could feel the blush start at the base of her neck and work its way up to her hairline. What on earth was he talking about, and what had Stephen said to them?

His mother swatted at her husband's arm. "Thomas, you're embarrassing the poor dear." She slipped her arm around Emily's waist. "Don't pay any attention to him. The Bridger men sometimes take a lot of training. I'm still working on this one."

Her gentle teasing didn't seem to put her husband off in the least. He clapped Stephen on the back. "But we know enough to pick women who will keep life interesting, eh, son?"

This time Emily could see a dull red flush creep up Stephen's neck. What a pair they must make!

Stephen's uncle hooked his thumbs in his vest pockets. "So you'll be ready to come join me next month as soon as this fair is over?" He added in an aside to Emily, "I've been waiting for him to join my architectural firm since his graduation. Going to be a full partner someday, this boy will."

Stephen stood a little taller at the praise. "Yes, and I appreciate your giving me a few months' grace to indulge in the opportunity to spend time studying such wonderful examples of architecture. I believe the knowledge I've gained will pay off handsomely for us both in the future."

The woman who had greeted them at the door appeared in the doorway and said, "Dinner is ready, Mrs. Bridger. Shall I serve it now?"

"Of course." Aunt Martha smiled at her guests. "We can continue our conversation over the meal."

They filed out of the drawing room and walked down the carpeted hallway to a richly appointed dining room. Though the table looked as if it would seat at least twenty, six places were clustered near one end, with Uncle Charles at the head. Aunt Martha smiled at Emily. "We thought it would be a little less formal this way."

Emily appreciated her thoughtfulness, even though the arrangements were much more upscale than anything she was used to. The last time she had seen a table that large was in the dining hall of the orphan asylum, with children seated elbow to elbow down each side. She shook the vision from her mind and took her seat on Uncle Charles's right. Stephen's father sat on her other side, with his aunt Martha on his right. Stephen's mother sat straight across the table from her, with Stephen on her left.

So much for the hope that Stephen would be seated next to her, where she could draw courage from him throughout the meal. She threw him a desperate glance, and he gave her an encouraging nod.

How she managed to survive the evening, she never knew. All four of the older Bridgers were friendly enough. More than friendly—almost effusive in their efforts to put her at ease and make her feel welcome. But Emily's ability to come up with polite responses was paralyzed by her fear of picking up the wrong fork or spoon. Once the meal ended, she still wasn't sure she had gotten it entirely right.

At the end of the evening, Stephen's parents and his aunt and uncle escorted them to the door, where Grace stood waiting with their hats and wraps. Stephen's father slipped Emily's cape over her shoulders.

Both Stephen's mother and Aunt Martha came over to give her a parting hug. Aunt Martha brushed her cheek with a kiss. "I truly enjoyed meeting you, dear. Do come again." Emily smiled and nodded, still at a loss for words.

Stephen's mother put her hands lightly on Emily's shoulders and gazed into her face. "I hope you'll visit us in Springfield whenever Stephen can bring you there. Let's plan an extended visit so we can really get to know one another. You still haven't met our other son and our daughter."

Emily swallowed hard and managed to get out the words, "Thank you. I'd like that." She cast a quick glance at Stephen, hoping she hadn't overstepped any bounds. He had brought her to meet his family, but she couldn't allow herself to read too much into that.

His family may have seemed to accept as fact the notion that she and Stephen were a couple who had intentions of building a future together, but the two of them had never discussed such a thing. She didn't want to build her hopes on something that might not have any more foundation than the sand castles built by optimistic children on the shore of Lake Michigan, ephemeral structures that washed away with the lap of the first big wave.

Again Stephen said little on the drive home. Emily sensed he was deep in thought, and she didn't want to do anything to disturb the hopeful mood that had enveloped her ever since his mother's parting words.

What was his purpose in bringing her to meet his family? Was it to see how well she would fit in or merely a social gathering? And if it were the former, had she passed muster? His family appeared to accept her readily enough, but Stephen was the one whose opinion mattered most. Emily still wasn't sure what effect the evening would have on his decision.

When the carriage rumbled up to the front of Mrs. Purvis's home, Stephen helped her out and escorted her up the walk, then up the steps to the front porch. Casting a quick glance back over his shoulder at the waiting carriage and driver, he opened the front door, and they both slipped inside the entry hall. Emily noted that he closed it behind them carefully, making no noise.

Stephen took both of her hands in his. "It has been a very special evening."

Emily smiled, her breath coming a bit more quickly. "You have a lovely family. I enjoyed meeting them." Despite the chill in the evening air, his smile warmed her through and through.

"They loved you from the moment they met you, I could tell. Just like—"

Emily waited, heart hammering, for him to finish the statement. His grip on her fingers tightened, and he bent toward her. His warm breath stirred the strands of hair at her temple as his lips grazed her left cheek.

Emily leaned her head to the side and pressed her cheek against his for a fleeting instant, aghast at her own boldness.

It didn't seem to put Stephen off in the least. He brushed his lips against her cheek once more before he straightened. "May I see you again tomorrow evening?"

Emily returned the pressure on his fingers before she slid her hands from his grasp and clasped them in front of her waist. "I'll be here," she said simply.

When the door closed behind him, she slid the bolt into place and floated toward the stairway, feeling as though her feet never touched the ground. At the foot of the stairs, she hesitated, seeing a faint glow of light emanating from the kitchen.

Emily made her way through the darkened parlor. As she suspected, Mrs. Purvis and Lucy were gathered around the kitchen table.

Lucy gave a little squeal when Emily stepped into the room. "How did it go?" Still caught up in her happy daze, Emily only smiled.

Mrs. Purvis patted the chair next to hers. "Did you have a nice time, dear? Let me get you a nice cup of tea, and you can tell us all about it." She picked up the flowered teapot and filled a cup that sat in front of Emily's place.

Lucy folded her arms on the table and leaned forward, her eyes aglow. "Did he kiss you?"

Emily felt her face color. She drew herself up with as much dignity as she could muster. "I'll have you know he was a perfect gentleman."

Lucy's shoulders slumped. "He didn't, then."

Mrs. Purvis made a tsking noise. "All in good time, my dears. All in good time. These things can't be hurried. Why, when my Randolph was courting me. . ."

Her voice trailed off, and her eyes misted. "You've had a busy evening. What makes me think you'll want to listen to an old woman's ramblings?"

"No, go ahead," Emily urged.

Mrs. Purvis needed little prompting. Her eyes lit up, and she scooted onto the edge of her chair. "We had both been married before and had each lost our spouse. Some people would have said that by the time we turned thirty, we should have been old enough not to worry about playing any silly, romantic games."

A tinge of pink colored her pale cheeks. "Thankfully Randolph never felt that way. He was the most devoted suitor a woman could ask for. It made me feel like a girl all over again, it did. Even today, I get giddy remembering the way he would woo me, bringing me flowers and little gifts just as if he were a young buck pursuing his first love."

Emily and Lucy exchanged glances and smiled. Seeing the light in Mrs. Purvis's eyes, Emily could almost picture the appealing young woman she had been.

"We had nearly two months of stepping out, attending parties and church functions together, before he even dared to bestow a kiss upon me." She sighed. "But that's what a gentleman does."

Emily shot a look of triumph at Lucy, who had the grace to look somewhat abashed.

"And he loved his little games, Randolph did. He would hide special gifts—treasures, he called them—here and there and leave little clues that would lead me to them. One time he left an acorn on my entry table. That was a clue to go look in the fork of the old oak tree. I found a lovely fan he'd hidden there." She leaned her chin on her hand and sighed. "It was so romantic. He knew exactly the way to win my heart."

Emily's throat tightened. Listening to the stories and hearing the tenderness in Mrs. Purvis's voice, she could easily imagine the love she and her husband had shared. How sad she didn't have that anymore.

The landlady's voice took on a dreamy tone. "He continued our little treasure hunts even after we were married. Some men grow stodgy and a little distant once they've said their vows, but not my Randolph. He kept hiding treasures and leaving me clues for as long as we were married."

Lucy sighed. "It sounds like you had a wonderful life together."

"Oh, it wasn't without its share of troubles," Mrs. Purvis said with a gentle smile. "No life ever is. We weathered a number of hard times together. We survived the Great Fire of '71 and another a few years after that. When we built this house, Randolph told me we would never again lose everything in a fire.

"We had just finished moving into this house, and he was as excited as a boy. He said he was planning one more treasure hunt, that he had something to show me that would put my mind at ease for the rest of our days."

Her normally cheery expression faded, and the light in her eyes dimmed. "Not long after that, he took sick, and it wasn't any time at all until he was gone."

Emotion clogged Emily's throat. Looking at Lucy, she knew her friend was fighting tears, as well. How she admired this dear lady for the way she managed to keep up such a sunny view of life after all she had endured!

Mrs. Purvis dabbed at her eyes and took a sip of tea. "I must have been in a daze for quite some time after that. It was all so totally unexpected. When I finally came to myself again and started sorting through Randolph's things, I looked for several things I wanted to keep as mementos. And would you believe it? I couldn't find a one of them!" She shook her head. "I must have put them somewhere without realizing, maybe even packed them up with the clothes I gave away. And so there I was, without my little treasures. . .or Randolph.

"But sometimes it seems like a part of him is still with me. I've never forgotten his promise that he had found a way to be sure

I would always be provided for."

What an inspiring story! Emily lifted her cup of tea to her lips and sipped.

Mrs. Purvis tilted her head to one side. "You girls may have noticed I do a bit of tapping on the walls from time to time."

Emily choked and sent a fine mist of tea spraying across the table. Lucy handed her a napkin without meeting her eyes. Emily took it, grateful for her friend's restraint. She knew if their gazes met, they would both break into peals of laughter.

Not seeming to notice, Mrs. Purvis went on. "Randolph told me he and the architect had worked an unusual feature into the plan for this house, and I never knew him to go back on his word. I have no idea what he meant, though, and the architect left town before Randolph passed away, so there's no one who can tell me what it might have been. I've been searching for it every way I could think of all these years."

Emily reached across the table and took one of Mrs. Purvis's hands in her own. "I'm sure you'll find it some day."

Mrs. Purvis beamed at them both. "Thank you, my dears. It's kind of you to say so. I don't intend to give up. Somehow it helps me feel that the connection between us hasn't been severed entirely."

Lucy stood and bent to kiss the landlady on the cheek. "I'll just clear away my cup and saucer, and then I should be off to bed." She set her dishes in the sink, said her good nights, and headed for the stairs.

Emily finished her tea and prepared to clear her own cup away. Mrs. Purvis seemed in no hurry to end their conversation. She laced her fingers together and leaned forward. "I didn't give you much chance to talk about your evening. Did you like Stephen's parents?"

"Very much." Emily's lips curved in a dreamy smile. "I met his uncle and aunt, too. They're all lovely people. It's just that. . ."

"What is it, dear?"

"I knew Stephen was a recent college graduate, but I didn't know anything at all about his background."

A tiny frown creased Mrs. Purvis's forehead. "Was something wrong with his family?"

"Far from it! They're some of the nicest people I've ever met. They made me feel so welcome."

"Then what could possibly be wrong? I sense you're distressed about something."

"It's just that I never expected them to be so well off. Stephen doesn't strike me at all as the type of person who comes from a wealthy family. He's so down-to-earth and easy to talk to. His uncle owns the architectural firm where Stephen plans to work as soon as the fair is over."

Mrs. Purvis perked up. "That sounds very promising."

"But I'm not sure. . . ."

"You aren't sure of your feelings for Stephen?"

Heat washed over Emily's face. "No, that isn't it. It's me. I don't know that I can live up to that kind of standard. Lucy and I not only grew up at the Collier Home; we stayed on to work there as helpers long after the others our age went on to make their way in the world."

She gave an embarrassed laugh. "We didn't get more than room and board, but at least we were able to stay in the only home we'd ever known. Until recently, that is. The benefactor who supported the home lost his money in the silver crash, and they had to close its doors."

"Oh my." Mrs. Purvis reached out to smooth a strand of hair off Emily's forehead. The gesture reminded Emily of the way she brushed Adam's hair back when he was fretting about something.

"Lucy and I are out on our own for the first time in our lives. I have no background, no family. What would make anyone think I'm good enough for people like the Bridgers?"

The landlady gave Emily a glance that seemed to look into her soul. "You're a believer, aren't you?"

The question brought Emily up short. "Why, of course. Ever since I was a young girl."

"And did you have to worry about being good enough for God, or did He accept you just the way you were?"

Memories of that wondrous discovery of God's unconditional love washed over Emily. She shook her head.

"Then you must know that God loved you enough to send His Son to die for you. If He could love you that much and accept you as you are, don't you think Stephen can love you enough to do the same? From what I've seen of that young man, he has a heart big enough to overlook the differences in your backgrounds and see the person beneath the surface."

Her gentle smile broadened. "And what I believe he sees in you, Emily, dear, is a priceless treasure. The man would be a fool not to notice that, and I don't believe your young Mr. Bridger is any kind of fool."

CHAPTER 13

Were you able to find out anything for me?" Stephen glanced at the pedestrians wending their way along the street outside the precinct house and kept his voice low, trying to look like a passerby asking directions from the uniformed policeman beside him.

Patrolman Elliott Ferguson nodded. "Somebody recognized her when they brought the body in. Her first name is Rosalee. We don't have a last name at the moment."

Stephen drew his brows together. "Recognized her? You mean she's been in trouble with the law before?" He thought about the fallen women who plied their trade in the Levee. Had she been one of their number? Surely not. Everything about Adam indicated a much more refined upbringing than he could possibly get in such a setting.

"Not in the way you're probably thinking. But some of the boys in the precinct know the man she kept company with."

A prickle of foreboding ran up Stephen's back. He braced himself, certain his friend was about to impart some highly unpleasant news. "Tell me more."

Elliott strode a few steps farther from the precinct house and pointed down the street, as if guiding Stephen to some fictitious destination. He spoke out of the corner of his mouth. "Have you ever heard of a man named Ian McGinty?"

Stephen's head whipped around. "McGinty?" At Elliott's stern look, he dropped his voice to a whisper. "Everyone in Chicago knows that name. He has his finger in every pie, from politics to prostitution. How the man maintains his social connections and keeps from being brought up on charges is something I've never understood."

Elliott grimaced. "You just answered your own question. If you have connections in high enough places"—he lowered his voice further—"including some in this department, you can pretty well consider yourself protected from prosecution. Grease enough palms, and you'll find people are willing to overlook almost anything."

"So this Rosalee was his—"

Elliott shrugged. " 'Kept woman' is probably the kindest term I can think of. He maintained her in her own home for the past five years. Didn't live there himself, but she was available as an ornament on his arm whenever he attended a social function. From what I've heard, she seemed surprisingly refined for someone in her position. But you can imagine how the hostesses in the social register felt about having to invite her to any of their soirees or about having their husbands anywhere near her."

Stephen searched for a question that wouldn't tip his hand. "Did she have any family that you know of?"

Elliott shook his head. "No one to come claim the body, if

that's what you're asking. And apparently McGinty is keeping a distance. There are rumors of a child, but I couldn't press for more without arousing suspicions."

"Is there any way to tie McGinty to her death?"

Elliott let out a short bark of laughter. "You know better than that. He never dirties his hands himself. If he ever did, maybe then we'd have the wherewithal to nab him and bring charges against him. No, if he was connected with this in any way, he had one of his underlings carry it out. But we'll never be able to prove it."

Stephen pondered the information for a moment. "No, I suppose not. Thanks for the help. I don't want to take up any more of your time. I'm just a poor lost visitor to this fair city, remember?" He strode along quickly, mindful of the time. He didn't want to be late this evening, not after he had spent the day looking forward to seeing Emily.

Keeping up the rapid pace for a couple of blocks, he turned the next corner and let his steps slow. Would Emily be glad to see him after he shared what he had just learned? He'd hoped to have good news for her, news that would help them find out who Adam was and reconnect him with his family.

Now they knew who he was, but it only made the situation worse.

This woman, this Rosalee—Adam's mother—was the mistress of one of the worst figures in Chicago's underworld, a man who ordered his henchmen to snuff out human life without a second thought. Did that mean...

He thought back, trying to remember Elliott's exact words. She had been kept by McGinty for the past five years. And McGinty was not the type of man to share what was his. Therefore...

Stephen felt as if the sidewalk were tipping beneath his feet. The nearby buildings seemed to sway, then right themselves. In that case, Adam was Ian McGinty's son.

His thoughts turned to the woman whose body had been discovered in the storage shed. An icy dread started in the pit of his stomach then threaded its way through his whole body. There might not be any proof, but Stephen felt sure McGinty was connected with her death. And if McGinty was willing to do this to the mother of his child, what would he be willing to do to a helpless little boy?

What would he be willing to do to Emily?

"How do these look?" Emily pulled a tray of macaroons from the oven and set them on top of the stove.

Mrs. Purvis lifted the edge of one with the tip of a knife and peered underneath. "Done to a turn. A beautiful golden brown."

Emily glowed with pleasure at Mrs. Purvis's approval. With her help, she set the dainty cookies on a rack to cool.

"It's a lovely idea you had about baking some treats for tonight," the landlady went on. "It doesn't hurt a bit to let your young man know you have some experience in the kitchen."

Emily thought back to the afternoon's first batch of macaroons, now laid to rest in the dustbin. That experience wasn't one she wanted to share with Stephen. Opening the windows had helped, but only after Lucy and Mrs. Purvis joined her in fanning the air with dish towels did the acrid smell of burnt cookies begin to dissipate.

Mrs. Purvis pulled out a delicate china tray and helped Emily arrange the macaroons on its painted surface. "You know what they say," she reminded Emily with a twinkle. "The way to a man's heart is through his stomach."

She cast a glance at the cupboard in the corner of the kitchen and smiled. "I wouldn't be surprised if I find myself adding another pair of names to my list before long."

Emily felt her pulse quicken, and she gave a nervous laugh. "Why don't we go back to what you said about letting things take their course, like they did with you and Mr. Purvis?"

She pressed her fingertips against her cheeks. Much as Mrs. Purvis's comments might stir hope, she couldn't allow her imagination to run too far ahead of reality. She carried the tray into the parlor, where Lucy helped Mrs. Purvis arrange a pair of chairs so that they faced the settee.

"A pleasant little grouping." Mrs. Purvis's voice held a note of satisfaction. "It will let us carry on a conversation quite nicely."

Emily breathed deeply, trying to quiet her nerves. She looked over at Lucy. "Did you check on Adam?"

"Right after you asked me to," Lucy assured her. "He was just as you left him, sleeping soundly."

"He and Matthew played hard this afternoon," Mrs. Purvis observed. "I think he was ready to drift off when I gave him his bath before supper. The poor little fellow is all tuckered out."

Emily noticed the way Mrs. Purvis and Lucy headed straight for the chairs, leaving the settee to her. Apparently all three of them hoped Stephen would join her there when he arrived.

Mrs. Purvis lifted her head. "I believe I heard the doorknob rattle. I'll just go see if that's him now."

"No wonder Adam is exhausted." Lucy picked up their earlier thread of conversation. "He's been through more lately than any adult would want to deal with."

Emily nodded. "What could be worse than being on the fairgrounds expecting a lovely outing and then having your mother disappear?"

Stephen stepped into the room just as Mrs. Purvis reached the doorway. "How about having one of the most vicious criminals in Chicago for a father?"

The landlady let out a yip and took a couple of steps back.

Emily looked at Stephen for some indication that he was making some sort of bizarre joke, but one glance at his somber face told her otherwise. "What do you mean?"

Stephen strode across the room and took his seat on the other end of the settee. He looked around. "Where's Adam?"

"He's upstairs sleeping," Emily said.

"Soundly," Lucy assured him. "I checked."

Stephen gazed at the three women in turn. "I was just talking to a friend of mine on the Chicago police force. The official word is that the woman whose body we found was the paramour of a man known as Ian McGinty."

Mrs. Purvis's hand flew to her mouth. "I've heard the name. You can't mean. . ."

Stephen nodded heavily. "I'm afraid so. She has been. . .with McGinty for a number of years."

Emily and Lucy exchanged glances. "I have no idea who you're talking about," Emily said. "Who is this man?"

Stephen's lips pressed together in a grim line. "Name an illicit activity anywhere in this city, and McGinty is sure to be part of it. More than a part, though. He's behind most of it and has raked in a considerable fortune through the degradation of others."

"But. . . ," Emily floundered. "I don't understand what this has to do with us."

Stephen looked straight at her. "It seems evident that Ian McGinty is Adam's father."

In the silence that followed, Emily could hear the measured beat of her own heart.

"I can't believe that," Lucy said.

Mrs. Purvis returned to her chair and sat shaking her head. "How could such a sweet little boy as our Adam have any connection with that man?"

A rushing sound filled Emily's ears, like the waves pounding on the shore of Lake Michigan. She became aware of Stephen's hand shaking her arm. "Are you all right?" he asked.

She looked up at him. "This horrible creature is really Adam's father?"

Stephen nodded, his face grim. "That certainly appears to be the case."

As if jolted out of its numbness, Emily's mind raced into a frenzy of activity. Thoughts tumbled through her head. Finally she looked up at Stephen. "We've been hoping to reunite Adam with his family, but how can we turn him over to someone who is no better than a common criminal?"

Stephen gave a mirthless laugh. "He's a good bit worse than any of the common criminals I've ever come across. I wouldn't turn a stray dog over to him, much less an innocent child."

"Then we won't," Lucy stated. "We'll keep him ourselves." Stephen looked at her without response, and Lucy jutted out her chin. "It's worked so far, hasn't it? And he doesn't know where Adam is."

Emily's hopes rose. "That's right. He has no idea we have Adam."

Stephen's mouth tightened. "I wouldn't count on that, not for long, at least. He may not know Adam's whereabouts now, but that could change at a moment's notice. The man has resources all over the city.

"You wouldn't believe what McGinty is capable of," he went on. "This man is evil personified, and his enemies have a habit of disappearing."

Lucy settled back in the chair, her enthusiasm apparently dampened by this revelation.

"But we can't just let him have Adam." Emily looked from Lucy to Stephen. "That would be wrong. God put him in our hands, and we can't turn him over to be sucked into that kind of life. Maybe this is God's provision to keep him from following in his father's footsteps."

"Hear, hear," chimed in Mrs. Purvis. "I couldn't have put it any better myself." She nudged the china tray toward Stephen. "Would you care for a macaroon?"

Stephen drew back and fixed her with a stern look. "I don't believe you understand the severity of this situation."

A serene expression spread across the landlady's features. "Remember, Randolph and I lived through the Great Fire. I saw God save us from an inferno that looked like hell itself. If He can do that, He is able to save us from the clutches of this man, as well."

She picked up the plate of cookies and held it out to him. "Now have a macaroon, dear. Emily made them."

CHAPTER 14

Your Mrs. Purvis was right. Our lives have meaning and purpose when we put them in God's hands." Stephen shortened his steps to match his pace to Emily's as they crossed the bridge that led to the northern tip of the Wooded Island. The gathering darkness settled over them like a soft gray blanket.

Emily nodded. "One thing I'm finding is that Mrs. Purvis is usually right about most things."

Stephen chuckled. "She may seem a little flighty on the surface, but there's a real depth of character and wisdom under those gray curls of hers."

Emily smiled in agreement, feeling more secure than she had since Stephen had stunned them all with his announcement that Adam was likely Ian McGinty's son. After two days of keeping the doors securely locked and waiting, watching, and jumping at every sound, she felt as though her nerves were strung as tight as piano wire.

She'd carried on a good many arguments with herself during that two-day period, each time trying to persuade herself that they had leaped to an unfounded conclusion. Maybe Stephen's friend was wrong. After all, he'd said it was only a rumor and not a certainty that McGinty's mistress had a child. They couldn't be 100 percent positive the man was Adam's father.

Part of her realized she was grasping at straws, but she needed to create some doubt in her mind in order to cope with her day-to-day life. Tonight she felt more relaxed. Perhaps one simply couldn't stay on that knife's edge of anticipation for too long.

She demurred at first when Stephen invited her to walk with him at the fairgrounds that evening, but she changed her mind after giving the matter some thought. After all, she and Lucy came to work at the fairgrounds every day, and nothing out of the ordinary had happened so far. Since this McGinty person didn't know she had any connection with Adam, the four of them had decided that as long as Mrs. Purvis was willing to keep Adam at home, Emily and Lucy should continue to go about their business as usual. Adam seemed perfectly happy under Mrs. Purvis's care, especially when his new friend, Matthew, came over to play. They shouldn't have any problem keeping him out of public view.

Emily took a long breath of the evening air, heavy with moisture from the lake, and let it out in a gentle sigh. They would take one day at a time and hope for the best. She turned her attention back to their surroundings.

The Wooded Island was a place she'd long wanted to explore, but she had only managed brief glimpses of the northern end as she dashed across the series of bridges on her way to and from her lunch breaks. This evening, though, Stephen told her he would take her on a grand tour down the entire length of the island.

Dusk faded into darkness, and the tiny fairy lights along the island's edge winked on, their soft colors adding to the feeling that they were walking through some wooded fairyland. When the thousands of incandescent bulbs came on, outlining every building in the Court of Honor, a collective gasp rose from the crowds on the shore. But here in their little pocket of shadow, she and Stephen strolled as though in a world apart.

Most fairgoers seemed to have gravitated over to view the dazzling white lights at close hand. She and Stephen nodded to the few they passed on the walkway. Other than that, it felt as though they had the island to themselves.

A glorious scent filled Emily's nostrils. "What is that?"

Stephen smiled and led her a bit farther until the path gave way to a rose garden. The heady fragrance of the massed flowers hung heavy in the still evening air. Emily drank it in, feeling light-headed. What a perfect evening! The calm, the quiet, the heavenly scent. . .and Stephen by her side.

She bent over to caress one of the blooms and bring it up to her face. She inhaled deeply and sighed. "I don't think I've ever smelled anything quite that delicious in my life." She straightened and took Stephen's arm again. They strolled on through the garden, with Emily stopping to sample the fragrance of different roses as they passed.

Stephen chuckled indulgently. "I take it you didn't get much of that at the children's home."

Emily's spirits drooped. One more reminder of the difference between her background and Stephen's.

"I got a letter from my mother today," he went on. "She's still raving about how much she enjoyed meeting you, and she wants me to assure you that she's looking forward to a visit as soon as it can be arranged."

Emily shook her head, a little bemused.

Stephen frowned. "What?"

"Your family. They're wonderful! They're so warm, so accepting. I don't quite understand it. It's still hard for me to believe."

Stephen tucked her hand closer inside the crook of his arm and covered her fingers with his other hand. "I don't see what's so hard to understand. They see the same lovely person, the same sweet spirit that I do."

They continued on toward the south end of the island, saying little. But even with the few words Stephen had spoken, Emily felt ready to float up on a rose-scented cloud of joy.

Ahead of them lay the bridge that connected the Wooded Island to the main part of the fairgrounds. On the other side, Emily could see people flocking to the grand buildings housing the mining and electricity exhibits.

Emily smiled. She had heard about the excitement generated by Tesla's display of the electricity powering the bulbs that lit the fairgrounds at night. But she didn't need to understand the theory of alternating current. With the tingle hovering in the air between her and Stephen, she expected to see sparks fly at any moment.

Just as they were about to step on the bridge, Stephen drew back and led Emily off to one side of the path and into the shelter of a pocket of trees. "Would you wait here just a moment? I'll be right back."

Here, away from even the fairy lights, Emily had to strain to see his face in the gloom. "Where are you going?"

She could hear the smile in his voice when he answered. "Just trust me. You'll be perfectly safe here. I won't be gone long."

Emily stood, more comforted than frightened by the veil of darkness that surrounded her. She gave herself the luxury of allowing her thoughts to run free for a moment.

"A lovely person," Stephen had said. "A sweet spirit." His words and the smile that accompanied them had given her the feeling that, in spite of her shortcomings, she hadn't been found wanting.

She wrapped her arms around her middle and hugged herself. Where could Stephen be?

The crunch of footsteps on the pathway signaled his approach. The steps hesitated, as though he was uncertain of where he had left her.

"I'm over here," she called softly. Her pulse quickened in time with his hurrying steps.

Without warning, a hand reached out of the darkness and grabbed her shoulder, then it slid around to grasp the back of her neck. A mouth, hard and unyielding, pressed against hers for a long moment then tore away.

A darkness deeper than nightfall threatened to blot out Emily's senses. She reached out and caught hold of a tree branch to steady herself. Bile rose in her throat, and hot tears scalded her eyes.

She couldn't deny she had wondered what it would be like to be held in Stephen's embrace. She had even dared to dream it might happen that very evening on the island, where every corner seemed to offer a perfect setting for romance.

This was not what she had expected at all. The disappointment almost drove her to her knees.

The gravel crunched again. Emily drew herself erect. She had been caught off guard before. He wouldn't find her so yielding this time.

Stephen's voice came out of the darkness. "Here, I brought this for you."

Emily flinched when he touched her hand and pressed something into it. Running her fingers along the length of the object, she felt the stem and then the downy petals of a rose.

With his hand at the back of her waist, Stephen ushered her back into the light and toward the bridge. "Don't tell anyone about one of the Columbian Guards breaking the rules. The flowers are not there for picking, but you were enjoying them so much I thought if I slipped around to the back that nobody would notice one missing. Do you like it?"

The boyish eagerness in his voice was in such stark contrast with his ungentlemanly behavior a moment before that Emily looked up at him in astonishment. How could he treat such a moment so lightly?

She held the rose up to her face. This time its fragrance made her stomach roil. "It's very nice," she managed. She walked beside him with a stiff gait. Stephen greeted her hollow response with a puzzled look.

Back on the bridge, they walked into the light again. Emily looked up at him with new eyes. *He's not the gentleman I thought he was.* The knowledge left her sick with disappointment.

Or were all men like that? Perhaps it was only her romantic, girlish dreams that had convinced her otherwise and given her such unrealistic expectations.

She studied the planes of his face, noting the strong brow, the firm chin, and the heavy dark mustache. His full lips. . .

No, she wouldn't think about them, not with the memory of that kiss with his hard upper lip crushing against hers with such force she thought they would be bruised.

Emily looked up at Stephen again, and sudden awareness made her head reel. The man who had kissed her did not have a mustache.

She stopped, struggling to breathe. If it hadn't been Stephen, then who? Who could possibly be audacious enough to dare such a thing and then slip back into the darkness when Stephen was so close by?

Stephen's brow puckered. "Is something wrong?"

Emily opened her mouth to tell him what had happened and then stopped. What would she say? That she had been kissing a strange man in the dark?

It had taken this long to get past the earlier half-truths and rebuild Stephen's trust in her. Would he look at her with the same eyes if she told him what had just occurred?

How would he feel if he learned that when—if—he did kiss her, his lips would not be the first to touch hers? She ducked her head, pretending to smell the rose again. "Nothing," she told him. "I'm fine."

It was better to keep quiet. She couldn't bear the thought of losing his trust again, perhaps forever this time.

They crossed a tiny scrap of land that lay between the island and the shore; then they continued along a second bridge. Emily concentrated on keeping pace with Stephen and trying to get her spiraling thoughts in order. When they reached the top of its gentle arch, she saw a figure step off the end of the bridge ahead of them.

The man stopped along the edge of the lagoon and put his hands in his pockets, looking over the nighttime scene with a proprietary air. Emily caught her breath. Even from a distance, she recognized the arrogant stance: Raymond Willard Simmons III, master of all he surveyed. In his own mind, at least.

At that moment, he looked up and saw them. In the bright light cast by the multitude of incandescent bulbs, Emily could see his expression harden. Her stomach knotted so tightly she was afraid she was going to be sick.

Raymond didn't have a mustache. Emily drew closer to

Stephen and saw the other man's face twist into a scowl. She held the rose tightly between her fingers to keep from swiping the back of one hand across her mouth.

CHAPTER 15

"Aren't we the very picture of domestic tranquility?" Mrs. Purvis picked up another stitch of soft blue yarn and went on with the cap she was knitting for Adam.

Emily looked around the parlor and smiled. She sat on the floor, on the parlor rug, Adam snuggled against her side, reading the story of Thumbelina from a volume of Hans Christian Andersen's works. Lucy sat in one of the overstuffed chairs, darning her stocking.

A smile curved her lips, and her heart swelled with contentment. Yes, they did look very domestic. It would be easy to become accustomed to this feeling of being home, being family.

A tap sounded at the front door. "I'll get it," Lucy volunteered.

"Don't bother." Mrs. Purvis set her yarn and knitting needles in the basket beside her chair and walked toward the front door with her usual springy step. "You girls work hard all day. It's a treat to see you have a chance to sit and relax for a bit."

Voices filtered in from the entry hall, telling Emily who their visitor was even before Mrs. Purvis caroled, "Look who's here!" and Stephen stepped into the parlor.

Mrs. Purvis followed right behind him, only to pivot and turn back when another knock rattled the door. She returned a moment later, her arms filled with an enormous spray of pink roses. Her eyes glowed with excitement and a touch of mischief. "Goodness, look what the delivery boy just brought." She crossed the room and held the armful of blooms out to Emily.

Emily gasped. "For me?"

"Look at the card," Mrs. Purvis urged. "It seems you have a secret admirer. Or maybe not so secret. I'd say the timing on that delivery was perfect." She flitted a coy glance at Stephen.

Emily got to her feet and held out her arms to accept the flowers. She looked at Stephen with a smile of gratitude, startled when she saw a frown darken his face.

Mrs. Purvis hurried toward the kitchen. "I'll fetch a vase so we can put these in water right away."

Emily laid the blooms on the table in front of the settee and pulled a small square envelope from between the stems. "Miss Emily Ralston" was penned neatly on the front of the envelope in a strong, masculine hand.

Once again, she shot a look at Stephen, hoping she had misread his earlier look of displeasure. His expression remained dark and somber. He crossed his arms and watched her without comment.

"I can't imagine who these are from." She heard the shakiness in her voice and cleared her throat. Taking a quick breath, she turned the envelope over and tore open the flap. A single sheet of stationery nestled within. Emily slid it out and glanced at the first line then froze.

"I hope you enjoyed our kiss as much as I did."

The pork chops she'd eaten for dinner turned over in her stomach. So it had been Raymond after all. She looked down at the roses again. It was just like him to do something underhanded like stealing that kiss and then bragging about it this way, without daring to face her. What a coward!

Her anger burned. She took hold of the note with both hands, ready to shred it into bits, when the second sentence caught her eye. She held the note closer and read the entire message through then went back to the beginning and read it through again.

"I hope you enjoyed our kiss as much as I did. Having now made your acquaintance, I have little doubt that you are well qualified to care for Adam, whatever your reason for taking him in the first place. Make sure nothing happens to my boy and know that I'll be watching."

The signature was a series of scrawls and curls, but Emily could make out the first letter in each word: *I* and *M*. She let out a cry and felt the floor rise to meet her.

The next thing she knew, she was stretched out on the settee, with Lucy patting her hand and Mrs. Purvis fanning her face with a dish towel. Stephen stood to one side, his face a stony mask.

Emily saw the square of stationery in his fingers and stifled a groan. He must have read the message by now. She let her eyes drift shut again.

Tiny fingers patted her face. "Miss Em'ly all right?"

She roused herself enough to open her eyes and smile at Adam. Pulling her hand from Lucy's grasp, she wrapped her arm around the little boy and held him close. There was no room for doubt now. Adam was Ian McGinty's son. She held him tighter and rubbed her cheek against his soft blond hair. How could such an angelic child be fathered by such an evil man?

She risked a glance over the top of his head. Stephen hadn't moved an inch since the last time she had looked at him. How was she ever going to explain that note to him? She pushed herself up off the settee and wobbled to her feet. Crossing the room with unsure steps, she took the offensive note from his hand and set it on the table next to the flowers.

"So you've met his father?" His voice was flat, empty of emotion. He nodded toward Adam, who had returned to the corner and was playing with the blocks Matthew had given him.

"No!" Emily reached out and touched the lapel of his jacket, willing him to believe her. "It happened last night while we were walking on the fairgrounds." She squeezed her eyes shut, remembering the shadowy paths, the fairy lights, and the heady scent of roses.

Roses. She cast another look at the mass of blooms on the low table. She would never think of them in the same way again.

"Do you remember when you left me to go pick the rose from the garden?"

He nodded abruptly. "It seems a pretty poor offering now. There's quite a difference between that one little bloom and what you just received."

"You're right. There is a difference. Yours meant something to me. These"—Emily swept her arm out to indicate the bouquet on the table—"mean nothing."

She took a shaky breath and forged ahead. "While I was waiting for you in the dark, I heard footsteps. I thought it was you at first. Someone came up to me and kissed me. Hard."

Emily saw the muscles in his jaw tighten. "It was horrible. I felt. . .violated. Back in that corner, it was so dark I couldn't see anything but the shadows. Just after that, there you were, holding out the rose you picked. I didn't realize until later it couldn't possibly have been you."

She squared her shoulders and looked up at him. "And I'm sorry I doubted you at all. I should have known better from the first. That kiss was the action of a cad. You would never do a thing like that." She saw his shoulders relax, and the planes of his face softened.

Emily turned to where Mrs. Purvis and Lucy stood listening openmouthed. "I don't understand any of it—the kiss, the flowers, the note. Why would he do such a thing?"

"I can tell you that." Stephen's voice was heavy. "He wields control over people through the use of power and intimidation."

Emily gave a shaky laugh. "I'd say he did a good job of both."

"Then that means he knows Emily has been keeping Adam," Lucy said. "Has he known that all along?"

Stephen raked his fingers through his hair. "There's no way of telling when he found out. The only thing that matters is that he knows now."

"That and what we decide to do about it," Lucy put in. "We need to find some way to make sure Emily is safe."

"As long as he's happy about Adam staying here, there shouldn't be a problem. The danger will come if we cross him in any way. What happens when he wants his son back?"

"He can't have him." The words burst forth from Emily's lips. "I won't let him."

Stephen gave her a long look. "And how do you propose to keep that from happening? He knows who you are. He knows where you live. The man has informants everywhere. Do you think you'll be able to make a move without him knowing?"

A chill ran from Emily's head to her toes at the thought of what had happened to the poor woman who tried to run from McGinty, only to meet her fate in a lonely shed on the fairgrounds. Did she want to come to a similar end?

A thin thread of panic crept into her voice. "Are you telling me the only way to keep myself from danger is to turn Adam back over to his father?"

Blocks clattered to the floor. She looked over to find Adam staring at her, his eyes huge in his pale face. "Da?"

Emily rushed to scoop him up and cradle him in her arms. She held him close and looked at Stephen over the top of the little boy's head. "I can't do that. I don't know what it's going to cost me, but God help me, I can't do it."

⌒

"Maybe we should just leave Chicago."

Emily stared at Lucy over the rim of her teacup. Surely she wasn't serious.

Lucy reached out to grip Emily's arm, sending a thin stream of tea sloshing over the rim of the cup. "If we leave in the middle of the night and get far enough away, he won't know where we are. You can't play games with a man like this, Emily. I'm frightened for you. You're the only family I've got."

The tremor in Lucy's voice made Emily soften her response to this wild scheme. "Think about it. A man like that—you heard what Stephen said about the resources he has. How far do you think we'd get?"

She used her napkin to dab up the spilled tea and leaned her head against the back of her chair, feeling unutterably weary. Her eyes were gritty from lack of sleep, but none of the three women felt ready to go to bed after Stephen left. Even Adam was restless. After two abortive efforts to put him to bed, Emily gave up and decided to let him play quietly on the parlor floor until he wound down enough to be able to sleep. She blessed Matthew's mother for the gift of the blocks. Adam knelt in the corner near the bookshelf, engrossed in adding another building to what looked like a small town.

"Where would you go?" Mrs. Purvis pulled her shawl farther up around her shoulders.

Lucy looked from Emily to Mrs. Purvis then held out her hands, palms up. "I don't know. Somewhere."

"And what would we use for money?" Emily pressed. "You have to think these things through, Lucy. We can't just jump and run."

"But you aren't safe here."

The chill of fear Emily had been fighting off ever since reading McGinty's note came back to coil itself around her heart. "At this point, he seems willing to let things go on as they are."

"But for how long?" Lucy persisted.

"Longer than if we uproot and take off. Think again. What would we do with Adam—take him with us? You heard what Stephen said. The man has informants everywhere. We'd never know who to trust. He'd be after us before we knew it. We could wind up like. . ." She nodded toward Adam and let the rest of the thought go unsaid. "If we stay here, at least we'll have a little time to make some plans."

Mrs. Purvis smiled at them from her overstuffed chair. "We may not know the answers, but we know Somebody who does. All we can do at this point is place this little boy in His hands—and ourselves, as well. The Bible talks about praying without ceasing. If ever there was a time to follow that advice—"

A soft thud from the far side of the room caught Emily's attention. She looked over to see Adam sitting in the midst of a pile of books. She got up and hurried over to him. "Are you hurt?"

His tired little face turned up to hers, and she could see his eyes fill with tears. "It fell down."

Emily knelt down beside him. He had apparently decided to expand his building efforts by using all the books from the bottom shelf to construct a bridge over the buildings in his make-believe town.

She sighed and started to put the books back in their proper places. "I'm sorry, Mrs. Purvis. I didn't realize what was going on. I don't know if you had these in any certain order, but I can at least clear them off the floor."

The landlady waved her hand. "It doesn't matter to me what order they're in. I seldom do more than dust them, anyway. I keep them there mostly for the use of my boarders."

Adam moved to help Emily, picking up the books with his chubby hands and passing them to her one by one. A slim blue volume slipped from his fingers and fell to the floor with its pages splayed across the rug.

"Oh dear." Emily picked it up and smoothed the pages.

Adam scooped something up off the rug and handed it to her. Emily took the yellowed envelope from his hand, memories of her recent experience with Ian McGinty's gift card making her shudder. This one, though, had one word written across the front in a bold scrawl: *Ethelinda*.

"What's this? Adam, maybe you'd better take this to Mrs. Purvis and see if it's something she wants."

She turned around and called across the room, "This fell out of one of the books. I don't know if it was marking a particular page or not. Do you want me to put it back where it was, or is it something you'd like to keep out?"

Adam trotted over with the envelope in his hand, and Emily went back to stacking the books on the shelf.

Mrs. Purvis caught her breath and gave a sharp cry. "Well, forevermore."

Emily placed the last two books on the shelf, stood, and dusted her hands. She went back to rejoin Mrs. Purvis and Lucy, taking a seat on the settee and lifting Adam up to sit beside her. Without a word, he curled up and laid his head in her lap.

"What is it, Mrs. Purvis? Are you all right?" Lucy bent toward the older woman, a look of concern shadowing her eyes.

Mrs. Purvis sat with her hand pressed against her chest, staring at the envelope. "That handwriting—I haven't seen it in years. It's Randolph's."

"Your husband's?" Emily's eyes widened. "How long has that envelope been down there?"

Mrs. Purvis shook her head slowly. "I have no idea. I don't even know that I've seen this before." She turned the envelope over, lifted the flap, and slid out a bit of pasteboard. An array of emotions flitted over her face. "Oh my, I do remember this. It's one of the little clues he used to leave about for me. I can tell you exactly how long it has been since I've seen it. I discovered it on the very day he took ill."

Her eyes misted over. "How strange to come across it again after all these years. It almost makes me feel like there's been a little bit of Randolph here all along."

Lucy gave a little bounce in her chair. "How exciting! I loved the stories about your treasure hunts. What did this clue lead to?"

Mrs. Purvis's face fell. She pressed the slip of paper between her palms and held it against her chest. "I guess I'll never know." She held it up to show a rough sketch, faded with the passage of years. "I remember looking at this one and trying to puzzle it out. It was right then that Randolph suddenly told me he wasn't feeling well." Her mouth twisted. "After that, my mind was on other matters. This was one hunt we never did finish." Her voice caught on the last few words.

Emily's heart went out to the older woman. "Do you think it's a clue to what you've been looking for all these years?"

Mrs. Purvis's face lit up for a moment; then the spark faded. She cleared her throat and straightened in her chair. "I've been thinking since our talk the other night. Maybe I misunderstood him. Maybe I assumed he meant his big surprise was ready when it wasn't finished at all. Perhaps it was still just a plan in his mind."

She stroked her thumbs along the faded drawing. "This may have been nothing more than a clue to one of the little treasures he used to leave lying around. It's possible I've built all these expectations up out of nothing but my own imagination. And even if this was supposed to lead me to Randolph's grand secret, I still have no idea what it means, and the other clues are surely gone by now."

Mrs. Purvis slid the drawing back into the envelope with an air of finality. She sighed. "I'll tuck this away as a final memento of Randolph and the love we shared. I'm afraid—sorely afraid— I've been wasting my time all these years. Surely he wouldn't have wanted me to act like such a foolish old woman."

She pushed herself up out of her chair. "It's time for me to go to bed. I'll bid you girls good night now, and it looks like that little tyke is fast asleep, too. Why don't we all get some rest? This has been a rather eventful day."

CHAPTER 16

Stephen trotted up the front steps of the house on Blackstone Avenue. He rattled the doorknob before tapping on the door. Good, they were keeping it locked. Trying to appear casual, he looked up and down the street, looking for anyone who seemed out of place in the neighborhood.

He heard the sound of feet crossing the entry hall toward the front door and tried to get his nerves under control. In recent days, he'd been as skittish as a cat on hot bricks, his every waking moment consumed with dreaming up ways to keep the occupants of Mrs. Purvis's boardinghouse safe.

The door swung open, and Emily looked up at him with the sweet smile he had become so fond of. No, his feelings had gone well beyond fondness. If he wanted to be honest, he was head over heels in love with this girl. Emily might worry about not knowing her family background, but her courage, her loyalty, and her willingness to sacrifice her own safety for the welfare of a little boy she barely knew were proof enough of her character.

As soon as things settled down to a more even keel, he meant to declare himself. But first he had to keep her alive to make sure they could have a future together.

She let him in and made a point of sliding the bolt home on the front door before ushering him into the parlor, where Mrs. Purvis and Lucy greeted him. Adam spotted him from the corner that had been designated as his play area. He sprang up and raced pell-mell to wrap his arms around Stephen's knees.

"How's my boy?" Stephen caught the youngster under his arms and tossed him into the air until Adam dissolved into a mass of giggles. The irony of it struck him, calling Adam "his" boy when he was, in fact, the offspring of a hardened criminal and a kept woman. He looked into Adam's clear blue eyes. He'd heard it said it was impossible to choose one's relatives. Never had he seen that thought illustrated more clearly than in Adam's case.

Stephen glanced into the dining room and saw trays heaped with an array of baked goods. He turned to Mrs. Purvis. "Am I interrupting anything? It looks like you're ready for company."

She beamed at him. "Indeed we are, and you're invited, as well. I heard from a former boarder today who asked if she and her husband could drop by this evening. Of course, I was delighted to have them over. They're one of my little success stories." She looked over at Emily and Lucy and gave them a quick wink.

Stephen turned in time to see a light blush tinge Emily's face. She ignored him, staring fixedly at the toe of her shoe.

"That's very nice of you to include me, but are you sure I won't be in the way?"

"Not at all." Mrs. Purvis continued to radiate goodwill. "In fact, I hear someone at the front door now. I'm sure it's them."

"Make sure of who it is before you open the door," Stephen

called after her retreating figure.

He looked at Emily, who had stooped to straighten Adam's collar. No matter what the little fellow wore, it always seemed his collar wanted to curl up. And just when was it, he wondered, that he had become so well acquainted with the mannerisms of the members of his little. . .

Family. The thought took his breath away. But that's what it was beginning to feel like.

If only he could always be around to protect them. But that wasn't possible. He had no right to stay with Emily night and day. Now, if he were her husband. . .

His pulse quickened as he turned the idea over in his mind. His parents had liked her right off, and his mother had already begun hinting that she wouldn't mind having Emily as a daughter-in-law. Maybe that's what he should do. Just take Emily along with him right now and hunt down some preacher who would be willing to marry them at a moment's notice.

"Here they are." Mrs. Purvis ushered in her guests. "Come right in, you two. I want you to meet my current boarders and a special visitor." Stephen stared at the young couple who followed Mrs. Purvis into the parlor.

She waved Emily and Lucy over to her. "Emily Ralston and Lucy Welch, I'd like you to meet Mr.—make that *Reverend*—and Mrs. Seth Howell. They've only been married a short time. They met while Dinah was rooming here earlier this summer."

Stephen hoped she didn't have any illusions about her actions being subtle. The way she waggled her eyebrows was enough to inform the densest person of her intent. He stared at the newcomers. Hadn't he just been thinking about going to look for a preacher? Maybe Seth's appearance was a sign, some sort of divine encouragement.

"This little boy is. . .Adam." Stephen noticed she avoided the use of a surname. "And this—"

"You don't have to introduce me to this big galoot," Seth Howell said. He punched Stephen on the arm and grinned, then lowered his voice so that only Stephen could hear. "What did I tell you? Your days are numbered. How often are you over here, twice a week? Three times?"

"I've been here every night this week so far," Stephen admitted.

Seth burst out laughing. "You've really got it bad. You might just as well give in. Let me give you a piece of advice. If you're looking for a romantic spot, I can highly recommend the gondolas on the lag—ow!"

He broke off, rubbing a spot on his ribs and giving his wife an unrepentant grin.

Dinah Howell glared at her husband then bestowed a sweet smile upon Stephen. "How nice to see you again." She turned to Mrs. Purvis. "Seth introduced me to Stephen while he was working at the fairgrounds earlier this summer. And I've met one of your charming boarders already."

Mrs. Purvis blinked, and Emily laughed. "That's right. Dinah stops by the Children's Building to pick up the daily reports."

"We haven't had a chance to do more than just exchange hellos, though. It will be a treat to be able to sit down and have a real visit."

Emily and Lucy helped Mrs. Purvis carry out the refreshments, and soon the four women were chattering away like old friends. Adam sat between Dinah and Emily, happily munching on cookies and drinking in all the attention lavished on him by the circle of female admirers.

Seth wandered over to the fireplace, where he leaned back against the mantel and watched the convivial scene. Stephen joined him and angled his body so the women wouldn't hear his part of the conversation.

"It's funny, but I was just thinking about hunting up a preacher when you knocked on the door."

Seth's eyes lit up. "So you've already popped the question?"

"No, but I'm thinking I need to do that soon."

Seth drew back and gave him a quizzical smile. "Need to or want to?"

"Well, both." Stephen glanced over his shoulder to where Emily sat talking to Dinah. He watched her animated face and the quick gestures she made with her hands. "Even though we haven't known each other all that long, she's bowled me over like a ton of bricks. This is the person I want to spend the rest of my life with."

"You've prayed about it, of course?"

"Ever since the first day we met." Stephen managed a sheepish grin. "There's something special about her. . . ."

Seth looked over at Dinah. "I know what you mean. All right, I can understand the 'want to' part. What about the 'need to'?"

Stephen hesitated. "I can't go into that right now. Let's just say I think it would be in Emily's best interests if she had a husband on hand to protect her."

Seth clamped his hand on Stephen's shoulder. "You haven't asked my advice, but I'm going to give it to you, anyway. You need to think this through. I don't know what kind of protection she needs, but that in itself is not a good foundation for a marriage. Do you believe God is leading you to rush into things like this?"

"No," Stephen admitted after a pause. "But it seems like the right thing to do."

Seth smiled. "Then my recommendation, unsolicited though it may be, is to keep on praying about it and wait until you get a definite yes. Wait until the other distractions are out of the way and you can both think clearly. Marriage is far too important to enter into it lightly."

Adam let out a shriek of laughter, and Seth grinned. "So that's the little fellow you told me about."

Stephen nodded. "He's a real charmer, isn't he?" He should have known Seth and Dinah would be drawn to the boy. They worked with children of Chicago's lower class and had a heart for needy youngsters.

"Wait a minute." A frown tightened Seth's forehead. "This is the boy who was abandoned at the Children's Building, the one whose mother was killed? Are you telling me you haven't been able to find his other relatives yet?"

The room grew quiet. Stephen looked over to find the women staring at them and realized he and Seth had forgotten to keep their voices down.

Lucy hopped up from her chair. "Adam, why don't I take you upstairs and get you ready for bed?" The little boy's mouth opened on a wail of protest.

Mrs. Purvis stepped over and took him by the hand. "How about if I come up, too, and read you a story about Jesus from the Bible?"

Adam gave in with relatively good grace. After bestowing good-night hugs and kisses around the room, he allowed himself to be led upstairs.

Both of the Howells stared at Stephen and Emily. "Did I say something wrong?" Seth asked.

Stephen crossed the room and took Emily's hand. "We already know who he belongs to."

Seth's eyes widened. "But you're still keeping him? I can see why you've grown attached to the little fellow, but a child belongs with his family. Perhaps you're worried about it being difficult to explain to them why you've kept him all this time. If so, I can understand your reluctance to step forward now. Maybe I can help in some—"

"His father is Ian McGinty." The words fell into the room like a stone dropped into a well.

"McGinty!" Seth's jaw tightened, and he put his arm around his wife.

"I take it you've heard of him."

Dinah nodded, her face ashen. "He's involved in. . .in. . . ." She looked at her husband.

"In more things than anyone should discuss in polite company." Seth turned back to Stephen. "I'm sorry for jumping to conclusions. You're in a difficult situation. I can see that. What can we do?"

Stephen leveled a solemn gaze at his friend. "You can pray."

~

Stephen seemed reluctant to leave after the Howells departed, and Emily couldn't help but be pleased. He lingered on, helping the women carry cups and saucers to the kitchen. He even proved to be handy with a dish towel, and with the added help, the dishes were washed and dried in no time.

Mrs. Purvis carried the largest of the trays to the corner cupboard and stood on tiptoe to fit it into its place.

"Let me do that for you." Stephen hurried over to take the heavy tray from her.

"Wait a moment." The landlady stared at the platter before relinquishing it to him. "That was one of my mother's trays, and I'd never want to get rid of it, but with it being so big and cumbersome, trying to get it out and put it away is such a struggle. If you don't mind, I think I'd like to put it in the cupboard under the stairs instead. That way it will still be available whenever I want it, but it won't be taking up space in here where I'd rather store the pieces I use more often."

"Your wish is my command." Stephen grinned and followed her out to the spacious cupboard where bric-a-brac was stored. Emily and Lucy trailed along behind. He set the tray in the spot she indicated then regarded the interior of the cupboard thoughtfully.

"It's an interesting place you have here," he told Mrs. Purvis. "The cupboard is a good use of space that would otherwise be wasted."

Her eyes sparkled, and she gave him a gentle smile. "Most of it was my Randolph's doing. He came up with the ideas for the floor plan and worked on them with the architect."

Stephen nodded. Emily watched as he stepped back and turned in a slow circle, studying the layout of the open space. "Was Ralph Armstrong the one he worked with?"

Mrs. Purvis brightened. "Yes, that was his name."

"I thought so. I studied his work at Cornell." Stephen continued his inspection. He leaned back into the cupboard and ran his hand along the left wall. "Pardon my curiosity, but I wonder why you decided to block this end off."

The landlady blinked. "Block it off? No, it's been that way since the day we moved in."

Stephen pulled at his chin. "Maybe I'm wrong, but I could have sworn. . ." He reached inside and started tapping along the cupboard wall.

Emily looked at Lucy, who edged over and whispered, "Maybe it's contagious."

Stephen straightened and looked at Mrs. Purvis. "What's on the other side of the back wall?"

Mrs. Purvis shrugged. "It's a spare bedroom. The door is just down the hall there."

"May I look at it?"

Emily could hear the excitement in Stephen's voice. She glanced at Lucy again, receiving a quizzical look in response. All three women followed Stephen as he strode down the hall and turned right at the door Mrs. Purvis indicated.

"See?" The landlady pointed at the corner nearest them on the right. "There's a closet there. It backs up to the cupboard on the other side."

Stephen opened the closet door and stuck his head and shoulders inside then turned back to Mrs. Purvis. "Not quite. It's a small closet, not nearly large enough to take up the space that's missing from the cupboard."

Mrs. Purvis's eyes grew round, and she clasped her hands under her chin. "You don't think. . . There couldn't be. . ."

Stephen grinned. "A secret room? Let's go take another look." He led them back down the hall to where the cupboard door stood open. "See?" He indicated the left-hand wall. "It doesn't make sense for this space to end so abruptly. I don't have a tape measure with me, so I can't take an accurate measurement, but my guess is there's a good three feet unaccounted for." He leaned back into the cupboard, examining the wall with care.

Mrs. Purvis peered over his shoulder. "I've lost track of the number of times I've tapped along this wall over the years. It sounded just the way I'd expect it to, with the closet on the other side."

Stephen nodded eagerly and continued to press his hands along the surface of the wall. "And I'm sure that's exactly what Armstrong intended. I believe you have some sort of hidden space back here. He didn't mean for it to be found by anyone who didn't know exactly what they were looking for."

Mrs. Purvis pressed her hands against her mouth and danced from one foot to the other. "This must be the surprise Randolph told me about. It has to be! But how do we get in?"

"Like this." Stephen pressed on a knot in the paneling almost hidden underneath the top shelf. With a soft *click*, the entire left wall swung back, revealing a sizable opening.

Emily gasped and clutched Lucy's arm. Beyond the doorway, a set of steps led downward.

"Oh my." Mrs. Purvis pushed past Stephen to stare down into the darkness. "We're going to need a lamp. Lucy, could you fetch one from the parlor, please? And bring some matches, too."

Lucy hurried off on her errand and returned moments later with the matches and lamp. Mrs. Purvis reached for it, but Stephen held out his hand to block her.

"I know you're aching to see what's down there, but I think you should let me go first. I want to check out the structural soundness so we don't have any unwelcome surprises."

Mrs. Purvis stepped back, although Emily could see it cost her an effort. "All right, if you think that's best."

Stephen descended the stairs one slow step at a time. Mrs. Purvis moved onto the top tread, giving Emily and Lucy room to crowd together in the doorway and watch his progress. He reached the bottom then moved out of their view. Emily took three long, slow breaths before they heard him give a low whistle.

"What? What is it?" Mrs. Purvis leaned forward so far it looked as if she might topple over at any moment.

"It's safe. I think you'd better come down here. You're never going to believe this."

Mrs. Purvis didn't need a second invitation. Emily followed her down the stairs, with Lucy at her heels.

"I'll need those matches," Stephen said to Lucy. Taking them from her, he lit a series of candles seated in brackets at intervals around the walls. The light grew with every one he lit, chasing the shadows away. Emily stared openmouthed, too thunderstruck to make a sound.

They stood in a furnished room about ten feet square. Stephen pointed to the brick-lined walls that met overhead, forming a vaulted ceiling. "Fire brick. And look at this."

He trotted over to a door that stood open at the foot of the stairs. "It's four inches thick and made of steel plates." Pounding on the door with the side of his fist brought only a dull thud. "My guess is that it's filled with sand to make it fireproof. This room would be totally safe for valuables—or people—in the event of a fire. It's a wonderful idea, and the execution is flawless, as far as I can see."

Emily looked around her. "It's amazing. Except for not having any windows, it looks like a small sitting room." A square wooden table and two chairs sat in the middle of the floor. Shelves lined one wall, and boxes of assorted sizes were arranged against another.

"What's this?" Lucy picked up a square of paper from the table and peered at it closely. Emily could see her blink rapidly then swallow before she handed it to Mrs. Purvis. "This is addressed to you, and I think I recognize the handwriting."

The landlady glanced at the page then sank into the nearest chair and fanned herself with her hand.

Emily hovered over her. "Do you want me to get you some water?"

Mrs. Purvis shook her head. "I'm all right. It just came as a bit of a shock, getting another message from Randolph this way." She opened the paper and began to read:

My dearest Ethelinda,

  Since you are reading this, I know you have discovered our secret room. You've become so adept at following my clues over the years that I had no doubt you would persevere until you found it.

  What do you think of my little surprise? I pray we never need the room as protection against another fire, but it will give us peace of mind to know it exists to guard our dearest possessions. Instead of having them on display upstairs, we can enjoy them down here, secure in the knowledge we won't ever lose them.

  You, of course, are the prize I value above all others. The years we've shared already count as my greatest blessing, to be surpassed only by the joys the future has in store for us.

       With all my love,
       Your devoted husband,
       Randolph

No one spoke for several moments after she finished reading the note. Emily dabbed at her eyes and heard a sniffle from the corner where Lucy stood.

"He was such a wonderful man!" Mrs. Purvis's breath came out on a long sigh. "So he planned to put our special things down here so they would always be safe."

"It looks like he already brought some of them down." Stephen indicated the shelves and boxes.

"So he did." Mrs. Purvis took a closer look at the nearest shelf and let out a gasp. Jumping up from her chair, she darted over to the shelf and scooped up a small, carved ivory fan. "Look at this! Randolph bought it for me on one of his business trips. I've always loved it." She spread the delicate vanes open and waved it back and forth in front of her face.

"What do you suppose this is?" Lucy poked at a bulky object wrapped in brown paper.

"I have no idea." Mrs. Purvis laid down the fan and started pulling at the paper. "Goodness, I feel just like a young girl on Christmas morning!"

She tore the last of the paper away and stared at the folded fabric within before sweeping it up and holding it tight against her. "It's my grandmother's quilt. She gave it to my mother, who passed it along to me. When I couldn't find it after Randolph died, I thought I must have given it away along with some of his clothing."

Handing one end to Emily, she held the other and backed away to spread the quilt open. Small hexagons of fabric had been pieced together to form a brightly colored design. "It's in Grandmother's Flower Garden pattern. Isn't it lovely?"

"It's beautiful." Emily's heart welled with joy at what this discovery meant to her landlady. "And now you can use it again."

"Here's something I expect you'll want to look at." Stephen held up a framed daguerreotype.

"Can it be?" Mrs. Purvis thrust the quilt at Emily and pulled a handkerchief from her sleeve to wipe the dust from the glass. "It is! Look, it's the portrait taken the day we were married."

Emily folded the quilt and moved to join the others. Looking over Lucy's shoulder, she could see the likeness of a couple dressed in their wedding finery. Though Mrs. Purvis's hair was darker in the picture, and fewer wrinkles lined her face, the air of goodwill and the sparkle in her eyes were just the same.

Emily studied Randolph's features. Even in the stiff wedding pose, she could see a glint of kindness and humor in his face. "He looks like a nice man."

"He was." The words came out in a whisper.

"What's that?" Stephen pulled a metal strongbox from one of the dark corners. He blew a fine layer of dust off the top then lifted the latches and raised the lid. Even in the lamplight, Emily could see his eyes flare wide.

"I think you'd better look at this." He carried the box to the table and set it in front of Mrs. Purvis. Both Emily and Lucy gasped when they saw stacks of banknotes lining the interior.

"Oh my!" Mrs. Purvis clapped her hand to her mouth.

"How much is there?" Lucy asked.

Stephen glanced at Mrs. Purvis for permission then lifted the banded notes onto the table. "There's something more under here." He pulled out a folder and spread it open.

Inside was a stack of papers festooned with gold leaf and curlicues. Emily couldn't make out the writing from where she stood, but she saw Stephen's mouth drop open.

"Stock certificates," he said. He inspected the top paper closely then sorted through the rest of the stack. He looked up at the three women. "They're worth a lot, all of them. There's a fortune in here."

Emily threw her arms around her landlady's neck and hugged her tight. "You've found it, Mrs. Purvis! Here's your treasure."

"No." The older woman cradled the picture and Randolph's note in her arms, not bothering to wipe away the tears that streamed down her cheeks. "My treasure is right here."

Ian McGinty pulled back the edge of the curtain from the grimy window and peered out into the night. Lights glittered on the barges that carried their cargo down the river toward Lake Michigan, and from there to points east. Heavy clouds pushed their way across the sky, obscuring the light from the moon and plunging the world into deeper darkness.

How fitting. The inky blackness suited his mood.

He turned away from the window, letting the heavy fabric fall back into place. The lamp on his desk sent out a comforting glow. He crossed the room and lowered himself into his chair with a heaviness more suited to a man twice his age. He felt old tonight, as old as the city itself.

He tipped back his chair and closed his eyes, still trying to come to terms with the message a wide-eyed informant had brought only an hour before: Flynn was dead, found murdered within view of Gilly's Pub.

Disturbing news, and something that would alter his immediate plans. He had little respect for Flynn's intelligence, but the man's usefulness in other ways couldn't be denied. And the fact that Flynn was recognized as one McGinty's lieutenants made the blow hit all the closer to home.

This time he had some idea where it came from. This interloper—the one who wanted to take over the territory McGinty had built up so carefully over the years—was a newcomer named Da Silva, according to reports Mort had picked up off the street. Little more was known about the man than his name. But a name could be enough, given McGinty's resources.

What to do? The rage that boiled up inside him upon hearing the news had subsided, leaving him feeling empty, hollow. He recognized Flynn's murder for what it was: one more step in Da Silva's escalating invasion. If things continued moving at this pace, it wouldn't be long before he became a target himself.

Knowledge was crucial in any sort of combat situation. He needed knowledge now—Da Silva's location, the names of the men loyal to him and which of them could be bought off.

He'd had rivals before, but they had been willing to come to terms after a certain amount of give-and-take, laying down boundary lines and agreeing to adhere to them. For the most part, it had worked well, with casualties limited to those he considered mere pawns instead of some of the major players.

McGinty would have been willing to discuss a similar agreement with Da Silva had the fellow shown the decency to come talk to him. But this opponent was different, apparently having his sights set on gathering all of Chicago under his control.

Choosing one of McGinty's well-known henchmen had been an overt display of arrogance. Leaving Flynn's body so close to one of McGinty's establishments was an intentional slap in the face. To come so openly into another man's territory was a bold move, and one he'd used himself in the past; he had to give Da Silva credit for that. But this was more than the death of a subordinate. It was a direct challenge and called for a direct response.

What should his next move be, and whom should he trust to carry it out? He thought again of Flynn, whose physical prowess couldn't be denied. It would have taken someone of equal or superior strength to bring the big man down. Though not blessed with great intellect, Flynn had been a cagey man with the survival instincts of a cat, always on the alert for danger. Even so close to Gilly's, he would have been on his guard.

What if it had been a setup? What if Flynn had been lulled into a false sense of security by the presence of someone he trusted? McGinty turned the thought over in his mind. It made sense. He had used the same ploy often enough himself to know the value of placing an informant within the enemy's camp.

The door of his office opened, and one of his guards stepped inside long enough to lay a stack of papers—receipts from the saloons—on the corner of the desk. He nodded and smiled briefly before exiting the room.

McGinty stared at the door after the man left. Had that been the smile of an obsequious underling or of one who knew more than he was telling? He shifted uneasily in his chair. For the first time since childhood, he felt the thin edge of fear.

A decisive move was in order, something to reestablish his position. But what? He had already sent a message of his own when he cornered that girl in the dark. The memory made him smile for the first time that night. It wasn't often he was able to demonstrate his power in such a pleasant way. A chuckle escaped his lips when he remembered her startled gasp and the yielding softness of her lips beneath his. He would have given a lot to have seen the look on her face when the flowers and note arrived. But it would keep her on her toes, and that was good.

He always enjoyed the sense of being a cat ready to pounce upon the cowering mouse in the corner. His anger flared again. Flynn's death put him in the unaccustomed position of feeling like the cornered mouse being toyed with by a faceless cat.

And that was going to prove dangerous for someone. He had resources, and plenty of them. He mustn't let this distraction put him off his stride. That was exactly what his opponent wanted.

A plan began to take shape in his mind. He would press harder, find out the location of Da Silva's headquarters. Then he would marshal his forces and send them out in a bold, strategic move, not waiting for the other man to seize the initiative and gain any further ground.

McGinty narrowed his eyes, welcoming the rising sense of anticipation. This time the mouse would kill the cat.

CHAPTER 17

WWould you like to walk out along the pier or farther down the beach?" Stephen paused at the edge of the Peristyle and waited while Emily scanned the pier that speared out into the gray green waters in front of them and the stretch of golden sand that bordered the fairgrounds on the east.

"Let's go this way." She turned south, following the lakeshore.

Stephen was happy to comply. That direction led them away from the hubbub of the fairgrounds to a quieter area where they could have some time to themselves. They walked past the models of the *Niña*, *Pinta*, and *Santa María* and the rampart-like walls housing the replica of the Convent of La Rábida to reach a spot where they could cross over the south inlet and continue on their way.

He'd often patrolled this same area as part of his duties as a guard, but today was different. When he was in uniform, he felt a bit constrained, always aware of people looking at him as a representative of the fair. In his street clothes, he was just a man out for a walk with his girl. It took little time to walk past Krupp's Gun Exhibit and the Leather and Forestry buildings and put the noisy scene behind them.

"You seem quiet today." He hoped it wasn't because he'd suggested their walk on the spur of the moment. It was a last-minute decision on his part, an effort to steal a few extra moments of time before she went home from work.

Lucy was great fun, almost like another kid sister; Mrs. Purvis was ever the gracious hostess; and he had no doubt about his feelings for Adam. But tonight, just for a while, he wanted Emily all to himself.

Beyond the southern tip of the fairgrounds, they came to a secluded stretch of the shore. A spindly tree spread its branches out above a large, flat rock. Stephen pointed to it. "Look, there's a bench just waiting for us. Shall we?" Emily smiled at his teasing tone and followed his lead. The sand scuffed under their feet as they made their way to the rock. Two seagulls hopped away and then took flight when they drew nearer.

Stephen helped Emily get settled on the rock's smooth, sun-warmed surface, happy to note there was just enough room beside her for him to sit. He could feel the pressure of her arm against his sleeve.

"This is a nice spot." Emily leaned back and sighed. As she did so, a twig from the lowermost tree branch caught the brim of her hat, knocking it askew.

Stephen scooted toward the extreme edge of the rock while she pinned her hat back into place; then he said, "Here, why don't you move over this way?" The maneuver put her even closer to him, but as she didn't seem to mind, he wasn't about to complain.

He looked down at her, and their gazes locked. "Funny, isn't it?"

he began. "Here we are, in the middle of an incredibly dangerous situation, yet lately I've been happier than I can ever remember."

A smile lit her eyes from within. "It is odd," she agreed, "but I feel the same way." She lowered her gaze, giving him the opportunity to study her close at hand.

Her eyelashes fanned across her cheeks, hiding her eyes from view. His gaze traveled across her upturned nose, the soft curve of her cheek, and those soft, inviting lips only a breath away.

Stephen caught himself and pulled back. Maybe it hadn't been such a good idea for them to sit this close. He thought back to his conversation with Seth Howell and his friend's advice to wait before bringing up the subject of marriage. Had he waited long enough?

More than anything, he wanted this woman to be a part of his life, a part of himself. And not only as a means of protecting her—he knew full well that was only a part of his desire to make Emily his wife. He wanted to see that sweet face every day of his life, to have the right to reach out and cradle her cheek in his hand, to run his fingers through that luxuriant red hair. His heart belonged to her and always would.

Was this the time? Seth had counseled him to wait until other distractions were out of the way and they could both think clearly. But they had no guarantee the pressure from McGinty would let up anytime soon and give them a chance to focus on things beyond their physical safety. Would the time ever be right?

With an effort, he tried to switch his thinking to a different track. Surely he could at least come up with something intelligent to say after asking her to spend time alone with him.

"Nice place, isn't it?" *Oh, now there's a brilliant remark!* Emily looked up expectantly, obviously waiting for him to say more.

He floundered ahead. "We'll have to come back someday. For a picnic."

Emily nodded and smiled. "That would be nice."

He watched the curve of her delicate lips, so irresistible, inviting him to come closer. He bent forward but held back when he saw her expression change. Apparently McGinty's forcible kiss was still fresh in her mind. Would kissing her now awaken that unpleasant memory, connecting the two events forever in her mind? That was the last thing he wanted to do.

She flicked another look at him. Did he read welcome in her eyes or caution? It took every bit of will he could muster to straighten and lean slightly away from her. He wasn't sure whether the expression on her face was one of relief or disappointment.

How did one go about asking a young lady whether she wanted to be kissed? She had been wounded, and he didn't want to compound that injury and perhaps forever ruin his chance of winning her.

He stood abruptly. "We'd better be getting back." He tried to ignore her startled look. Maybe he was making a fool of himself, suggesting they spend time together and then ending it almost before it began. But he had to get out of there now, before his all-consuming desire to hold her in his arms and cover her face with kisses became too much for him to control.

The light in her eyes dimmed a bit. "All right."

He held out his hand to help her to her feet. She started to rise then plopped back down on the rock with a look of dismay. She put her hand to the back of her head. "My hair. It's caught in these branches."

She reached back with both hands and tried to free herself. The look on her face went from one of embarrassment to irritation and then to mild panic. Her fingers worked frantically, sending a couple of hairpins flying to the ground, but the more she struggled, the more tightly entangled she became. She jerked at the branch, and her hat tilted down over her eyes.

Emily yanked the hat pin loose and pulled the straw hat from her head. She looked up at Stephen, mortified. "I hate to ask you, but—"

"Allow me." He stepped in, glad to be able to do something besides stand around and witness her distress.

It wasn't as easy a task as he expected. In her struggle, she had managed to work some of the tiny twigs deep into the auburn mass. Stephen wasn't sure how he was going to get them loose. He tugged experimentally. "Am I hurting you?"

Emily closed her eyes. "No, go ahead."

He went about it methodically, pulling the twigs free of the coppery strands. "I'm sorry, I'm knocking some of your hairpins loose."

"That doesn't matter. Just get me out of this."

He worked his fingers through the silken tresses. "I'm going to have to break these twigs off. There isn't any other way."

"Do what you have to." Her voice revealed she was on the verge of tears.

"These pins are getting in the way. They're holding everything so tight I can't pull the twigs loose."

"Then let's get them out of there." Emily reached back and tugged at the remaining pins. With the last one removed, the heavy coils of hair cascaded over his hands.

Stephen stared at the silken mass. From the day they'd met, he'd wondered what it would look like hanging free. Now it tumbled through his fingers like folds of satin. For a moment, he couldn't move. The warmth of the sun was in her hair. Without thinking, he ducked his head to inhale deeply and drink of its perfume.

His breathing quickened. Touching her hair brought back the feelings he had been trying to quell. But he had gotten himself into this; he had to see it through. He fumbled to break away the last of the twigs and worked them free of her hair.

Emily turned then and gazed into his eyes. Stephen stared into those emerald pools and felt like a drowning man.

He couldn't help it. He leaned forward as though drawn by a magnet.

Emily watched Stephen's face move closer until it filled her vision. His eyes, the color of rich coffee, grew even darker. Still entwined in her hair, his hands cupped the back of her head and pressed it forward.

She struggled to think, to breathe. When he drew nearer still, she let her eyelids drift shut and tilted her face up, surrendering her lips to his.

They pressed against hers, softly at first, then with more assurance. The taste of his lips was sweet as warm honey. Her hands crept upward of their own accord, her fingertips running lightly over the smooth weave of his broadcloth jacket. Her hands reached his shoulders and linked together behind his neck.

A well of joy sprang up within her, and her heart cried, *Yes!* This was the way it was supposed to be, everything she had dreamed about and more. She melted into his arms, feeling as though her soul had somehow joined with his.

Gulls sent out their keening cries as they swooped overhead. Emily's heart soared with them as she lost herself in the wonder of Stephen's kiss.

Emily made a final notation on her report and slid it into its folder then placed the folder neatly at the corner of her desk. The great fair seemed to move more slowly every day as it neared its end, like a clock winding down. In the middle of the week, attendance tended to slump a bit. Today the spate of parents bringing and collecting children had dwindled down to a bare trickle.

She looked around at her tidy work space. The reports were finished; the ledger was up-to-date. Nothing remained to claim her attention. She linked her fingers and stretched her arms out in front of her. It wasn't often she had time on her hands, but it would be nice to have a chance to catch her breath and relax a bit.

The door swung open. Emily wrinkled her nose and hurried to resume her businesslike demeanor.

A lone man approached her desk. Well dressed and neatly groomed, he crossed the reception area with an air of authority.

He stood before her desk, commanding her attention without a word. Emily looked up at him, startled by the intensity of his clear blue eyes. She tilted her head and studied him from under her lashes, observing the square face, the uncompromising jaw, and the dark hair that lay smooth against his head. A hint of a wave in his hair made her suspect that if it didn't receive frequent trimming, it would soon become an unruly mass. Johnny Meacham's hair had been like that.

He wasn't as tall as Stephen, but his shoulders were broader. He had a stocky frame, but she saw no sign of a paunch or any other hint of softness about him. Before he spoke a word, Emily felt sure that this was a man who knew exactly what he wanted and was sure of getting it. Perhaps he was one of the fair officials.

She lifted her chin and gave him her most pleasant smile. "How may I help you?"

"Good afternoon, Miss Ralston." His voice held a rolling lilt. "What a pleasure to see you in the daylight."

Emily held her smile in place, trying to give no hint of the sudden tension that gripped her. Should she know this man? He knew her name. What was he talking about?

"The last time we were together, I had to leave so abruptly that we didn't have time for a civil greeting."

Emily's thoughts bounced around like a child's rubber ball. She didn't have any recollection of meeting this man before. Was he demented? She cast a surreptitious glance over her shoulder, hoping to see Lucy or one of the other workers in the hall. No one was there; she was quite alone with her strange visitor. She turned back around and saw that he'd noticed her unease. The corners of his mouth tilted up slightly.

Needing something to do with her hands, she slid the ledger over to her. "Did you come to pick up a child?"

His smile widened. "No, I'm not ready to lay claim to my son. . .just yet."

A horrible suspicion started forming in the back of Emily's mind. At the same time, the man inclined his head and said, "Allow me to introduce myself. My name is Ian McGinty."

Emily shot up from her chair, sending it toppling over to clatter against the floor. She whirled, but before she could take more than two steps, he moved around the desk with the speed of a cat and blocked her way.

Fear engulfed her. The man was a killer. What was he going to do to her?

He pinned her with his gaze as he bent to pick up her chair and gently set it upright. He put it back in its place behind her desk and gestured for her to resume her seat.

Emily complied, knowing her legs were too tottery to carry her any distance. She clasped her hands tightly together on top of the desk, hoping he couldn't see the tremors that rippled through her body. "What do you want?"

His deep chuckle rolled around the reception area. "Ah, Miss Ralston, I want so many things. Sadly, only a few of them pertain to you."

Emily lifted her chin, attempting a bravado she was far from feeling. "Adam isn't here."

"I know that. He's at home with your Mrs. Purvis, just as he is every day. But as I said, I'm not here to take him with me. I have other matters to deal with first. One day, perhaps soon. . ."

He dropped his easy manner, and his tone became brisk and businesslike. "I'm here to make you a proposition."

Emily gripped the edge of the desk with both hands.

"The fair is ending in just a few weeks," he went on. "You'll need to find new employment. Since you have appointed yourself as my son's caretaker, I'm offering to let you keep that position on a permanent basis."

Emily made no outward move, although her mind raced madly, trying to discern his meaning.

"On the day I'm ready to reclaim my son, I would like you to come with him. You would make a lovely addition to my household."

Emily gasped and shook her head from side to side so rapidly the room seemed to spin.

Adam's father tilted his head to one side in a gesture she might have found appealing in anyone else. "You may have heard stories about me, but I am primarily a businessman. I'd like you to look at this as a business proposition."

Emily finally found her voice. "I couldn't possibly—"

He held up his hand, cutting her off. "I can see refusal in your eyes. I'll give you awhile to ponder my offer before you give your answer." He planted his palms on her desk and leaned forward until his face was only inches from hers.

"You want to do what's best," he said. "For yourself, for Adam. . .and for your friends. Think about it. If you come with me, I'll see that you are well paid. You'll never want for anything." The keen blue gaze bored into hers until Emily felt like a bird being hypnotized by a snake. "I've heard how fond you are of my son and heir. I believe having to say good-bye to him would cause you some distress, am I right?"

Emily willed herself not to answer but realized her head was nodding in mute agreement.

"This way, you won't have to. You'll be able to have him with you every day with my blessing. Adam will be well cared for, you will be happy to be with him, and your friends will be able to go about their business as usual. I'm sure you want Mrs. Purvis and Miss Welch to remain safe and well, don't you?"

Emily stared into the piercing gaze that seemed to speak volumes without words. A whimper rose from her throat, and she bit back a cry, hating the show of weakness.

McGinty straightened and smiled as though her anguish pleased him. "Think it over. I'll be back for your answer later, when these other matters have been dealt with." Without further comment, he turned on his heel and strode out of the building as jauntily as if he were out for a Sunday stroll.

Emily struggled to draw air into her lungs. So that was the infamous Ian McGinty. She wasn't surprised he had the reputation he did. The man exuded a sense of power like no one she had ever met.

"Are you all right?" Lucy's concerned voice broke into her thoughts. Lucy bent down to peer into Emily's face. "Answer me, Emily. You're as white as a sheet. What's wrong?"

"Where were you?" The cry burst forth from Emily's lips.

Lucy's frown deepened. "I was right down the hall. Did you need me for something?"

Emily seized both of Lucy's arms. "He was here. Adam's father." She loosened her hold, taking some satisfaction from Lucy's look of utter astonishment.

"Have you called the Columbian Guards? Where's Stephen?"

"It's too late. He's already gone. There was nothing I could do to call for help while he was here."

Lucy crouched down in front of Emily and gripped her hands tightly. "What did he want?"

"Me."

"You can't be serious." The look of shock on Lucy's face would have been amusing had the situation not been so dire.

"He said he's willing to leave Adam in my care until he takes care of some other business. But then he plans to take Adam back, and he wants me to come with him."

Lucy looked around wildly, as though McGinty stood right there, threatening to drag Emily from the building at that very moment. "What are we going to do? We can't let that happen."

"I don't know. If I don't, he implied he'd do something to hurt you or Mrs. Purvis. I don't know how to refuse a man like that." The trembling took hold of her again as his words replayed in her mind. She spoke her thoughts aloud. "Villain or not, the man has a right to his own son. But how can I bear turning Adam over to him, knowing what he's like?"

Tears thickened her voice. "It's one thing to pretend things will go along as they have been, but he made it clear that his son is in our care only because he allows it. We'll never be able to stop him from taking Adam whenever he chooses."

Lucy looked at her as though she thought Emily had lost her mind. "But that doesn't mean you have to go with him."

Tears spurted from her eyes, and Emily dashed them away with the back of her hand. How could she explain to Lucy the feelings she had developed for Adam? She couldn't love him more if he had been born of her own flesh.

Lucy folded her arms. "You can't imagine he only wants you there to care for his son. You're an attractive woman. Think where that will lead. This is not just about Adam; it's about your own safety."

Emily eyed her steadily. "And yours."

"Miss Welch!" Miss Strickland's voice echoed down the hallway.

"I'm coming," Lucy called. Turning back to Emily, she said, "You're not thinking straight after meeting that evil man face-to-face. Don't give up hope; there's always a way. Haven't you told me that God always has a plan for us?" She sniffled and gave Emily a watery smile. "You can't tell me this is His plan for you."

Miss Strickland called again. With a quick parting hug, Lucy hurried off to find the supervisor.

Emily wrapped her arms across her chest and rocked back and forth. Lucy was right—she couldn't think of agreeing to go along with such an outrageous scheme.

Or could she? If she refused, he had all but promised to bring harm to the people she loved most. She could bear the thought of something bad happening to her more easily than she could contemplate some terrible fate befalling one of them.

She suspected McGinty was well aware of that.

And if the unthinkable happened, the fault would lie at her door. Could she live with herself, then?

She rested her elbows on her desk and cradled her head in her hands. Was there any bright spot in this nightmare? If she did agree to go with McGinty when he came for Adam, she could at least be sure the little boy stayed safe and well and hopefully steer him away from following in his father's footsteps. That in itself would be worth a good deal of self-sacrifice.

But the price would be high in other respects. She remembered McGinty's compelling gaze, and her mind flew back to that demanding kiss taken without her consent. Whatever her official title might be, she had no doubt he would consider her his property to do with as he willed. She shuddered.

But God worked in mysterious ways. Miss Pierce, the matron at the Collier Home, had quoted those words often enough to sear them in Emily's mind forever. Could this be one of those ways? She found it hard to see how God could have anything to do with a man as depraved as this one.

"For God so loved the world. . ." Surely that included Ian McGinty. God had reached down at a low moment in her own life to accept her, to save her, and to make her His child. According to the Bible, He wanted to do the same thing for everyone, even for this man. But would He ask Emily to play some role in that?

She thought about the way the man's blue eyes, so like Adam's, softened when he spoke of his son. Maybe at the core, he wasn't completely evil. There might still be hope for him. Did that mean she was expected to help bring it about? Had she, like Esther, been placed in her situation for such a time as this?

The thought chilled her.

But would God ask her to go against His other teachings to try to redeem this man? Would He ever ask her to disobey Him in one area in order to bring about a good result? Did the end ever justify the means?

Deep in her soul, she knew the answer. "Thank You, Lord," she whispered. "I couldn't do that. I just couldn't."

CHAPTER 18

"W"e're going to ride the train!" Adam danced from one foot to the other, his eyes bright with excitement.

Emily knelt in front of him while Mrs. Purvis and Lucy laughed at his antics. "We won't be able to leave until I can fasten your shoe, so you'd better hold still."

Stephen corralled the youngster and dropped to one knee, seating Adam on the other. "Let's help Miss Emily so we can get going. What do you say?"

Adam contented himself with bouncing gently on Stephen's knee while Emily worked on his shoe. With a sweet smile, he began singing, "Jesus loves me, this I know. . . ."

A lump formed in Emily's throat. This was not the same child they'd brought home from the fairgrounds. Adam had lost his haunted look and was now an exuberant, playful little boy, to all appearances quite happy in his new setting.

As always, Emily marveled at the way he trusted her. When

she gave him her word, he had no doubt she would follow through. She wondered how many promises to him had been broken in his young life.

She finished fastening the shoe, and he hopped down off Stephen's knee. "Ready! Let's ride the train!"

Stephen reached out a hand to help her to her feet. Emily stood and smoothed her skirt. "All right, young man. Let's go."

"Don't you think you'd better wear a coat?" Mrs. Purvis urged. "I was out sweeping the front stoop earlier, and the air is turning quite nippy. Cold weather will be upon us before we know it."

"I'll get Adam's," Lucy volunteered. "I remember where we put it the first day we brought him home."

Stephen pulled Emily's dark blue cape from its hook on the hall tree and placed it over her shoulders, while Lucy clattered back down the stairs and helped Adam into his coat. Emily smiled when she saw Lucy stoop to smooth the stubborn collar into place. Then she saw a frown cross her friend's face. "What is it?"

"I can't make it stay down," Lucy responded. "There's something crinkly in his collar. See for yourself."

Puzzled, Emily went over to check and felt the back of Adam's collar. Sure enough, something was between the layers of heavy fabric. "What is it? Do you suppose it's a stiffener of some sort?"

"If it is, it isn't doing a very good job of it." Lucy tried to turn the collar down in the back, but it sprang straight up again. "See?"

Emily pressed her fingers along the rest of the collar, expecting to find more of the peculiar stiffener all down its length, but she felt nothing.

She turned to Stephen. "Would you mind waiting a few minutes? I can't take him out in public like this. I'll go fetch my scissors, snip the seam open, and take out that ridiculous lump, whatever it is."

Stephen nodded and helped Adam out of the coat while Emily ran to her room for her sewing basket. When she returned, she sat on the bottom tread of the stairs and carefully snipped the stitches holding that part of the collar together. When the opening was wide enough, she pulled the layers of fabric apart, slipped her fingers inside, and drew out a small packet of folded papers.

"What on earth?" She held it up for the others to see.

"How very odd!" Lucy said. "Do you suppose it was put in there by mistake?"

"How could it have been?" Emily countered. "Somebody had to put it there intentionally, but for the life of me, I don't know why."

She turned to Stephen and Mrs. Purvis for help, but the landlady shook her head. "I can't imagine a seamstress or tailor putting a wad of paper in a collar like that."

Emily fumbled with the papers until she could tease the edges apart. Several thin sheets lay bundled together. She smoothed them open on her lap and looked at the top page. She frowned as she moved that page to the bottom of the stack and picked up the second sheet. She sucked in her breath.

"What is it?" Stephen asked.

Emily put her finger to her lips and gestured toward Adam.

Lucy picked up on her signal. "Come on, Adam. Do you want to play with blocks?"

The little boy shook his head so hard his hair formed a blond cloud around his head. "No. I want to ride the train."

Emily looked up helplessly, and Mrs. Purvis went into action. "I think Miss Emily and Mr. Stephen need to talk privately for a moment. Why don't you come back to the kitchen with me and help me stir up some of those oatmeal cookies you love so much?"

Adam looked at her dubiously but allowed the landlady to lead him toward the back of the house.

"I'll give you a hand," Lucy called and followed them.

"Can you tell me now?" Stephen knelt in front of Emily and put his hand on her arm.

For a long moment, she couldn't move. Finally, she met his eyes. "You're not going to believe this."

She pulled the first page from the bottom of the stack and read it aloud:

> "If anyone is reading this, it means that I have failed in my effort to dispose of these papers myself. In that case, I beg whoever is in possession of them now to turn them over to Mr. Gerald Cavender of the district attorney's office. He will know what to do with them."

"What?" Stephen's eyes grew wide.

"That's not all." Emily indicated the rest of the pages, filled with writing in a small, neat hand. "I've only seen the first few lines, but I think we should both hear this." She licked her lips and began:

> "My name is Rosalee Sawyer. I am known in many circles as Ian McGinty's companion. Not so many know that I am also the mother of his son, Adam. Lest you judge me too harshly or have doubts about accepting the testimony of a ruined woman, let me give you a history of how this situation came to be.
>
> "I wasn't raised to be this type of person—far from it! My dear parents would be mortified if they knew of the life I have lived for the past five years. My father always had an

adventurous streak, a somewhat unlikely trait for a banker in Baltimore. When he heard of an investment opportunity in Chicago, he leaped at the chance, liquidating all his assets to put into the new venture and cutting ties with his business connections back home. All of us—my parents, my brother, and I—boarded the train filled with excitement at the turn our lives were about to take.

"But Papa took sick along the way. Along the route in Ohio, he became ill enough for the conductor to request the help of a fellow passenger who was a doctor. He said my father had contracted cholera and recommended we be put off the train at once. They set us off, bag and baggage, at the next stop. Papa grew worse, and by morning, it was obvious my mother had caught the disease, as well. My brother fell ill that evening. Over the next three days, I lost everyone in my family."

Tears blurred Emily's vision. "How awful! She must have been devastated."

Stephen nodded. "Go on."

Emily wiped her eyes and continued:

"People said I was the fortunate one. I wondered then—and now—whether that was truly the case. After the burial expenses, I barely had a penny to my name. The only possession of any value was my ticket to Chicago. I boarded the next train and continued the journey, planning to meet with Papa's new partner and beg him to return the money my father invested.

"But that was not to be. The man had the audacity to tell me Papa owed him money beyond that which he had already

paid, and he wanted the rest of it immediately. When I told him I had no money, he threatened to sell me to the owner of a local brothel and take those funds as his payment.

"A friend of his, Ian McGinty, stepped in at that point, saying I looked too refined for the brothel trade and he would be willing to give his friend the money to pay my debt and take me under his wing. My gratitude knew no bounds! At that time, I saw him as my rescuer, but that happy state didn't last long.

"I soon realized I had leaped from the frying pan into the fire. Degradation of one sort had been averted, but I had stepped into a new role, that of Ian McGinty's mistress. As bad as that was, it soon became even worse. When he visited the house he provided for me, he would often drink heavily and talk about the people he did business with. I noticed that often the people he named as competitors disappeared or turned up dead, and I wondered what kind of man I had linked my lot with."

Emily's hands shook so hard she could barely focus on the words.

"Would you like me to read for a while?" Stephen asked. She nodded and placed the thin sheets in his hand. Then she covered her face with her hands as he read more of Rosalee's story:

"For the most part, he tended to be a reasonable man when we were together, not given to violence or fits of rage, but one day I asked him what it would take to fulfill my part of our bargain and bring our arrangement to an end. He squeezed my arm and backed me into a wall. A look of cold steel came into his eyes, and he told me I belonged to him

and there was no point in discussing any other arrangement. From that day on, fear became my constant companion. I never found the courage to bring up the matter again.

"I wept for three days when I learned I was with child, but my biggest heartache turned out to become my greatest joy. Adam is the most precious creature in the world, bearing little resemblance to his father in looks and none in temperament. His birth gave me a purpose for living. But as he grew, I found myself concerned about his future. How could I hope to instill any morality or sense of decency in him, living the way I do? As a child, I had given my heart to Jesus and promised to follow Him always. How far I have strayed from that vow!

"While I knew there was no hope left for me, I didn't want my son to grow up in the shadow of his father's wickedness. I prayed for the first time in years, asking God to show me a way to leave this life of shame and escape McGinty's clutches. I never expected the answer to come as it did.

"The neighbor lady who sometimes watched Adam when McGinty and I went out invited me to attend one of the tent meetings held by Mr. Moody. I had little hope of gaining anything from the service, but I was so starved for the companionship of more congenial people that I went with her. And there God reached out to me, and I discovered He hadn't turned His back on me after all. I knew at that point that my life could not go on as it had."

Emily's cheeks were wet with tears. "What an amazing story! God never gives up on us, does He?"

Stephen shook his head, his expression solemn. "Do you want

me to keep reading?" At Emily's nod, he went on:

"*That same week, McGinty's carriage delivered me to his house, where I was supposed to meet him to accompany him to some social function. He took so long in coming out to the carriage that I went in to see what was causing the delay. I heard voices and followed them down the hallway. The voices grew loud, and I realized a heated argument was in progress.*

"*I thought about returning to the carriage to wait, but the door was partly open, so I peeked through the crack. McGinty faced a man I recognized as Arthur Long, a city alderman. On his face was that same steely look that always paralyzed me with fright. 'You shouldn't have crossed me,' he said in a tone that chilled me to the bone.*

"*Long tried to bluster his way out, saying McGinty didn't know what he was talking about. He moved to one side, blocking my view, and I heard him cry out, 'No, don't!' The next thing I knew, he lay on his back on the floor, and McGinty bent over him, pulling a silver dagger from his chest. Then he reached into Long's jacket and took out a folded sheet of paper. When I heard him call for one of his henchmen, I ran back to the carriage.*

"*McGinty drank more than usual during the party, while I tried to behave as if I didn't know anything out of the ordinary had happened. When he took me back to my house, I dreaded having to keep up a conversation. I needn't have worried—it wasn't long before he passed out on the sofa. I kept staring at the pocket where I'd seen him slip the paper he took from Long and finally got up enough nerve to reach in and take it. I am enclosing that paper with this letter. It names the people McGinty controls in city government, from patrolmen on up to men on the mayor's staff.*

"And I found the knife, as well. For whatever reason, he slipped it into his pocket along with the paper, probably meaning to dispose of it as soon as he got home. The knife is hidden beneath a loose floorboard under the head of my bed. It is still stained with Arthur Long's blood and will serve as proof of what I have written here.

"When he came to, he was too drunk to notice the paper and knife were missing or to care about anything but climbing back into his carriage and going home. He has never asked me whether I've seen these pieces of evidence, but there is a watchfulness in his eyes that makes me think he suspects.

"I swear all this is true, as God is my witness. I will leave it to the district attorney and the courts to determine what happens, because once I have placed this in the hands of Mr. Cavender, I can no longer stay in Chicago. My intention is to get my son and myself to safety in a new place where we can start our lives over again."

Silence filled the room when Stephen finished. When Emily looked up, she could feel the tears spill over to wend their way down her cheeks. "Then she wasn't a bad woman at heart, was she?"

"No," Stephen said slowly. "It sounds like someone who had to choose between two unspeakable options and took the one that seemed less evil."

Emily folded the papers in quarters and smoothed them against her knee. When Stephen stood, she pushed herself to her feet and took hold of his arm. "But I still don't understand. Why would this be in Adam's coat, of all places?"

Stephen slipped his arm around her shoulders and pulled her to his side. "We'll never know the answer to that for sure.

My guess would be that she hid it there as a safeguard in case something happened to her."

"And it did," Emily whispered. She shuddered and pressed closer against him. "And that means she knew someone was after her. Then that's why she ran away. She didn't abandon Adam, after all."

"No, it was like a mother bird drawing the attacker away from her nest. She was willing to lay down her life to keep Adam safe."

"While still preserving the evidence." Emily choked on the words. "Do you think she meant to meet this Mr. Cavender on the fairgrounds?"

"It would make sense. Think about it—thousands of people milling around, and nobody really notices who is contacting whom. Sometimes the easiest place to disappear is in the middle of a crowd."

"But it didn't work this time."

"No," Stephen said flatly. "It didn't."

Emily rubbed the folded papers between her thumb and fingers. "She gave her life trying to bring this evil man to justice. And she died not knowing if these papers would ever get to the authorities." She turned in the circle of Stephen's arm and tilted her chin to look into his face. "That makes us responsible for getting this evidence to them, doesn't it?"

"I don't see anything else we can do. We certainly can't just toss them away and pretend we never saw them."

Emily straightened. "I already have my hat and coat on. I guess that means we're making a trip to see Mr. Cavender. I'll go let Mrs. Purvis know." She moved toward the kitchen, but Stephen caught her arm.

"Wait a minute. Let's think this through. If Rosalee was

caught and murdered before she could meet with this man from the district attorney's office, there was evidently a leak somewhere that got the word back to McGinty."

Emily sagged against his arm. "You're right. I hadn't thought about that."

"We need to handle this in another way. I'll take it to my friend Elliott Ferguson. He'll know what to do with it."

Emily lifted her chin. "You mean *we* will take it to him. We're in this together. I'm not letting you take all the risks alone."

Stephen looked at her steadily, but she thought she saw the corners of his mustache twitch. "All right, you're going with me."

"I'll tell Mrs. Purvis and Lucy. Oh. . ." Emily clapped her hand to her forehead. "I'll have to tell Adam I can't take him to the train today. And he was counting on it so! I'll promise to make it up to him soon." She stopped in the doorway and turned back to give Stephen a searching gaze. "Are you sure this Elliott can be trusted?"

Stephen nodded. "He's an honorable man. I would stake my life on that."

Emily gave him a long, searching look. "I hope you're right, because that's exactly what we're doing."

~

"I'm not sure how to tell you this." Mort looked even more nervous than usual without his partner, Flynn, there to back him up.

"Just tell me straight out." McGinty sighed. Would the man never learn?

"Our snitch downtown tells me the district attorney's office just got hold of some very interesting information."

McGinty schooled his face to mask the anxious thoughts that stirred within him. "What exactly are we talking about?"

"You know that stuff you thought the woman took with her?"

McGinty's stomach tightened. "All right," he said, although he felt sure he knew the rest of the story.

"Well, somebody got it into the hands of a cop—a clean one. And he got it to the district attorney. Word is he's planning to make a move as soon as he's sure he has everything he needs to make an indictment." Mort shrugged. "You know he's thinking ahead to the next election, so he'll want to do something that will stick in the minds of the voters."

McGinty breathed heavily through his nostrils. "And where did this evidence come from?"

"That I don't know." Mort's Adam's apple bobbed up and down. "Neither did my informant. He told me everything he knew, boss, and I brought it along to you as soon as I heard."

McGinty jerked his head toward the door. "Get out."

"Where? Anything you want me to do?"

"Just wait outside. I'll let you know."

With Mort gone, McGinty remained in his chair, letting the news sink in. While his body sat motionless, his mind darted from one thought to another. That speed, that ability to see many facets of a situation at once had helped him get where he was, letting him forge ahead in one area while warding off danger in another.

But he hadn't warded off danger completely, had he? His plan for mounting a counterattack against Da Silva's continued encroachment had proved more disastrous than he ever imagined. Da Silva had someone in his camp; he felt sure of it. Someone who leaked word of his intended coup in time for Da Silva to marshal his own forces and lie in wait, resulting in a bloodbath that decimated all but a handful of McGinty's troops.

So much for his plan for the mouse to kill the cat.

He had been weighing his next move when Mort burst in,

carrying this latest bit of news. McGinty shoved his chair back and paced the room. He needed to move, to unleash some of his pent-up energy.

He had an overwhelming sense of too much coming at him too fast. With this new threat following on the heels of Flynn's death and Da Silva's mounting attempts to take over, he felt backed into a corner, with everything he valued threatening to come crashing down around him. His breathing grew shallow, his thoughts more scattered. He stopped to examine the unfamiliar sensation. Was this what panic felt like?

He tried to shake off the weakness by sheer force of will, but the walls of his office seemed to be closing in on him. His breathing became more labored, and he felt a tightness in his chest.

He clutched the back of his chair in both hands and watched his knuckles turn white. *I will not let this get the best of me. Think. Think! This is no time to lose control.*

He had to make a decision and make it now. He had always prided himself on the ability to analyze a situation quickly and take immediate action. Now it seemed as if his thoughts were mired in the mud.

He sat in his chair again and scooted into its place behind his desk, feeling more confident in his throne, his seat of command. He needed to look at the situation like a general waging a battle, assessing his next move. And that was exactly what he faced. He had moved from being the undisputed ruler of his domain to being thrown into the middle of a war, one that could prove disastrous. A wise general knew it was a bad move to fight battles on two fronts at the same time. It would be impossible to win both, and a loss on either front would be fatal.

Yes, that was better. He was back on track now, his mind moving along more smoothly, able to assess the moves available to him. And the conclusion seemed inevitable: It was time to withdraw from the field.

He could hear the voice of his father as if he were there in the room: "A McGinty never gives up."

Right, Da. But sometimes a McGinty may choose to relocate.

With his mind made up, relief flowed through him like a balm. He felt like himself again, sure of his next step and ready to take action. . .only not in the direction anyone expected.

He walked to the painting that hung on the wall behind his desk. Pulling the painting aside, he spun the dial on the safe concealed behind it. He swung the door open, revealing stacks of bills secured with paper bands. He had spent plenty of time and effort accumulating his wealth, so much time that he'd barely spent a fraction of it. Now it was time to rest on his laurels and enjoy the fruit of his labors.

His fingers riffled through the bills as he sorted through them quickly, looking for those of larger denominations. He couldn't stuff it all into his pockets—it would be too bulky, too visible— but he would need some cash on hand until he got settled again.

He closed the door, spun the lock, and put the painting back, leaving the rest of the cash in the hidden safe. He had long suspected Mort and the others were aware of its existence. Once they knew he was gone, he felt sure they'd try to rifle the contents. Let them have it. They could think of it as a parting gesture, something to remind them he'd always treated them fairly.

Resuming his seat at the desk, he pulled open the bottom drawer on the left side and released a hidden latch, allowing the false bottom to spring free. A smile curved his lips. Down there, unknown to anybody but himself, was where the bulk of his fortune lay—stock certificates worth many times the amount of cash in his safe. He folded the papers into a slim leather case and slipped it into his breast pocket.

One more item to attend to. He slid his fingers into the farthest recesses of the drawer and drew out a chamois bag. Loosening the drawstring, he spilled the contents into his cupped hand. The diamonds caught the lamplight and winked up at him. He poured them back into the leather pouch, refastened the tie, and tucked it into an inside coat pocket.

It had been worth his while to maintain contact with his boyhood friends in New York. They had proven quite useful over the years, none more than those who had connections with the jewelry trade and were willing to act as go-betweens to purchase the valuable stones for him without asking where the money came from.

McGinty grinned. Da might not have approved of his method of making money, but he knew the old man's eyes would have lit up at the sight of the wealth he had amassed.

And now he was ready to go...where? He hadn't thought that far ahead yet. But did he need to make up his mind immediately? After all, he was about to cut all ties with his present life. The world was wide open to him!

A sense of anticipation and freedom filled him at the prospect of a new beginning. He could use the knowledge he'd gained in building up this business to start over and...

Realization struck him full force. He didn't have to do that. He had enough to his name to allow him to go anywhere he chose and settle down to life as a wealthy gentleman, without a secret side he had to keep hidden from public view.

The notion appealed to him. Maybe the very thing intended to bring him down would turn out to be the best thing that ever happened to him. He could have a fine life wherever he decided to go. He could see it now. He would buy a suitable house—no, build one, a home to fill his every desire and inspire envy among the gentry, the perfect setting for a gentleman of means.

He smoothed his jacket, checking for any telltale lumps or bulges that might give away his intention to cut and run. He would find a woman—a decent one this time—maybe even marry her and settle down to a life of respectability and ease. He reached for his hat and his walking stick. He could see it now. . .Ian McGinty, family man.

His hand froze in the act of reaching for the doorknob. Instead, he drew out his wallet and removed several bills. He replaced the wallet and folded the cash in his hand; then he opened the door and called for Mort.

He had one last job for the man to do.

CHAPTER 19

Y ou have to be joking." Stephen's dark eyebrows drew together, daring her to disagree.

Emily jutted out her chin and planted her hands on her hips. "I most certainly am not. I told Adam I would take him to ride on the elevated railway, and I intend to keep my promise. It's bad enough I had to put him off after we found that evidence in his collar, but I told him then we'd go on my next day off. Which is today. Just because you have to attend a meeting and can't go with us doesn't mean I'm going to put him off again."

"I didn't plan for things to go this way." Stephen kept his tone even, but she could see the frustration that blazed in his eyes. "My uncle and his partners are meeting with a client today, and he wants me to be there so I can begin doing some preliminary work on the project before the fair ends. That way, I'll have some momentum built up by the time I'm ready to start working at his firm full-time."

He ran his fingers through his hair. "I admire the fact that you always want to do the right thing, but you need to think again about what the right thing is in this case. We sent evidence to the district attorney that could bring McGinty down once and for all. Do you have any idea what a man like that is capable of doing when he's been crossed?"

He took one step toward her, bridging the gap between them. "Do you have any idea how many people who angered him have just disappeared? This is not a good time for the two of you to go about in public."

Emily stood her ground, although she had to tilt her head back in order to look up into his face. "I don't see that there's going to be any good time to take Adam out if we're going to do it according to Ian McGinty's pleasure. Just when would that be, do you suppose? We've been keeping Adam hidden away most of the time, anyway, and a child can't be cooped up forever. I know what it's like not to have a chance to play outside and do things like a normal child."

She moved over beside the hall tree to put some distance between them. "I don't see that it makes any difference. McGinty knows Adam is with me, and he knows where we live. And as you keep reminding me, he has his spies everywhere. So what does it matter where we are at any given time?" She flung her arms out to her sides. "He'll know it, anyway. We can't live our lives cowering behind locked doors, afraid of what might happen."

Stephen set his bowler atop his head and placed his hands on her shoulders. "I'm not asking you to spend the rest of your life in hiding. I'm only asking you to put off Adam's excursion a little while longer." This time he used the softer tone that usually turned her legs to butter. "Surely you can understand my concerns."

Emily swallowed. "I understand."

He smiled and bent to press a quick kiss on her lips before he trotted down the front steps and climbed into his uncle's carriage.

Emily leaned back against the doorjamb and watched the carriage set off north along Blackstone Avenue, her heart swelling with love for this man who cared so much about her safety. She knew his request didn't stem from a desire to control but from a desire to protect her and Adam.

She thought back to the day she'd told Adam she would have to go off with Stephen to run an errand instead of taking him to the fair as planned. He had straightened his little shoulders stoically and tried to be brave, but she'd seen the way his lower lip quivered.

Emily knew what it was like to live with disappointment day after day. She couldn't bear to do that to him again.

What if. . . Emily brightened as a thought took form in her mind. She calculated rapidly, accounting for the time it would require for Stephen to travel to his uncle's office and back and the time he would be involved in the meeting.

She nodded, feeling like giving a victory whoop. Even if the meeting proved to be a short one, it would still give her plenty of time. She and Adam could go to the fair, take the promised ride on the elevated train, maybe even take in a few of the other sights, and still be back before Stephen even knew they'd been gone.

A flicker of guilt stirred. Was this another one of those half-truths that had gotten her into trouble before? Emily mulled it over a moment then smiled. No, she'd only said she understood his position; she never said she agreed with it. Her alternate plan hadn't come to mind until after he left, so she hadn't deliberately misled him.

In any case, she would rather face Stephen's irritation than hurt Adam again.

With her mind made up, Emily closed the front door and hurried into the house to get Adam ready to go.

———

Stephen tried to pull his mind back to thoughts of architecture instead of dwelling on the mental image of a young woman with stormy green eyes. The conversation he'd just had with Emily was the first one that came near to being an argument, and he couldn't say he'd enjoyed the experience.

Nor could he say he'd come out the clear victor, either. Emily might have accepted his reasoning, but he could tell she didn't like it. If this meeting weren't so important to his future, he gladly would have skipped it to spend time with her and Adam.

The horses' hooves beat in quick rhythm as they clopped along, bearing him toward his uncle's office. He hoped everything would go well. Though he said otherwise, Stephen's uncle had stretched his neck out a bit by giving this job to someone fresh out of college. If Stephen could prove himself with this first project, he could assure his uncle he had made the right decision and demonstrate to the partners that he owed his hiring to something more than nepotism. A success now would smooth the way for the future, bringing the day closer when he could ask Emily to be his wife.

Once the situation with McGinty was resolved. He sighed, remembering Seth's advice.

Still, he felt encouraged to know he was getting his house set in order to be ready when the time came. And the moment that happened, he meant to lay his heart at Emily Ralston's feet and ask for her hand in marriage.

Would their life together include many more discussions of the kind they'd had today? The question brought a chuckle. He wouldn't doubt it. Not too far below that sweet surface lay the heart of a spitfire. He leaned back against the tufted cushions and smiled. Ah well. Life with Emily would never be dull.

The carriage pulled to a stop before the imposing brick structure that housed the architectural firm of Bridger, Caldwell, and Morrison. The driver waited at the curb while Stephen mounted the front steps and made his way to his uncle's spacious office.

"Ah, there you are, my boy. I sent a messenger to try to intercept you, but he said he couldn't find you at home."

Stephen warmed under his uncle's shrewd gaze. "I asked the driver to stop by Emily's boardinghouse for just a moment. I hope that was all right." He looked around, puzzled when he didn't see any of the other partners. "I'm not late, am I?"

A smile creased Uncle Charles's round face. "To the contrary. I was trying to get in touch with you to let you know our client took ill in the early morning hours. He sent word that we would have to postpone the meeting."

Stephen's shoulders slumped. If only he had known, he could have accompanied Emily and Adam to the fair and spared their altercation. Then he brightened. He had the rest of the day ahead of him. There was no reason they couldn't still do as they'd planned.

"I'll take my leave, then." He started toward the door then paused. "Would you mind if I borrowed your carriage to take me back to Emily's? We had to alter our plans for the day, and I may be able to salvage them after all."

Uncle Charles laughed and clapped him on the back. "I'll go you one better. Have my driver take you to pick up the young lady and then consider him at your disposal for the rest of the day. That's a fine girl you've got, and I'm happy to do whatever I can to help further this romance of yours."

Stephen thanked him and hurried back to the carriage. He ordered the driver to return to Blackstone Avenue then settled back in the seat, letting happy images of the afternoon ahead play through his mind. He could picture Emily's pleasure and Adam's delight when he showed up at the boardinghouse and told them they could go ride the train after all.

He leaned forward with his elbows on his knees, wishing he could make the horses go faster.

"Up there!" Adam pointed to a platform high overhead.

Emily started to let him pull her along to the steps leading to the elevated railway station but stopped when she realized the train had already departed. It would be several minutes before another came along, and she didn't think Adam would be able to contain his pent-up excitement during a period of forced inactivity.

"The train just left. Why don't we go look at some of the other exhibits?" When Adam's face fell, she pointed east toward the other side of the fairgrounds. "Would you like to go see an aquarium with some big fish? Then maybe we'll go out by the lake and look at the Viking ship." Detecting a spark of enthusiasm, she set off across the plaza fronting the Illinois Building before Adam lost interest.

Their adventure wasn't turning out to be as much fun as she'd hoped. First there was the guilty sense of letting Stephen down, though he had no idea she had circumvented his request to forgo the outing until a later date.

Second. . . Emily looked back over her shoulder and felt the skin between her shoulder blades tighten. Stephen's concern had left her with a sense of foreboding she hadn't been able to shake.

They passed the Merchant Tailors" Building and walked across the bridge that spanned the waterway connecting the North Pond with the lagoon.

"There!" she announced, her voice far brighter than her mood.

Adam eyed her dubiously. "Where's the fish?"

"In here." She led him to one of the circular pavilions that flanked the main Fisheries Building and went inside.

The boy's reaction was everything she had imagined, boosting her spirits for the first time since they had hurried away from Mrs. Purvis's house. He walked up to one of the heavy glass panels and stared raptly as gar and rainbow trout swam by. The designer's ingenious use of lighting made it seem as if they were part of that underwater world. Emily could almost pretend she and Adam were walking along the ocean floor as they passed by displays of sheepshead and striped sea anemones.

Adam's interest was short-lived, though. After one brief circuit, he turned back to Emily with a hopeful smile. "Can we ride the train now?"

Emily knew determination when she saw it. "All right. Let's go find the nearest station." They walked out onto the Fisheries porch and paused while she got her bearings.

Adam quickly became fascinated by the decorated columns covered with bas-relief representations of marine life. Grateful for the distraction, Emily let him slip free of her grasp and watched as he circled a column covered with rows of starfish.

"Emily!"

She gave a guilty start. Stephen must have changed his mind about the meeting and somehow caught up with them. She turned, braced for his reprimand, and flinched when she saw Raymond Simmons approaching.

She swallowed hard. "Good afternoon, Mr. Simmons." She put all the frostiness she could into her tone.

The aggravating man didn't seem to notice. He continued walking toward her, swinging his walking stick with a jaunty air. "How nice to see you here. . .alone." His smile was in marked contrast to the scowl he'd worn the last time she'd seen him, the night she and Stephen had walked across the bridge from the Wooded Island.

Emily had to make an effort not to stamp her foot. This was supposed to be her day to enjoy the fair with Adam, but everything seemed to be conspiring against her. She moved aside while a chattering group of fairgoers mounted the steps to the porch and continued on into the Fisheries Building. "Hardly alone in the midst of a crowd like this."

Raymond came closer, and Emily had to steel herself to keep from taking a step back. "I think you know very well what I mean." He gave her a tight smile. "It's unusual to see you anywhere without that Columbian Guard who seems to persist in showering you with his attentions."

"At least Mr. Bridger has had the courtesy to find out first whether his attentions would be welcome," Emily retorted. "He does not—"

"When can we ride the train?" Adam, satisfied with his examination of the starfish, emerged from behind the column and took hold of Emily's hand.

She squeezed his fingers and smiled down at him. "In just a moment." Looking back at Raymond, she continued. "He does not insist on accosting me at every turn."

Adam tugged at her hand. A broad grin covered his face. "Let's ride the train now. Come on, Mama!"

Emily ruffled his hair, laughing at the way he had slipped a second time and called her by his mother's name.

One look back at Raymond's face told her he didn't find Adam's misstatement amusing in the least. His pale features stiffened, and he took a step back. "Now I understand."

Emily started. "Excuse me?"

Raymond's nostrils pinched together as if he had encountered a nasty smell. "No wonder you didn't want to go out with me. Or was your coy behavior part of a plan to entrap me? Perhaps I should be grateful you kept putting me off so I didn't wind up entangled in your snare."

Emily stared at him, wondering if he had lost his mind.

He pointed to Adam. "Who is his father? That guard of yours?" His strident tone attracted the notice of people passing by.

Emily fought to maintain her composure. "Please lower your—"

"Or does he even know you have this child?" Raymond's voice rose higher with every word. "Does he know you're nothing more than a strumpet?"

The rest of his words faded into a blur. Emily darted a glance from side to side, praying no one else was paying any attention. Hope died when she saw the shocked gazes riveted upon the little drama being played out on the Fisheries porch. Several women pulled their skirts aside and hurried away as if afraid they would be contaminated by breathing the same air as a fallen woman.

Raymond spun on his heel and stalked away. Emily stared at the disapproving faces around her and opened her mouth to make a response, but what could she say? Instead, she gripped Adam's hand. "Come on."

She hurried down the porch steps and plunged blindly down the nearest walkway, wanting to put as much distance as possible between herself and the judgmental crowd of witnesses.

To her right stood the Swedish Building. Emily skirted one of the round towers at the nearest corner and ducked behind it, where a stand of trees screened her from the view of passersby. She leaned back against the ornamental brickwork, her arms wrapped tightly across her chest, and rocked back and forth. Her breath came in shuddering gasps, and she shut her eyes as though by doing so she could block out the memory of Raymond's accusation.

What a hateful, odious man! How dare he make such insinuations! Tears slipped down her cheeks, and she dashed them away.

"Miss Em'ly?"

She looked down to see Adam looking up at her, his face crinkled with worry. Having gained her attention, he shook his head solemnly. "He's a bad man, isn't he?"

Emily stooped to wrap him in her arms and hold him close, breathing in his little-boy scent and letting his presence wash away the ugliness of Raymond's words.

A wave of sympathy for Adam's mother washed over her when she thought of the scorn Rosalee Sawyer must have endured being known as "McGinty's woman." Whatever benefit she had derived from their arrangement, it couldn't have been enough. No amount of material goods could ever erase that sense of degradation and shame. Emily had just received a taste of it, though totally undeserved. The idea of living with that from day to day—no, it just couldn't be borne.

"That fellow was pretty hard on you back there." The voice came from just inside the cluster of trees.

Emily released Adam and rose to her feet. A man stood

between the building and the tree on the end, blocking her escape. She took a closer look at him and felt her mouth go dry. It was the man who had come to the Children's Building looking for a lost little boy.

The one who claimed to be Adam's uncle.

CHAPTER 20

S he did *what?*"

Seeing the startled look on Mrs. Purvis's face, Stephen attempted to bring his voice from a roar to a more reasonable tone. He swiped at his forehead with the sleeve of his jacket. "I'm sorry. I didn't mean to bellow at you like that. I'm just concerned for their safety. How long ago did she and Adam leave?"

Mrs. Purvis took a moment to think. "Let's see. He'd managed to get into some jam, and he had it smeared all over the front of his shirt. She had to take time to change his clothes and try to do something about that stain on the fabric. I'd say it was at least thirty minutes after you left."

Stephen closed his eyes, estimating the time it had taken to travel downtown, talk to his uncle, and come back in the carriage. Emily had been traveling on foot instead of in a wheeled conveyance. She was probably just reaching the fairgrounds.

"If she returns before I catch up with her, please let her know

I was here. And ask her to stay put this time until I get back."

Stephen hurried back to the carriage and called out instructions to the driver, who set the horses moving down Blackstone Avenue at a brisk clip. It wouldn't take long to reach the fairgrounds at this rate. He would ask the driver to drop him off at the entrance Emily usually used and wait until he returned with her and Adam.

He tried to shove down his irritation. He'd already detected a stubborn streak in Emily, but he never realized she could be so intent on having things her own way. Once he found her and gave her a piece of his mind, perhaps they could salvage the rest of the day. They might take Adam for a ride in Uncle Charles's carriage. Inside its enclosed coach, it should be safe enough for the three of them to go about. Maybe he would tell the driver to roam the streets of Chicago without any particular destination in mind. It would give both Emily and Adam a different view of the city than they'd seen before.

She couldn't be too far ahead of him. As soon as he reached the fairgrounds, he would check the nearest elevated railway station. Since she couldn't walk too quickly with Adam in tow, he might even catch up with them before they boarded the train. The three of them could ride it together before returning to the carriage. At least that way, he would have them under his watchful eye and could make sure nothing happened to them.

Whether Emily took the threat seriously or not, Stephen could never rid himself of the worry that somehow McGinty would learn of their part in supplying the evidence and seek retaliation.

———

One corner of the wiry man's mouth quirked up, and he tipped his bowler hat back on his head. "The kid looks like he's in good shape. The boss will be glad to know you've been taking such good care of the little guy."

Emily moved instinctively to put Adam behind her, gripping his shoulder so tightly the little boy yelped.

The man shook his head and gazed at her mournfully. "We've had such good reports about you all along. Don't ruin your record now." He moved inside the group of trees, nearing the spot where she stood.

Despite the man's slight build, Emily felt a prickle of fear. She darted a quick look around, but with the building behind her and the trees surrounding her on three sides, she had no place to run.

The slender man continued his slow advance, coming ever closer. He reached out one hand, and a smug smile spread across his face, as if he was pleased to think that Emily would be easy prey.

His outstretched fingers were a mere inch away from the fabric of her sleeve when Emily's foot lashed out, connecting squarely with his shin. While the man howled and clutched at his injured leg, Emily grabbed Adam's hand and set off at a run, practically yanking the little boy off his feet.

Dashing past the man, she cleared the opening between the wall and trees and turned right onto the walkway in a headlong flight. Ahead, she could see the tip of the North Pond. The Palace of Fine Arts lay on its farther shore. If she could make it that far, surely she would find a guard or some other official she could turn to for help.

She looked back over her shoulder and saw the man coming along behind her, though he moved at a walk instead of a run. Emily felt a grim satisfaction. At least she had slowed him down a bit. The shin was a surprisingly tender area. That same maneuver had always worked on Johnny Meacham.

She slowed enough to catch her breath. All she had to do now was maintain the distance between them. Maybe when he realized he couldn't overtake her, he would give up and go away. No, another glance showed her he was still coming after them, though limping and moving slowly.

"Come on, sweetheart," she said to Adam and hurried along, moving to one side to avoid the stream of pedestrians merging onto the walkway from an adjoining path on the right.

She checked again. This time it took a moment to spot her pursuer, who had dropped even farther behind. Emily wanted to cheer aloud at their victory. Just before she looked ahead of her again, she saw him raise one arm and wave, pointing toward her with his other hand.

She whipped her head back to scan the walkway ahead of her and saw a dark, burly man nod back and start toward her. Adam's so-called uncle had a confederate.

Emily swiveled her head back and forth, trying to decide which one of them was the lesser of two evils and praying for a way to avoid them both.

The answer to her prayer lay just before her—the pathway that veered off sharply to the right. She made the turn and fled down the gravel path, shooting a quick glance over her shoulder as she sped away.

The burly man moved faster than his counterpart. Emily watched with a sense of dread as he picked up his pace, advancing steadily, implacably. She swept Adam up into her arms and balanced him on her hip then put on a burst of speed.

Twenty yards farther down the pathway, she risked another look back. Hope fluttered within her when she saw that the heavy man's progress, while steady, hadn't kept pace with hers. For the first time, escape seemed like a real possibility. And now she had only one of them to deal with. She couldn't even see the would-be uncle in the distance.

Straining for breath as Adam's weight began to take its toll, Emily glanced around to get her bearings and found she was angling back in the general direction from which she had come.

Good. If she could regain the safety of the Fisheries Building, she should be able to find someone to come to her aid.

A crossroads lay ahead. A swift look at the sleek, white building to her right told Emily she was almost even with the India Building. Beyond it, she could see the towers of the Swedish Building. Elation seized her—they were almost there.

Emily started to round the corner to her right. Without warning, the man who had accosted her back in the trees moved onto the path and smiled.

Emily stumbled to a halt and whirled to look behind her. The burly man had somehow gained ground while her back was turned. When he caught her gaze, he grinned and gave her a mocking salute.

Panic clawed at her stomach. While she had been distracted by the new threat, the man she had kicked had circled back, ready and waiting for her to do exactly what she had done. Instead of outsmarting them, she had fallen right into their trap.

She couldn't go back, couldn't go to the right. To her left lay the lake. No possibility of escape there. Emily's breath tore in and out of her lungs in ragged gasps. She clutched Adam closer to her, and the little boy whimpered against her shoulder.

These men weren't only after her; their presence here meant no good for Adam. She had to find a way to protect him, but how?

Jesus, help me!

Overhead, she heard a low rumble. She looked up to see the elevated train passing on the track above her. Quickly she traced the track and spotted a station across the plaza, just beyond the east pavilion of the Fisheries Building.

Gulping back a sob, she set Adam on his feet. "Are you ready to ride the train?"

He gave her a tentative nod, though confusion clouded his features.

Emily summoned up a smile. "We're going to have to hurry if we want to catch it. Let's run." She seized his hand, and together they dashed across the open plaza, focusing only on the goal of the elevated platform.

Had their two pursuers spotted them? Probably, but it didn't matter. The moment they gained the platform, they would worm their way into the middle of the crowd waiting for the train. Surely even these two thugs wouldn't try anything in a setting like that. Her feet pounded across the pavement, and she set her sights on the stairs leading to the platform, only yards away.

Pain stabbed at her side like a hot knife. Emily ran on. Once they were able to board the train and elude their pursuers, she would have a chance to rest. They would ride the train to the western edge of the fairgrounds and get off at the station near the Midway. From there, it would be a simple matter to leave the fair behind and head back to the safety of Mrs. Purvis's home.

At the bottom of the stairs, she scooped Adam into her arms again and hurried up the flight. She winced at the way her feet clanged against the metal treads, feeling as though she were sending out a signal saying, "Here we are. Come find us."

It couldn't be helped. They had to get away.

Was this how Rosalee Sawyer had felt in her last few moments—running, trying to escape, being pursued like a hunted animal? The unbidden thought chilled Emily. She didn't want her lifeless body to be found in some remote storage shed. And what would their capture mean for Adam?

She floundered up the last few steps and stumbled onto the platform with a sob of gratitude. Ready to bolt for the nearest car, she looked up to find the train already in motion.

"Nooo!" The cry tore from her throat. She lunged ahead, only to pull back when she realized how foolish it would be to throw herself against a moving train. Emily watched helplessly as her hope of escape glided out of the station.

Tears pooled in Adam's eyes. "When can we ride the train?"

"Soon," she said distractedly. How long would it be until the next one arrived? Too long. She had to figure out what to do next.

Adam was too exhausted to run any farther, and she couldn't continue to bear his weight. She gripped the railing at the edge of the platform and looked down. A sick agony spread through her chest, and her limbs trembled.

The two men, now reunited, stood talking directly below her. The smaller one pointed toward the stairs.

~

Stephen turned in a slow circle atop the platform of the elevated railway station that fronted the Fifty-ninth Street entrance. He'd been sure Emily would have used her regular entrance to the fair, and this station was the closest to that point. Against all reason, he had hoped he might catch up with her and Adam there. He should have known better, but the disappointment was unexpectedly crushing. Now what?

He glanced toward the north and stepped back from the edge of the platform when he saw a train pulling into the station.

His pulse quickened while he scanned each passenger who disembarked, but he saw no Emily, no Adam. Just to make sure, he walked along the platform, gazing through the glassed-in sides of the cars at the passengers who remained on board.

Stephen descended the steps to the ground with a heavy heart. He hesitated, uncertain whether to keep looking or go back and dismiss the carriage driver.

Ten to fifteen trains ran along the railway at any given time. He could go back up on the platform and wait until every one of them came and went, but the prospect galled him. He couldn't stay still that long; he needed to be out and moving.

He tried to put himself in Emily's place. What was she thinking? What was she planning to do? Stephen took off his hat and ran his fingers through his hair. The only place she had mentioned taking Adam, the reason for this whole outing, was the elevated railway. Where else could she be?

He started south toward the Children's Building then stopped. It was her day off, after all. She wouldn't be likely to choose to spend any more time with Miss Strickland than necessary. Besides, she had Adam with her.

The Wooded Island, maybe? It offered endless possibilities for a little boy to run and hide among the trees. But Emily's last experience there hadn't been a pleasant one. Stephen doubted that even Emily would venture there without an escort.

A new idea popped into his mind, and his lips parted in a broad smile. Their time together out on the shore had been a much more enjoyable experience. Perhaps she'd taken Adam out to the lake. Stephen brightened. They might even have ridden the elevated train that far and gotten off, planning to finish their tour later.

Stephen retraced his steps to the plaza that lay between the

Illinois Building and the lagoon, feeling somewhat more hopeful. He walked along, continuing to scan the crowd for a woman with a little boy.

Near the Merchant Tailors" Building, he saw a man in a guard's uniform and recognized his friend Bill Watson. Stephen grinned. No one knew better than he that the first thing people did when trying to reconnect with a missing loved one on the fairgrounds was to talk to one of the Columbian Guards. He strode over and tapped the stocky man on the shoulder.

Bill chuckled when he turned and saw Stephen. "I thought this was your day off. What's the matter? Just can't keep away from the place?"

Stephen waved off his friend's teasing. "Actually, I was going to ask for your help in finding someone. Have you seen a young woman around twenty years of age?"

Bill adjusted the chin strap of his hat and looked at Stephen with renewed interest. "Lots of them. You're going to have to narrow that description down just a bit."

"She's small." Stephen held up his hand to indicate a height just below his shoulder. "Red hair, green eyes. Probably wearing a pale green outfit," he added, hoping she hadn't changed her clothes before leaving the boardinghouse.

"She would have a little boy with her, too. Cute little fellow—blond hair, blue eyes. Seen anybody answering that description?"

A look of concern shadowed Bill Watson's face. "Did Colonel Rice send for you on your day off? This isn't another missing woman report, is it?"

At Bill's words, a sense of dread settled over Stephen like the mist that shrouded Lake Michigan on a foggy morning.

"No," he said, hoping he was right. "I'm just looking for a

friend. If you see anyone fitting that description, would you let her know I'm on the grounds and trying to find her?"

Relief erased the worry on Bill's face. "Sure. I'm glad to hear it isn't anything more than that. If I see her, I'll tell her."

Stephen walked away and looked back toward the elevated train platform. Still no sign of Emily. Beyond the platform, he could see the entrance to the Midway, and beyond that, the Ferris wheel circling up into the sky. A metallic taste filled his mouth. That wasn't too far from the place where they'd found Rosalee Sawyer's body. Bill's casual comment had brought the connection all too close to home.

He strode toward the edge of the lake with a sense of urgency quickening his steps. His frustration mounted. It wasn't as though Emily had been forced to come down here without him. Hadn't he hurried back from the canceled meeting as quickly as he could? He was here now, ready to protect her. But it wouldn't do a bit of good if she wasn't there to be protected.

———

Emily looked around wildly. The benches and chairs lining the center of the platform offered nothing in the way of a hiding place. At the left end, a steel girder stretched up to the roof. It might be enough to conceal either her or Adam, but not both of them. Its twin stood in its place at the far right, with a stack of wooden crates at its base. Emily headed toward the pile. It wasn't much, but it was all she had.

Emily pulled Adam along to the end of the platform and shoved him behind the crates. She squatted down beside him and made herself as small as possible, feeling like a rabbit diving into its burrow with a hungry fox close behind.

Adam blinked up at her, his face a mask of confusion. Emily

put her finger to her lips. "Remember how you played hide-and-seek with Miss Lucy? Well, we're hiding again. Can you be very, very quiet?"

"Okay." He placed his fingers across his mouth.

Heavy footsteps vibrated on the metal stairs. Emily scrunched down, scarcely daring to breathe. She heard the steps approaching their end of the platform, and her heart hammered so hard she thought it would burst from her chest.

Emily held Adam close with one arm and balanced herself against one of the crates with the other. Shifting her position with infinite care, she pressed her face up to the narrow space between two crates and peered out through the crack. Fear gripped her when the burly man stopped within two feet of their hiding place.

After a brief pause, the man continued his circuit around the platform then rejoined his companion at the far end.

Please let them think we got on the train.

After an exchange of words too low for Emily to make out, the men walked down the stairs with no sign of their former haste. Emily kept hold of Adam, not daring to move until the sound of their footsteps faded into silence.

She waited a moment longer then forced her muscles to uncoil and got to her feet. She stepped from their hiding place with Adam beside her.

He looked up at her, his eyes shining. "We hided good. Did we win?"

Relief swept over her, leaving her weak. "We won," she assured him. "You were a very good boy. Let's go sit on one of these benches and wait for the train. How does that sound?" They had only taken two steps when she heard the scrape of a boot against the platform floor.

"I'm afraid you're going to have to alter your plans." A shadow emerged from behind the girder at the far end, and Ian McGinty stepped out into the sunlight.

CHAPTER 21

S tephen took a moment to stop at the top of the bridge spanning the waterway that led into the lagoon. He looked to the north—left past the Illinois Building, then across the North Pond to the Palace of Fine Arts. No sign of Emily.

Surely she wouldn't have ventured to the state buildings on the far side of that edifice. He couldn't imagine what would be over there to tempt the interest of a little boy.

Continuing his survey, he turned his gaze farther to the east, studying the walkways in front of the buildings that housed exhibits from various countries—Brazil, Turkey, Venezuela. Stephen's shoulders slumped. He didn't recognize a soul.

No, wait. He narrowed his eyes. Along the walkway just past the Japanese Tea House, he spotted a vaguely familiar figure.

Stephen looked again and pressed his lips together when he recognized Emily's would-be suitor. What was his name? Ah yes. Simmons.

The fellow strode along with his shoulders hunched and his hands jammed deep in his pockets. With his gaze focused on the ground, he shouldered his way past pedestrians who strayed into his path, heading straight toward the bridge where Stephen stood.

Stephen stepped forward to intercept him. "Excuse me."

Simmons's head jerked up, and his expression darkened. "Oh, it's you. What do you want?"

Stephen swallowed his distaste. Much as he disliked the man, he was the only person within view in this crowd of thousands who knew Emily. Like it or not, Stephen needed his help.

He tried to arrange his features into a more cordial expression. "I'm trying to locate Miss Ralston. Have you seen her, by any chance?"

Simmons's upper lip curled. "She and her brat were over there in front of Fisheries a few minutes ago. You're welcome to her, for all I care. I want nothing more to do with her."

Stephen's hand snaked out and grabbed the shorter man by the front of his tailor-made shirt, lifting him up onto his tiptoes. "I'll thank you not to impugn Miss Ralston's character in that way. She's a finer person than a worm like you could ever hope to appreciate."

He pulled his hand away and left Simmons gasping and tugging at his shirt collar. If this lout had dared say anything of that sort to Emily, he would be tempted to come back and finish throttling the man.

The certainty that Raymond Simmons had the gall to do exactly that spurred Stephen's steps. If he had crossed paths with Emily and flung such hateful words at her, what must she be feeling now?

More than ever, he wanted to find her.

"Da?" Adam's tremulous whisper sent a chill up Emily's spine. She felt him press his little body tight against her leg.

Keeping her body between McGinty and Adam, Emily edged away until she came up against the edge of the railing. She flitted a quick glance to each side, noting the distance to the stairs that led to the ground and safety. He was still some distance away. If she snatched Adam up and made a run for it. . .

As if reading her thoughts, McGinty shook his head. "I wouldn't try that. They're still down there." He strolled over to the far end of the railing and looked down.

Without taking her attention away from him completely, Emily followed his gaze. She saw the man who claimed to be Adam's uncle look up. McGinty nodded, and the other man smiled and sketched a salute before he sauntered away and melted into the crowd.

Emily's jaw went slack. "Then he really is your brother?"

McGinty's soft chuckle lacked humor. "No, Mort works for me. He's a loyal employee—he did exactly what I paid him to do. He brought you here to me." He thumped his walking stick gently against the platform. "I told you I'd be back for your answer."

The moment she dreaded had arrived without warning. Emily shook her head and slid farther away, still shielding Adam from him.

"My answer is no. I can't possibly go along with what you suggested." She heard the quaver in her voice and lifted her chin. "You might as well accept the fact that I'm not going with you, and neither is Adam."

She shot a glance at the track. "Another train will be coming along soon. There will be too many witnesses around. You won't be able to do anything then." Relief danced through her as she spoke the words. It was true—if she could just hold out a little while longer, she would win. This round, at least.

McGinty gave her a smile that chilled the blood in her veins. "The witnesses are a part of my plan. You and the boy and I are going to board the next train—in full view of whoever happens to be here—and take our leave like a happy little family."

Emily recoiled and felt the steel railing dig into her back. "A family? Are you out of your mind?" Her gaze swept the area below them. "There are plenty of people within hearing right now. All I have to do is scream."

"I don't think so." McGinty slipped his right hand into his coat pocket and tilted it toward her. "It's a small pistol but quite effective at this range."

Emily felt her mouth go dry. "You wouldn't risk it. A shot would bring every guard in this corner of the grounds on the run."

"Are you willing to risk your life on that? And surely you don't want to endanger the boy in the event my aim is a trifle off." His shoulders shook with laughter. "I think we have reached what is called a standoff, Miss Ralston."

He removed his hand from his pocket and took a step toward her. "Now that we understand each other, let me explain what we're about to do. When the next train arrives, the three of us will get on it, quietly and without any fuss. You will do nothing—absolutely nothing—to arouse the suspicions of our fellow passengers." He patted his pocket. "Remember, I will be sitting right next to you."

He continued as if describing the itinerary for a pleasant outing. "We will get off when the train reaches the platform above Terminal Station. From there, we will go down and take our seats on the Limited." He leaned to one side, looking past Emily. "A nice train ride, Adam. You'd like that, wouldn't you?"

Adam cowered and clutched Emily's skirts more tightly.

"And then what?" Emily's voice came out in a hoarse rasp.

McGinty rested both hands on the knob of his walking stick. "Curious, are you? It's nice to see you're getting into the spirit of things at last." He reached into the breast pocket of his coat and pulled out an envelope. "I purchased these tickets this morning."

He slid the envelope back into his pocket. "I hear California is a wonderful place to make a new beginning."

Emily's knees gave way. If not for the railing at her back, she would have fallen. She gripped the steel pipe to hold herself upright. This couldn't be happening.

But it was. Panic rose, threatening to choke her. Emily drew in a quick breath of air. She had to keep her head clear. She looked around the platform. Was there anything she could use as a weapon?

Nothing—only the chair and benches and the crates they'd hidden behind. Emily fought down her rising despair.

Where were the passengers for the next train? Why weren't they climbing the stairs to the platform even now, milling around and giving her a chance to escape? As much as she wished for it, no one came to her rescue. It was up to her. She had no one to rely on but herself.

She had never felt so alone.

Her first and foremost thought was to protect Adam. If she cried out now and drew the attention of the passersby below, would McGinty shoot as he threatened? Emily stared into the steely eyes of the man who held her future in his hands and felt sure he would. A shudder coursed through her body.

But if she did as he said and went along with his plan, what value would her life have? Would it be worth saving her physical body only to have her soul crushed? She weighed the thought carefully, aware that she stood on the brink of taking an irrevocable step.

Emily drew in her breath and watched McGinty's eyes narrow. She hesitated. If she screamed and died in her effort to call for help, that would provide no surety of deliverance for Adam. A man like Ian McGinty was capable of twisting the facts and slipping through the noose again, as he had so many other times. There had to be another way.

She let her shoulders sag into a submissive posture. "You make a compelling case, Mr. McGinty. I don't see that I have any other option." She turned and knelt in front of Adam, wiping his tears away with the flat of her fingers. "It looks like we're about to have a great adventure. Do you think you're ready for that?"

The boy looked at her dubiously.

Emily forced a smile, trying to give him the encouragement he needed. She gripped his shoulders firmly. Looking into his eyes, she spoke distinctly, pronouncing each word with precision. "Listen to me, Adam. You need to be ready, because the train will be here in a jiffy."

His shoulders tensed under her hands, and she could see the question in his eyes.

"That's right." She nodded and gave him the tiniest of pushes. "In a *jiffy*."

Quick as lightning, the little boy spun on his heel and darted down the nearest set of stairs like a scared rabbit. Emily whirled and braced herself for the onslaught that was sure to follow.

McGinty started to lunge forward then held himself in check. Emily could see the muscles bunch along his jaw. He took one measured step toward her, then another. "That was not a wise move, Miss Ralston. It would have been much more pleasant for both of us if you had agreed to go along with my plan."

He stopped and regarded her with a gentle smile. "You expected me to go dashing after the lad, didn't you? But there's no hurry. I need to attend to things here first, and then I'll go looking for him." A laugh rumbled deep in his chest. "After all, we both know where to go to find a lost child."

His face grew stony again, and he continued his relentless advance. "Such a shame that the child became so excited up here on the platform. How he managed to duck under the railing and onto that dangerously narrow ledge before you could reach him is a mystery."

What was he talking about? Adam had already left the platform. Emily edged backward until she felt another railing at right angles to the first and knew he had her cornered.

"Everyone will admire your bravery in climbing through the rail yourself to keep him from falling to a certain death when his body met the pavement." He seized her wrist in an iron grip and pulled her to him. "What a shame that you slipped as you were lifting him back over the bar and lost your life while saving his."

CHAPTER 22

E mily wasn't there.

After a quick search of the main building, Stephen had checked the aquarium. Still no sign of Emily. He slapped his hand against one of the columns that bordered the Fisheries porch.

He might as well give up. It had been a foolish idea from the start. Even if Raymond Simmons was telling the truth and Emily *had* been there earlier, there was no reason to assume she would have stayed at the Fisheries Building. She and Adam could be anywhere by now.

Stephen stepped off the porch, ready to go back and have the carriage driver take him home. Or maybe he would ask to be let out at Mrs. Purvis's. He could wait there until Emily got home so they could talk things over.

He paused at the foot of the steps to let two middle-aged matrons go by. They both stopped right in front of him. One pressed her fingers to her mouth. "What is wrong with that poor child?" She pointed toward a clump of bushes near the edge of the lagoon.

Stephen swiveled around in time to see a small figure dive under the concealing branches. A small figure who looked very much like. . .

"Adam!" Stephen sprinted toward the little boy's place of concealment, knelt down, and parted the branches.

Adam shrank back, his eyes puffy and his face splotched and contorted with fear. He stared at Stephen for a moment; then he gave a glad cry and launched himself into Stephen's arms with enough force to knock him backward. The two of them toppled over onto the grass.

Stephen picked himself up and bent down to lift Adam. The little boy twined his arms around his neck, almost cutting off his air. "Whoa, there!" Stephen gently loosened Adam's stranglehold and held the boy back so he could study his face. Tears streaked his cheeks, and his breath came in shallow gasps. Stephen could feel the little boy's body tremble from head to toe.

Memories of the first time he had seen Adam, alone and frightened near the bandstand, rushed at Stephen full force. A sense of foreboding gripped his heart. "Where's Miss Emily?"

Adam's lower lip quivered so he could hardly form the words. "Jiffy, run, hide."

"Wha—?" The statement might make perfect sense in a three-year-old's mind, but not to Stephen. Cupping Adam's chin gently in his hand, he looked straight into the clear blue eyes. "Where is Miss Emily, Adam? Tell me."

The little boy drew a shuddering breath then turned and pointed to the platform of the elevated railway. "Up there. With Da."

Da? Emily was with McGinty? Stephen shook his head. He

didn't understand what was going on, but he had no time to sort things out. If McGinty was on the scene, Emily was in terrible danger.

Stephen tucked Adam firmly under his arm and sprinted for the platform stairs.

McGinty shifted his grip to Emily's upper arm and began to drag her toward the far end of the platform. "We'll have to go down here, I'm afraid. Otherwise, you might land in the lagoon instead of on the pavement, and that wouldn't suit my purpose at all."

"No!" She dug in her heels and wrapped her free arm around the railing. No longer weighed down by the responsibility of protecting Adam, Emily wasn't about to surrender her life without a fight.

McGinty raised his walking stick and used it to give a sharp rap against the point of her shoulder. Pain exploded down the arm clutching the railing, and it dropped limply to her side.

A sardonic smile curved McGinty's mouth. "A little technique I learned in my early days back in New York. Effective, isn't it? You may as well accept your fate, Miss Ralston. You lost the battle the moment you decided to cross me."

Emily looked up at his granite features. He wasn't any more disturbed by what he'd just done than if he had whisked away a pesky fly. Johnny Meacham, the orphanage bully, had made her younger years miserable, and Raymond Simmons was a boorish cad. But they both paled in comparison with Ian McGinty. Seeing his utter disdain for human life, she knew she stared into the very face of evil.

She wanted to close her eyes to blot out the sight but couldn't make her body move enough to perform that small task. It wouldn't be long now. McGinty wore the look of a man sure of imminent victory.

Emily drew a long breath, wanting to savor what might well be her last intake of air. McGinty's lips curved upward ever so slightly, and she knew he took pleasure at the thought of what he was about to do.

Help! Her mind cried out for rescue, but she couldn't scream, couldn't make a sound. She couldn't do anything but stand there and wait for the inevitable.

Rapid footsteps clanged against the metal stairs. An instant later, Stephen appeared, holding Adam in his arms. Quicker than thought, McGinty spun Emily around and pulled her tight against him with his left arm around her throat.

Skidding to a halt, Stephen seemed to take in the situation with a single glance. He took a slow step back and set Adam down in the shelter of the girder. "I want you to sit tight there and don't move. Will you do that for me?" Instead of answering, Adam tucked his knees up under his chin and put his hands over his eyes.

Stephen faced them and stretched out one arm. "Let her go."

"I think not." McGinty moved back, dragging Emily with him. She detected an edge in his voice she hadn't heard before, and the hint of underlying emotion frightened her even more. She clawed at his sleeve but stopped when his arm tightened, threatening to cut off her air.

"She's made her choice," McGinty went on. "There's nothing you can do to save her."

Stephen continued to advance.

"Stay back!" McGinty shouted. Emily felt his right hand fumble in his coat pocket. "Stay back, I said. I have a gun."

Stephen took another step toward them, never taking his eyes from the man's face. "A hand in the pocket? That's the oldest trick in the book."

McGinty thrust his hand forward, and Emily felt hard metal jam into her spine.

"Believe him, Stephen!" Her cry brought him up short. Mc-Ginty's arm tightened around her throat again, pulling her back against the gun's unforgiving barrel. With a flash of clarity, Emily knew his mind in that instant: He was going to throw her over the railing and then shoot Stephen. And she was powerless to stop him.

Lord, help us! Show me what to do.

She read the look of agonized indecision on Stephen's face. Looking into his eyes, she tried to convey all the love she'd hoped to express to him over a lifetime.

McGinty pulled her closer to the railing. Emily dug in her heels and twisted her body in a desperate attempt to break his hold. He snugged his arm around her throat and held it tight. Emily felt her world growing black.

Through the dark mist, she could hear Stephen's voice. "Think about it, McGinty. If you kill us both, then what? There's no place for you to go. You'll never get away with it."

Emily made one final effort, clutching her captor's arm with both of her hands, pulling with all her remaining strength to rid herself of the awful pressure. His grip loosened a fraction, and she gulped in a lungful of precious, life-giving air.

They reached the edge of the platform. McGinty put one booted foot on the bottom rail and stepped up, lifting Emily off the floor. She twisted in the air, kicking wildly and fighting to breathe. She could see Stephen crouch, ready to rush McGinty, even though doing so meant inviting certain death. Emily knew Stephen was going to charge and knew he was too late to help her.

Emily felt the top rail through the back of her skirt. All that McGinty had to do was twist and release her, and she would plummet to the unforgiving pavement.

Still holding the gun, McGinty pulled his hand from his pocket and encircled her waist with his right arm. Emily shut her eyes, not wanting her last sight on earth to be that of the ground rushing up toward her.

Time slowed down. Emily could hear McGinty grunt as he lifted her a few inches higher. The railing was at her knees now. She had no hope of avoiding a fall once he turned her loose.

She heard Stephen's shout and the sound of his boots pounding across the platform. Emily felt the impact when his body slammed into McGinty's, and her whole body flinched when she heard the gun go off. McGinty twisted and flung Emily aside with his left arm. The next instant, she was dropping through space.

Emily fell, arms flailing wildly. One outstretched hand struck one of the posts holding the railing upright, and she wrapped her fingers around it, hanging on with all her might while her body dangled in the air. Below her, someone screamed, and she heard the sound of voices raised in alarm.

A strong hand clamped around her wrist, and Stephen's head appeared over the railing. "Give me your other hand."

With the last bit of strength she had left, she raised her other hand and gripped his, tight. She could see his shoulders strain against his jacket as he drew her up and pulled her over the railing.

Emily collapsed on the platform, exulting in the solid feel of the planking beneath her. Stephen dropped down beside her and gathered her in his arms. She buried her head against his chest and waited for the trembling to stop.

When she could manage to speak, she lifted her head. "I heard a shot. Are you hurt?"

Stephen shook his head. "The bullet went wild. I grabbed his gun hand just before I hit him."

At the reminder of McGinty, Emily jerked to attention and looked about the platform. "Where is he? Did he get away?"

Stephen's expression hardened. "No. He lost his balance when I ran into him. He went over the railing at the same time you did."

Emily scrambled toward the edge of the platform. Stephen caught her by the shoulders and pulled her back. "You don't want to look."

She caught the lapels of his jacket in her hands. "Is he—?"

"He's never going to bother you again." Stephen's mouth was set in a grim line. "He managed to escape the law, but now he'll have to face God's judgment."

"What's going on up here? Is everyone all right?" A man in the uniform of the Columbian Guards burst onto the platform. He stopped, his chest heaving, when he saw Stephen cradling Emily in his arms.

"Bridger?" The guard narrowed his eyes. He looked at Emily then back at Stephen. "I see you found your lady friend."

Stephen rose and pulled Emily to her feet, wrapping one arm around her waist to steady her. "Everyone's all right up here, Bill. And thank God for that. Do you realize who you have down there? That's Ian McGinty."

The guard's eyes widened. "You don't say!" He eyed the point on the railing where McGinty fell. "I have a feeling there's quite a story behind this. Do you two feel like coming down to the guard station and filling me in on what happened?"

"Miss Ralston needs a few minutes to collect herself. Give us a little time, and we'll be along."

The guard nodded and went back to deal with the scene on the ground.

Stephen helped Emily to the nearest bench then walked toward the far girder. "You can come out now, Adam."

Emily saw the little blond head ease past the edge of the steel upright. Adam looked from Stephen to Emily. His mouth twisted. He scrambled to his feet and dashed headlong into her arms. Burrowing his head into her lap, he clung to her as if he would never let go again.

CHAPTER 23

Gulls wheeled overhead, uttering their shrill, plaintive cries. A light breeze stirred Emily's hair as she looked out over the sand to the point where gentle waves lapped the lakeshore, leaving trails of white foam behind.

She rolled up a checkered cloth containing the remnants of their picnic meal and placed it in the basket Mrs. Purvis had loaned them. Curling her feet to one side, she leaned her weight on her right arm and closed her eyes to savor the utter stillness. Her fingers traced over the stitches in the Grandmother's Flower Garden quilt Mrs. Purvis had insisted they bring along.

It had been a good day. Emily opened her eyes to smile and wave at Stephen, who walked along the shoreline where the sand was wet and firm. From time to time, he picked up stones or bits of shell and pitched them out into the water. He waved back and continued his trek along the water's edge.

Such a peaceful scene, so different from that awful day a week ago when she had felt sure she wouldn't live to see the sky, the lake, or Stephen again. Amazing though it seemed, peace had begun to return to her life once again. She reveled in the knowledge she no longer had to keep looking over her shoulder or bear the constant pressure exerted by McGinty's unseen presence. She wouldn't have thought it possible, but already the memories of that horrible time were beginning to fade.

Stephen picked up a fist-sized rock and flung it far out into the lake. Emily watched it arc over the water to land with a splash thirty yards away. What a perfect time for him to remember his comment about returning to the lakeside. She was glad he'd found a new spot for today's outing, far away from the distractions of the fairgrounds.

Emily thought back to their previous visit to the shore and let those memories play through her mind. That day had turned out to be. . .rather nice. A slow smile curved her mouth when she remembered the touch of Stephen's lips on hers.

Emily stretched her legs out in front of her and leaned back on her hands. Bringing up those memories might have been a mistake. All afternoon, she'd found herself half expecting something similar to happen. But so far, Stephen had acted the perfect gentleman.

She closed her eyes again, tilting her face back to catch the waning rays of the sun and let the peace seep into her soul. The breeze, the sun, the lapping of the waves, and the gulls' lonely cries all combined to act as a balm to her healing spirit. After the turmoil of the past few weeks, this day had been blessedly quiet.

Maybe a little too quiet.

Emily opened her eyes and looked back at Stephen. They had talked through the beginning of the meal, discussing Lucy's new job at one of the downtown department stores, Mrs. Purvis's joy in discovering the treasure room, and the results of the belated meeting with his uncle's architectural client. But by the time they had started on the apple pie, Stephen had become unusually quiet, as though he had something on his mind. She sat up and wrapped her arms around her knees. Was it because of anything she had said or done?

She remembered how buoyant he'd been when he'd come to get her at the boardinghouse. He had savored the smells emanating from the basket Mrs. Purvis had helped her pack, declaring them so delectable that he didn't think he could wait to eat until they reached their destination. As far as she could tell at that point, everything seemed perfectly fine, as it did when he looped the basket over his arm and escorted Emily out to the curb, to a waiting cab this time instead of his uncle's carriage.

She could still feel the warmth of his hands on her waist as he lifted her up to the seat. They'd both laughed when Mrs. Purvis burst out of the house at the last minute, calling for the cabdriver to wait and running after them with the quilt in her arms.

She'd pressed the quilt into Emily's hands, telling her they would need something to sit on. Recognizing the quilt as the one they'd found in the treasure room, Emily tried to hand it back, saying it was too precious to spread out on the sand, but she gave in to the older woman's insistence.

After that, the cabdriver drove north at Stephen's direction, bringing them to this lonely stretch of sand where he dropped them off, agreeing to return for them at sunset.

Emily looked away from the lake to the west, gauging the sun's position. It wouldn't be much longer now. Their idyllic day was nearly at an end.

Tomorrow morning she would return to work to spin out her

days in the Children's Building until the fair wound down to its end. And then what?

Lucy, at least, had a new job to look forward to. Between caring for Adam and spending time with Stephen, Emily hadn't found time to go job hunting, something she needed to correct at the first opportunity. So far, she had managed to push away her doubts about finding employment that would pay enough not only to meet her needs but to provide sufficient income for raising a child.

For a moment, she envied Stephen, who already had a job, a family who loved him, and abundant opportunities for a bright future. He would no longer be a Columbian Guard patrolling his area on the fairgrounds but a professional man with a promising career ahead of him.

Would they continue to see each other? No longer would Stephen be able to wander into the Children's Building whenever he wanted to visit. Soon he would have to make a special effort to break away from the demands of his work and travel to Blackstone Avenue to see her.

Emily felt a tightness in her chest. And what was the likelihood of that happening? Once the fair was over, he would step right into his new life. . .and away from her.

A puff of wind stirred her hair, and she tucked a stray wisp back behind her ear. She looked down at the quilt, admiring the blend of colors and the evenness of the tiny stitches. Mrs. Purvis had said her grandmother had made it. What hopes and dreams had filled that long-ago woman's mind as the stitched the pieces into place? Had she found the peace and joy so evident in her granddaughter?

Emily knew those attributes didn't come from leading a charmed life. Mrs. Purvis had experienced her share of heartache, yet she seemed to find happiness in life in spite of it. Emily sighed.

Would there be joy and fulfillment in her own future, as well, or more pain and loneliness?

For a time, she had dared to hope she and Stephen might build a life together. But since McGinty's death, Stephen had seemed withdrawn, almost distant. Maybe his interest in her had been based on protective instincts rather than affection. He had put his life on the line in order to rescue her, but wouldn't he have done the same thing for Lucy or Mrs. Purvis?

Emily bent forward and scooped up a handful of sand then held it up and watched the grains trickle out between her fingers. At least she had Adam. She could take comfort in that fact. They were both orphans now, and she would never abandon him to life in an institution.

She brushed the sand off her hands. Could that be the cause of the distance she felt between her and Stephen? Or did the idea of "her and Stephen" exist only in her imagination, like some fanciful castle in the air?

If that was the case, it would be hard to understand that amazing moment the last time they'd come to the lakeshore. The feeling of her heart taking flight when Stephen's lips met hers would be etched in her memory for all time.

Stephen was a man of integrity. She knew him too well to think that kiss meant nothing to him. But did it, as she hoped, signify something that would last, or was it only a fleeting attraction?

Had her determination to keep Adam created a wedge between them? Perhaps Stephen was in the market for marriage but wasn't interested in a ready-made family. If that was the case. . .

Emily felt as though she stood at a crossroads, faced with an impossible decision. But she knew her mind was made up already. Even for love, she wouldn't abandon Adam. If need be, they would be a family, just the two of them.

And a family of two would probably be the case not only for now, but for the rest of her days. Emily remembered Raymond Simmons's reaction when Adam had called her Mama. She could expect most other eligible men to react in the same way. Tears stung her eyes, and she blinked them away.

She knew how she felt about Stephen. She didn't want to lose him, but she couldn't force herself upon him if he didn't love her the way he would have to for this to be a love that would last a lifetime.

Near the water's edge, Stephen picked up a chunk of driftwood and hurled it into the lake then walked over to her and dropped down on the other end of the quilt.

"It's been a nice day, hasn't it?" He sat with his knees bent, his hands linked loosely around them, staring out over the lake instead of looking at her.

Emily felt a wave of loneliness that nearly choked her. The sun dropped lower in the western sky, tinting the clouds in hues of crimson, orange, and violet. The vibrant colors reflected off the water in front of them.

Stephen picked up a small stick and trailed it through the sand. "It's getting late."

Emily nodded. The cabdriver would be back to pick them up shortly. Their day would soon be over. Would there be any more times like this?

She studied it all—Stephen, the quilt, the basket, and the rainbow-hued lake—wanting to imprint the scene on her memory so she could treasure it through all the years ahead.

Stephen tossed the stick, watching it flip end over end until it landed on the sand. A sigh escaped his lips. "It seems a shame to have to say good-bye to a day like this, but I guess all good things come to an end. The year is nearly over, and the fair is about to close."

Emily looked down and realized she was clutching a corner of Mrs. Purvis's quilt in her fist. Was their relationship just one more thing about to come to an end? Had he brought her out here for the purpose of telling her good-bye?

She braced herself for the blow, determined that when it came, she would accept it with good grace and not do anything to embarrass him or herself. She drew in a ragged breath and firmed her chin. At least she would have her memories.

She just hoped they would be enough.

———

Stop babbling, you idiot! Stephen winced as he heard yet another inane comment roll off his tongue. Could he have possibly chosen any less romantic topic than a discussion of the time of day?

He sent a quick glance Emily's way. Apparently she felt the same way. She sat quiet and still with a stoic look on her face, as though she could hardly wait for the day to be over. And could he blame her? He hadn't been the world's best company.

Stephen looked around. The setting was perfect, the day idyllic. Even the weather cooperated, sending a welcome Indian summer to give them a reprieve from the chill breath of autumn.

Now, with the sun lingering low in the western sky, he felt a bit of a nip in the air, just enough to put a hint of roses in Emily's cheeks. She would probably need her cloak before the cabdriver returned. Or maybe he could just scoot across the quilt and put his arm around her shoulders to warm her.

He might have done exactly that if he hadn't just made such an idiot of himself. And that cabdriver would be along any minute. He didn't have much time to get things back on track, but he could try.

"My uncle is pleased with the preliminary ideas I have for the new project. In fact, I'm thinking about quitting my job early, before the fair is over."

Emily looked stunned, and he thought he detected a trace of moisture in her eyes. That wasn't exactly the response he was hoping for. He had made the statement intending to reassure her that he would have a steady income soon, something more substantial than a guard's pay. Enough to start a new life together.

But that would never happen if he couldn't find a better way to lead into that subject. He stretched out his hand, but there weren't any stones, shells, or sticks within reach. This business of working up to asking one small question was proving to be far more difficult than designing the plans for the building he and his uncle were working on. He already had a vision of the structure in his mind. If he had a drafting pencil and a sheet of paper, that mental image would move from his brain through his fingers and onto the paper in a smooth flow of creativity.

How he wished he could find a way to draft a proposal as easily!

He had chosen his setting carefully, hoping it would trigger pleasant memories of another afternoon when he freed Emily's hair from the grasping tree branch and they shared their first kiss. It seemed to Stephen that a connection like that would set the mood so he wouldn't have to fumble around to create a romantic atmosphere.

At the beginning, she had seemed eager enough about the idea of a picnic, but as the day wore on, she'd become edgy and watchful.

Stephen dug the heel of his boot into the sand. His friend Seth had counseled him to wait before offering Emily his hand in marriage. But he hadn't mentioned anything about how long to wait, and Stephen hadn't thought to ask.

None of them had expected such a horrific ending to the whole affair. Was waiting a week sufficient? Or should he hold off longer?

The vision of Emily going over the platform railing still haunted his dreams. What must it be like for her, having actually experienced the terribly certainty that her life was about to end?

The moment when he had seen her small white hand clinging to the supporting post would forever rate as one of the happiest moments of his life. The glimpse of McGinty's twisted body lying half in, half out of the lagoon with his head on the rocks near the shore had given him the strength he needed to pull her up and over the railing until she tumbled onto the platform floor. He hadn't ceased to send up heartfelt prayers of thanks for her deliverance.

If he had followed his instincts, he would have laid his heart at her feet right then.

But Seth was right. That was not the time, and proposing then would have been unfair to Emily. She deserved the chance to recover enough to think the matter through clearly.

How long? Feeling the need for more godly counsel, he'd tried to locate Seth several times over the past few days but seemed to miss him at every turn.

He watched the smooth, deft movements of her hands as she stowed the plates and napkins in the basket and brushed crumbs off the quilt without saying a word. She had made great improvements already this week, no longer jumping at unexpected sounds and seeming much less nervous than she had during the first two or three days following her ordeal.

Stephen had hoped to bring up the subject once they reached their picnic spot, but it appeared he'd been overly optimistic. After some inane chitchat that must have bored her to tears, he'd gotten up and paced the shoreline, reduced to flinging sticks and stones out into the water like a twelve-year-old.

With their picnic things picked up and stowed away, she now sat staring down at her hands clasped loosely in her lap. It looked as though the day had been a disappointment for her, too.

"I suppose we'd better head on back to meet the cab."

Emily shot a look of surprise his way; then she nodded and retreated into herself again.

Stephen picked up the basket while she shook out the quilt and folded it. Their shadows stretched out long across the beach. Swinging around to check the western sky, he saw that the sun had dropped almost to the horizon. He cupped Emily's elbow in one hand to help her across the sand and scanned the spot where the cabdriver had promised to meet them.

An anxious feeling settled in the pit of his stomach. The fellow should have been there by now. In his excitement over what the day might hold in store, Stephen had made the arrangements in a hurry, taking the man's agreement for granted and never dreaming they might wind up being stranded. He glanced at Emily, hoping she hadn't yet noticed their plight. He needed a few more minutes to think the situation over and come up with an alternate plan.

Like what? In only a short while, it would be fully dark, no time to be wandering around trying to hail another cab. Even getting back to an area where they might find a cab to hail would mean an arduous walk. He didn't want to contemplate the prospect of having to travel all the way back to Mrs. Purvis's on foot.

Please, Lord, get that cabdriver here. I don't want to make this day worse than it's been already.

When they reached firm footing, Stephen led Emily into the

shelter of some trees. He set the basket down and scanned the road ahead. Still no sign of the cab.

Some of his inner tension must have communicated itself to her. She followed his gaze out to the road and then turned to him with a concerned expression. In the twilight's glow, shadows played across her face. Her eyes, so solemn, gazed up at him with a look that made him want to gather her into his arms and bury his face in her hair.

Stephen took a deep breath. Maybe he'd been wrong about waiting any longer.

Hope stirred within him as the idea took hold. He reached down and took both of Emily's hands in his. How foolish to think he could ever wait long enough for all their problems to vanish! One danger was past, but who knew what difficulties might lie ahead? No life was ever free of trouble.

If he could just get the words out—and if she would accept—they could at least face their troubles together.

He looked around through the gathering darkness. In the distance, a pinpoint of light bobbed along the road, heralding the cab's approach. At least he knew their future problems didn't include trying to figure out how to make their way back to Mrs. Purvis's. Freed of that concern, he turned back to Emily.

Say something! He swallowed and licked his lips. Now that the moment had arrived, every approach he had rehearsed fled his mind. He wrapped his hands around her fingers. "There's something I've been wanting to talk to you about all day." He watched her closely, trying to gauge her reaction.

She closed her eyes then looked up at him and lifted her chin. "Yes, I thought you had something on your mind."

Stephen gulped. It wasn't quite the reaction he'd been hoping for, but he'd committed himself now. The only thing left to do was

271

CAROL COX

to forge ahead. Even if she rejected him, at least he would have told her what was on his heart.

"Emily, I have truly enjoyed the time we've spent together."

Her lower lip began to tremble. This wasn't going right at all. He raised his left hand to cup her face and stroke his thumb along her cheekbone.

Stephen felt the tremor that ran through her at his touch. Was that a good sign? He didn't know, but he pressed on.

"It has been a very special time to me. . .and I'd like it to go on forever. Will you do me the honor of becoming my wife?"

Emily's lips parted. Her eyes grew huge, and she stared at Stephen without saying a word. His heart sank, knowing he had just made the biggest blunder of his life.

Without warning, she pulled her hands from his grasp. The next thing he knew, she had flung her arms around his neck, nearly squeezing the breath out of him.

She pressed her petal-soft cheek against his and whispered, "Yes." He could hear the laughter bubbling up in her voice. "Oh yes!" she whispered again, her breath warm against his ear.

Stephen wrapped his arms around her waist and lifted her into the air, holding her close as he tilted his head and sought her lips with his.

Long moments later, the *clip-clop* of horses' hooves filtered into his consciousness, and a cheery voice cried out, "Hello! Are you there?"

Stephen pulled his lips away from paradise and set Emily down on the ground with tender care. "We're here," he called.

The cab drew up beside them. "Sorry to keep you waiting. One of the harness straps broke, and I had to take time to make a quick repair. I hope you didn't mind the wait too much."

Stephen looked down at his future wife. In the glow from the cab's lantern, he could see the love shining in her eyes. "No. We didn't mind at all."

———

Emily crossed the parlor and settled onto the floor near the bookshelf. A few feet away, Adam pushed a block boat down an imaginary river. Fresh from his bath, his face looked flushed and rosy, and damp hair clung to his forehead.

She found it hard to believe how much her life had changed since she'd left the house that afternoon. In that short time, she'd gone from feelings of impending loss to the knowledge that Stephen wanted her to be his, now and forever.

Lucy and Mrs. Purvis had received the news with happy cries and congratulatory hugs. Now there was one more important person to talk to.

"Would you like to come over and sit with me?" Adam put down his block and climbed into her lap. Emily pressed her cheek against the top of his head and breathed in the scent of the little boy, thinking of the way his whole existence had been turned upside down over the course of the past month. At least this time, he was about to hear some happy news.

Stephen leaned against the mantel, having agreed she should be the one to talk to Adam. Through the dining room, Emily could see Mrs. Purvis and Lucy hovering in the kitchen doorway.

She brushed the soft blond hair back from Adam's forehead. "You know your mama's gone to be with Jesus, don't you?"

His clear blue eyes held her gaze, and he gave her a solemn nod.

This was going to be more difficult than she thought. Emily glanced over his head at Stephen, who nodded and gave her an encouraging smile.

"Stephen and I decided something tonight," she went on.

Flutters of joy danced in her heart when she spoke the words. Even now she could scarcely believe it was true. "We're going to be married soon. Would you like to be part of our family?"

Adam looked up at her and patted her cheek. "Will you be my mama now?"

Emily thought her heart would burst. She pulled him close and rocked him back and forth. "Yes, sweetheart. I'll be your mama, now and always."

Beaming like a proud father, Stephen crossed the room and squatted down in front of them. He ruffled Adam's hair. "I guess that will make me your dad, won't it?"

Emily felt the little boy's body stiffen. She met Stephen's startled gaze and realized the same thought was running through both of their minds. The term *Da* was too deeply ingrained for anything resembling it to carry a good connotation for Adam. She licked her lips and tried to think of some way to rescue the moment.

Adam pulled his head away from her and looked up at Stephen. "Matthew has a papa," he said.

Stephen's face lit up. "Then *Papa* it is." Getting to his feet, he scooped Adam up and tossed his new son into the air. The little boy shrieked with laughter.

"It sounds like a celebration is in order." Emily looked up to see Lucy carrying a plate of cookies.

Mrs. Purvis followed, bearing a tray laden with five cups of steaming hot chocolate. She blew across the top of Adam's cup to cool his drink before handing it to him. Lifting her own cup, she said, "Here's to the happy family."

Stephen picked up a cup of the hot cocoa and gazed at Emily. Raising the glass to her, he said, "To us."

"To us," she whispered.

Mrs. Purvis chuckled. "I knew I was doing the right thing when I brought that quilt out to you."

"The quilt your grandmother made?" Emily tilted her head. "What do you mean?"

The landlady beamed upon them both. "I brought it along on a picnic I took with Randolph many years ago. It was while we were sitting on it that he proposed to me." She shook her head. "I thought he would never get around to it."

Emily grinned. "So it worked twice, eh? It looks like you'll have another set of names to add to your list."

"You're a little late." Lucy giggled. "She did it while the milk was heating for our cocoa."

When the laughter died down, Lucy asked, "Have you set a date yet?"

"We really haven't gotten that far." Emily sent Stephen a questioning look.

He moved next to her and put his arm around her shoulders. "I suppose tomorrow is too soon?"

Emily felt a delicious shiver run through her, followed by warmth rushing to her face. She gave a shaky laugh and pressed her hands against her flaming cheeks. "I don't know. There's so much to think about. You're starting the job with your uncle's firm soon. Do you think it would be best to wait until you've had a chance to get settled there?"

The expression in Stephen's dark eyes turned her knees to jelly, and Emily felt the heat flood her cheeks again. "We'll need to find a place to live," she reminded him.

"That's right." The light in Stephen's eyes dimmed. "I haven't made a huge sum as a guard. Once I finish a project or two for Uncle Charles, we'll be on solid footing financially. But until then and considering that we're going to need a place big enough for three. . ." He sighed and leaned forward to kiss Emily on her forehead. "Much as I hate to say it, we may have to put the wedding off a little while."

"Maybe not." Everyone turned to look at Mrs. Purvis. "I've been thinking about something ever since you sprang the news on Lucy and me."

She stepped over to Stephen and Emily and took each of them by the hand. "What would you say to my giving you this house as a wedding gift?"

Emily felt her eyes grow as round as saucers. Beside her, Stephen bent to give Mrs. Purvis a peck on the cheek. "That's very generous of you, but it's far too—"

The landlady raised her hand. "You didn't let me finish. I am offering you the house as a wedding gift. . .with the provision that I can go on living here for the rest of my life."

Emily glanced at Stephen, who looked as dumbfounded as she felt.

"I'll keep my quarters on the ground floor, so I won't be in your way," Mrs. Purvis explained. "The house is big enough for the two of you and Adam. And there's plenty of room for any other children who may come along," she added with a twinkle in her eye.

Stephen shook his head slowly. "I don't know what to say."

"Say yes!" Mrs. Purvis's face softened. "It isn't all generosity on my part. I've spent ten years of my life searching for Randolph's treasure. Now that I've found it, I realize it doesn't mean anything if I don't have someone to share it with. Having you here would bless me far more than it will you."

Emily saw the corners of Stephen's mustache lift upward. He raised his eyebrows, and she nodded.

"In that case. . ." he began.

"We accept," Emily finished. "Thank you so much." They both wrapped their arms around Mrs. Purvis.

"Just a minute." Lucy faced them, her hands on her hips. "I think you're missing something. You have the child, the parents, and the grandmother all lined up, but it seems to me this family needs an aunt, as well."

Emily looked at Stephen, who grinned and shrugged. "There's plenty of room."

Lucy whooped and flew across the room to sweep Adam up into her arms. "I'm going to be your aunt Lucy now. What do you think about that?"

Adam threw back his head and laughed then reached for Stephen, who took him in his left arm, keeping his right arm snug around Emily's waist.

Once again Emily studied the faces of her little family: Adam, the most precious child who ever lived; Mrs. Purvis, who had become like a mother to her; Lucy, her best friend. . .

And Stephen. Emily's heart swelled as she gazed at the man she loved. After weeks of fear and worry, her life had been transformed in one sweeping moment, giving her everything she ever dreamed of.

Thank You, Father. I asked You to show me Your plan and to straighten out my life, and You've done it far better than I ever could have imagined.

CHAPTER 24

D o you remember what you're supposed to do?" Emily bent forward carefully, so as not to create the slightest wrinkle in her snowy white dress, and adjusted the golden rings anchored to the pillow Adam held in his hands.

He looked up at her, eyes shining, and nodded.

Emily dropped a quick kiss on his forehead. "I know you'll do a fine job. You're my big boy, aren't you?"

Adam grinned. "And you're my new mama."

Tears stung Emily's eyes. She stood and touched her fingertips to her eyelids. The last thing she wanted was to have puffy red eyes on her wedding day.

Just then Lucy and Mrs. Purvis burst through the door, dressed in their finest. Mrs. Purvis stopped in the middle of the room, located off to one side of the church sanctuary, and pressed her hand to her bosom. "Don't you look lovely!" She turned to Adam and grinned. "Both of you."

Emily twirled in front of them to show off her dress; then she took Adam's hand and spun the giggling boy around.

Peering into the mirror, Lucy twisted a tendril of blond hair around her finger and then patted it into place. "It's hard to believe your big day is here already."

Emily murmured agreement, although over the past two weeks, she had wavered between feeling this day would never come and thinking it was bearing down upon her like a rushing train. Did all brides feel this way?

There had been even more details to attend to than she had expected. If she'd had to continue working full-time, she never would have managed it. But Stephen insisted she resign from her job so she would have time to enjoy the wedding preparations, instead of stewing over them. With the fair nearing its close, the number of youngsters being dropped off at the Children's Building grew smaller every day; she didn't feel she was leaving the rest of the staff in a lurch, and Miss Strickland didn't seem grieved at the idea of her leaving.

The door opened, and a smiling woman looked in. "Am I disturbing you?"

"No, come right in." Emily smiled as Stephen's mother entered the room, followed by his sister, Beth. Even without any work-related responsibilities, she never would have been able to pull everything together without their help. Between the two of them, Lucy, and Mrs. Purvis, they had managed to make all the arrangements for the invitations, decorations, and reception.

The day after Stephen told his family about their engagement, his mother and sister had boarded the train, and they had been staying with Uncle Charles and Aunt Martha ever since so they could direct operations at close hand. In anyone else, the eager help might have seemed overbearing, but Emily welcomed the assistance, recognizing it as an offering of love rather than an attempt to control. Mother Bridger had even insisted on taking Emily to her favorite seamstress downtown, where she helped plan the design for Emily's lavish wedding gown.

Emily smoothed her hands over the cool white satin, still in a state of awe at the idea of wearing such a lovely creation. Wide lace trim capped the sleeves of the frothy confection and added a pinafore effect to the bodice. The long full skirt flowed out to form a train behind her, finished with ruching of the same fabric as the gown. A coronet of crystal-beaded flowers and leaves sat atop her auburn hair, holding the floor-length veil in place.

It was the dress of her dreams. No, more than that. With no family to help with expenses and no savings of her own, she never would have allowed herself to dream of anything so grand. Besides, the whole point of this day was to be joined together with Stephen as husband and wife. A simple ceremony in Mrs. Purvis's parlor would have been enough.

But Mother Bridger had plans of her own. From the moment she stepped in, insisting on paying for all the wedding expenses like some benevolent fairy godmother, Emily found herself swept along on a current of elaborate preparations. She balked at first, but once she realized Stephen was happy to see her being cosseted and cared for this way, she let herself relax and enjoy the elegant proceedings.

Emily studied the dress in the mirror then looked over at her future mother-in-law. "Do you think Stephen will like it?"

Mrs. Bridger laughed and walked over to give her a gentle hug. "My son would love you even if you wore a potato sack. But yes, darling, he'll approve. You look absolutely radiant.

"Everything is ready," she went on. "It's so nice of Charles and Martha to arrange for us to use their church for the ceremony."

Emily nodded. Once she'd seen the Bridger side of the invitation list, she knew she would have to alter her plan of holding a quiet service in Mrs. Purvis's parlor. She was grateful for Uncle Charles and Aunt Martha's help and doubly grateful to Mrs. Bridger for being willing to allow the guests to sit on either side of the aisle. With Adam acting as the ring bearer and Lucy standing up with Emily, holding to the more formal seating arrangement would have meant only Mrs. Purvis sitting on the bride's side.

A quick tap sounded on the door, and Dinah Howell poked her head into the room. "They're ready to seat you now, Mrs. Bridger." She grinned. "And you're next, Mrs. Purvis, as acting mother of the bride."

Mrs. Purvis trotted over to give Emily a kiss on the cheek; then she and Stephen's mother smiled at each other and linked arms as they went out to the sanctuary.

Dinah followed, leading Adam by the hand. She stopped in the doorway and looked back over her shoulder at Emily. "You only have a moment longer. It's almost time."

Lucy picked up the bouquet resting on a nearby table and handed it to Emily. "Are you ready?"

Was she? Emily closed her eyes. She and Stephen hadn't known each other very long, but their souls seemed to connect from the moment they met. In a few minutes, she would say the words that would give her not only the husband God meant for her to have, but a wonderful family, as well.

She opened her eyes again and smiled at Lucy. "I'm ready. Let's go."

⌣

Stephen's father waited for them in the foyer, with Adam at his side. He stepped forward when they entered the small room and bowed with courtly grace. "Thank you, Emily, for asking me to stand in your father's place today. It's a privilege to welcome you into our family."

He stepped back and took in the picture she made and gave her a smile that reminded her of Stephen's. "I must say the boy has excellent taste. He's a chip right off the old block."

From inside the sanctuary, the organ notes swelled into the opening strains of the wedding march. Mr. Bridger pulled the door open and nodded to Adam. "I believe it's your turn, young man."

The little boy squared his shoulders and marched off with measured steps, carefully holding the ring pillow in front of him.

When he was halfway down the aisle, Lucy caught Emily by the hand and said, "I couldn't be happier today if you were my true sister. I love you, Emily, and I wish you all the best."

Unable to speak, Emily blinked back happy tears and nodded. Lucy turned and took a deep breath; then she stepped forward to follow Adam. Mr. Bridger extended his left arm, and Emily tucked her hand into his elbow.

Every person in the sanctuary turned to face her when she stepped into the doorway, but they all faded into a blur as Emily focused on the only one who mattered to her at the moment. She heard the soft rustle of her satin dress as her feet glided along the aisle, carrying her toward the man to whom she would pledge her heart. In his black frock coat and pin-striped pants, he looked handsomer than ever.

Beside him stood his brother, Philip, whose clean-shaven features were almost a mirror image of Stephen's except for the mustache. Seth Howell waited behind the pulpit, Bible in hand. Mr. Bridger led Emily to the front and placed her hand in Stephen's then seated himself beside his wife.

Seth looked out over the assembled guests and smiled. "Dearly beloved, we are gathered today in the presence of God and of these witnesses to join this man and this woman in holy matrimony. Marriage is a sacred covenant, and all who enter into it must recognize the seriousness of these vows. Let us ask God to bless this union."

They bowed their heads, and Emily felt Stephen's fingers tighten on her hand. After the "Amen," she looked up into his dark brown eyes, and the rest of the room seemed to fade away.

Seth's next words brought her attention back to the moment.

"Stephen and Emily, as it is your stated intent to enter into the covenant of marriage, please join your right hands and repeat these vows."

Tears welled in her eyes as Stephen repeated the words after Seth. Never again would she worry about being a person of value. The look in his eyes told her she was truly cherished and loved.

Seth led her through her own vows as she promised to love, honor, and obey Stephen until they were parted by death. The solemnity of the moment took her breath away. They were a part of each other.

"I now pronounce you man and wife. You may kiss the bride."

Emily tilted her head back to share her first kiss with Stephen as husband and wife, dimly aware of the applause that erupted throughout the sanctuary.

Philip pumped Stephen's hand then smiled down at Emily. "Is the best man allowed to give the bride a kiss?"

"Just one," Stephen growled, giving his brother a mock glare.

Philip laughed and leaned forward to brush a kiss on Emily's cheek. At the same moment, Lucy reached over to give Emily a hug, and Philip's arm collided with hers. Lucy gasped and backed away.

Emily noted the pink spots on her friend's cheeks. Glancing over quickly, she saw a dull red flush suffuse Philip's face. Stephen looked at her with raised eyebrows, and they both smothered grins. It seemed as though romance might be in the air for more than her and Stephen. After all these years of claiming each other as sisters, was it possible she and Lucy might one day share the same last name? Maybe she should point Mrs. Purvis in their direction.

Seth looked out over their heads and spoke to the congregation. "Ladies and gentlemen, I take great pleasure in presenting to you Mr. and Mrs. Stephen Bridger."

As she turned with Stephen to face the smiling well-wishers, Emily felt something catch her by the knees. She looked down to see Adam, his arms stretched wide enough to wrap them around both her and Stephen.

He looked up with a joyful grin. "I have a mama *and* a papa!"

Stephen bent to gather the little boy in his arms. Laughter shook in Seth's voice as he added, "Let me correct that last statement. I am pleased to present to you Mr. and Mrs. Stephen Bridger. . .and son."

About the Author

Author of thirteen novels and eleven novellas, Carol Cox's love of history, mystery, and romance is evident in the books she writes. A pastor's wife, Carol has a passion for fiction and is a firm believer in the power of story to convey spiritual truths. She makes her home with her husband and young daughter in northern Arizona, where the deer and the antelope really do play—often within view of the family's front porch. To learn more about Carol and her books, visit her Web site at www.CarolCoxBooks.com. She'd love to hear from you!

OTHER BOOKS BY CAROL COX

Ticket to Tomorrow
Fair Game

Arizona Brides
Sagebrush Brides